I0668129

A trail of red led up to and beyond the front door. Megan followed it to the top of the stairs. The long, long way down – flight after flight of steep stairs – taunted her weakened legs. Light in the hallway flickered, showed her the red trail going down in sickening strobes. The strength and speed she had found faltered, leaving room for the ache of her middle to announce itself. Could she really make it down the stairs?

She extended her foot and took a step down. She'd grasp the handrail with all her might and move down as steadily as she could, fast but not so fast that her feet would slip out from beneath her. Caitlin would get no help if Megan ended up unconscious. On the second step she realized how slippery the blood had made the stairs. She squeezed the handrail until the bones in her hand felt like they'd crack in protest. Down, down, another step, then another. Down to floor six. Floor five.

The scene at the fifth-floor landing stopped her, knocked her backward, connected her backside with a slippery step. She recognized the man, plump and middle-aged, as someone who had lived in the building longer than they had. Quite a few times he had helped her lug groceries, and once or twice she had returned the favor. His hair was shoulder-length, usually tied back in a ponytail. He had once said that his job involved computer programming. She couldn't remember his name. He was lying near the door to his apartment.

Something had torn off most of his face and split him down the middle. The gashes on his tattered chest and stomach looked like claw-marks. A five-fingered claw.

Carter? Impossible. But...

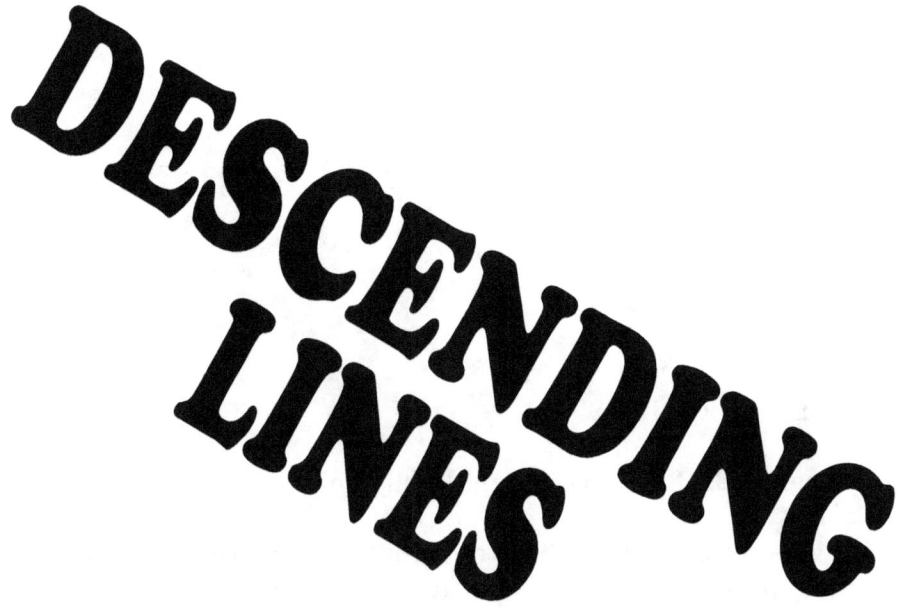

DESCENDING LINES

by L. Andrew Cooper

a BlackWyrm book
Louisville, Kentucky

DESCENDING LINES

Copyright ©2013 by BlackWyrm Publishing

All rights reserved, including the right to reproduce this book, or portion thereof, in any form. Written permission must be secured from the publisher to use or reproduce any part of this book, except for brief quotations in critical reviews or articles.

The characters in this novel are fictitious. Any resemblance to actual persons living or dead is purely coincidental.

A BlackWyrm Book
BlackWyrm Publishing
10307 Chimney Ridge Ct, Louisville, KY 40299

Printed in the United States of America.

ISBN: 978-1-61318-150-8

Cover Design by Dave Mattingly
Edited by Debbie Kuhn

First edition: October 2013

This nasty little story, unlike most of the characters in it, received a lot of nurturing along the way, and I can't possibly thank everyone. Like much of the universe haunted by Dr. Allen Fincher, the roots of *Descending Lines* go back to when I was living in New Jersey and taking the train the New York whenever possible, so to all my friends and supporters from that difficult time in my life—you know who you are—thank you. On a more practical note, strong women in those social circles as well is in my own family (yeah Mom, face it, you're a strong woman) offered me factual and personal insight far more valuable than all the books I read on pregnancy in order to give Megan's experiences authenticity. Also practical is thanking the folks responsible for putting this book in front of you: Deborah Kuhn, my editor, has been creative and precise, and Dave Mattingly at BlackWyrm has got to be one of the Best Publishers Ever.

I'd also like to thank Michael Williams and other supportive present-day colleagues at the University of Louisville. The greatest thanks, as always, go to my partner James Chakan.

All that aside, this book is dedicated to Mary Lawless and Caroline Shriner, who, North or South, have long given me delightful places to run and hide.

Book One

Ruin

Vector

"My knee hurts, Mommy," Megan's daughter said.

Of course Caitlin's knee hurt. Megan left the hospital and went home to her husband, her heart aching.

If they had stopped the first tumor earlier, if they had gone to the right doctor first, if they had paid more attention – but they hadn't. Their obligation was clear.

Carter stared at her intently as he told her his plan.

"You're crazy, Carter. I won't listen to this."

His blue eyes, framed by oval lenses, were calm. His hair, short, blond, and straight, formed a neat ridge across his forehead. She wanted to tousle it. They sat in the living room of their seventh-floor apartment. They sat talking about murder, and she wanted to muss his hair. They were both crazy.

"You said you'd do anything to save her," Carter said. His gaze narrowed.

Megan nodded. "I know. And I would. I'd do anything, but *come on*. What you're saying is ludicrous, absurd, monstrous, cra—"

"Crazy, yes, you mentioned that. But you know it'll work."

He was right. She hadn't experienced all the things that Carter had, but she had seen enough to believe it would work. *It.* She couldn't say what *it* was, not even in thought, but he could.

"Say it again," Megan demanded.

Carter's eyes lost a little of their warmth, and she was glad.

"Say it again," he echoed. "Say what?"

"State your *proposal*. I need to hear it again." She leaned back on the sofa, waiting.

"My *proposal*." Carter laughed. It sounded cold, humorless. "I propose that there is something you and I want more than anything else in the world. We want our daughter, Caitlin, to grow up and be the bright, beautiful, healthy woman she ought to be. The question is, how far are we willing to go to make that happen?"

Megan blinked.

"I propose," Carter continued, "that either one of us would do anything in our power to save her. *Anything*. We'd kill for it, wouldn't we?"

Megan's neck was rigid. She didn't breathe again until Carter resumed talking.

"Of course we would," Carter said. "Who wouldn't kill to save their own child?" He paused. "I propose that saving our daughter's life is more important than morality. I can't think about her lying in that hospital bed and worry about whether or not saving her is the *moral* thing."

Megan heard him. What did morality have to do with the cancer that was destroying their baby's bones, lungs, and lymph nodes? It had already been a year. It could be two, even three more. With new treatments, with new clinical test groups, anything was possible. The shreds of hope the doctors gave them were supposed to be comforting. Recurrent synchronous multifocal osteosarcoma. Bone cancer. She hated the doctors' idea of hope. Of course she'd kill to save her little girl. She'd do it if she had to. She'd do it because she *wanted* to.

"I propose that anybody who had the power to save their child from that bed and those tubes and the pain and the hair loss and the infected incisions and...." Carter dabbed a finger in the corner of one eye. "The thing is," he began again, "most people don't have that kind of power." He cleared his throat. "We do."

Yes, they had the power. A decade of wishing couldn't take it away.

"We have the power," Carter said, "and you know how it works."

Megan grabbed a sofa cushion and hugged it tightly to her chest. Her lips did not move.

Carter looked at her, assessing, before he continued. "To get something, you have to give something up. That much isn't supernatural at all. It's just how life goes. We have to make a sacrifice if we want our daughter to live."

Megan thought about how she hated the doctors. She looked at the ridge of hair on her husband's forehead and thought about hating him, too.

Carter laughed again. "It sounds so *empty* when I say it, doesn't it? Sacrifice. Like the 'sacrifice' of working so many hours a week to put food on the table. Like the 'sacrifice' of choosing the lesser career so you have time to be home with your family. It's just not that easy, not for us."

Megan twisted her bare heel against the carpet until it burned. *Say it, Carter. Say* human *sacrifice. Say that you want to kill a baby. Our baby.*

"I propose that I go into that closet and find that book, the one we pretend not to think about. It has the exact prescription for saving our daughter's life. It's got details about a tribal ritual that restores the life of a first-born child through the 'intervention' of a 'disembodied will.' The 'intervention' requires the sacrifice of another child from the same parents. We don't need all the fun tribal facts, though. We just need the description of the ritual – the words to say, the way to do it."

Carter looked at Megan, and she looked away. The turn of her head acknowledged his victory.

"We'll save her, Megan. It'll work."

"Okay," Megan said. "But you have to do it. I have to do everything else, but you have to do *it*. I'll go through forty weeks of hell, but that last moment, that last step, is yours. Do you understand me?"

Carter nodded, and Megan sighed. They didn't have a second child, so to save Caitlin, Carter wanted her to get pregnant. Forty weeks, nine months, a lifetime. A life.

And what if Caitlin died before the baby was born?

Don't call it a baby, Megan. It's just...something we're making, a cure. Don't think of it as a baby.

But *what if*, Carter, what if? Carter never said, "Then we'll already have another one." A *replacement*. Either way, they would have one living child. Unless, of course, it didn't work – unless they killed one child to save another and both ended up dead. But it *would* work. Carter was certain. Megan was just as certain as he was. Their certainty was absolute will. It was power.

When Megan's reasoning diverged from his, Carter told her that the ritual was usually used to save first-born sons. It would work to save daughters, too, but traditionally it involved the killing of daughters to save sons. Wasn't Megan supposed to be a feminist? Wouldn't a reversal be a form of cosmic justice? Carter read the book between the lines to get at its implicit sexism. He was getting close to a PhD. If Carter said the ritual was used to save first-born sons, then it was. Think about all the daughters, Carter argued, the daughters killed for the sake of sons – not just in rituals like this one, but in China, in every part of the world in every era of history where boys are worth everything and girls are worth less than dirt. Our daughter is worth more than that, Megan. Our daughter is worth anything.

Murder. To conceive, carry, and bear a child for the sake of murdering it. It, her, or him. *Don't think of it that way. Not a baby. A cure. It.* Forty weeks.

It would take longer than forty weeks. Calculating the exact timing of ovulation without the help of a doctor was tricky. Even with perfect timing, there were no guarantees.

Megan's mother, Susan Penser, had warned Megan and Carter to "maintain an active sex life." Unaware of the irony, Susan had said, "It's important for the two of you to stay close, for my granddaughter's sake as well as your own." Intimacy was an effort, but it had purpose.

In January, Megan's trip home from her office at the Penser Foundation was always after dark. The crunch of human bodies into subway cars and the treachery of ice-slicked sidewalks brought her home. Carter was usually either there when she arrived or on his way back from the library. When they were together, they could turn on lights and music and talk, but there was always an empty room with pink curtains and a big Barbie townhouse. Their apartment was cold. Tall buildings surrounded them and blocked out the sun.

The first time they tried to conceive their second child, Carter was waiting when Megan got home. He had made dinner and lighted candles. He wore his green sweater, Megan's favorite, the heavy one that fit snugly through the chest, making him look strong but soft. Occasionally Megan could look at her husband through the candlelight without remembering the dinner's purpose. She could spear lettuce with her fork, put it in her mouth, and chew without thinking about what the hands that had made the salad would eventually do.

The next morning, Megan wanted to take a pregnancy test. She knew it was too soon, but she needed to take it anyway. The night had been fine, even good, but she wanted it to have been *effective*. She took a test, and it was negative. Carter said nothing. They knew the result was meaningless as far as actual pregnancy was concerned, but the result did have meaning: they would have to try again that night – and the next evening. Soon the illusion that they were having sex because they wanted to or because it felt good faded. They were having sex for their daughter. For Susan's granddaughter.

A guilt like the guilt she had felt when she had first learned to masturbate accompanied each tingle. Carter made references to the well-established link between sex and death, to the French habit of calling an orgasm *la petite mort*, and he tried to laugh at his own cleverness. The laughter twisted Megan's stomach.

Megan closed her eyes while Carter was on top of her. She closed them and let her mind go anywhere but the bedroom, trying to avoid pleasure. Carter's grunts and moans followed her into mental darkness like cawing crows, pecking reminders of the act.

"Was that...was that *good* for you?" she asked.

Carter sat on the edge of the bed with his back to her. His bare shoulders were slumped, rising and falling with quick shallow breaths.

"*Good?*" He made a low sound in his throat, more like a hiccup than a laugh. "I can't say that it was what I call *good*."

"But you did...finish...didn't you?"

"As long as the equipment is functioning properly, hundreds of thousands of little soldiers are on a forced march right now."

Megan got her period in late January.

They asked each other, "What am I doing wrong? What are you doing wrong?" But neither of them had an answer.

"I can't do it anymore! I can't!" Megan curled up on the sofa, crying. She closed her eyes and wished she were far away from the snow and honking taxis and Carter – beautiful, brilliant, terrifying Carter. He haunted her body, a bogeyman with an invitation.

"Then don't. I won't make you. I'm not going to *rape* you, Megan. It's your choice. You can choose whether Caitlin lives or dies."

Megan sat up, wiping her eyes. "Don't put it all on me. It's not fair. You don't have to do anything."

"I don't have to do anything? That's right. I'm *enjoying* myself. I'm having the time of my fucking life. Do you have any idea what it's *like* for me? You just have to lie there, but I have to trick myself into thinking I'm doing something I want to do. Do you realize that I have to *work* to get an erection? Oh, it's a fucking *joy*! Clenching every muscle in the hope that I'll come soon so I don't have to keep pumping away at this—"

"STOP IT! I...I..." Megan knew she had been unfair. "I didn't mean that it was *easy* for you." She reached for the box of tissues on the end-table. She blew her nose and studied Carter while he cooled down. "What I meant was that it's not fair for you to say it's up to me whether Caitlin lives or dies. It's not up to me. It's not my fault." She thought of an argument worthy of Carter: hadn't kings punished and even executed their wives for failing to conceive? She ended up saying nothing.

They took a week and a half off from their obligation. They ate their dinners in silence. For the first few days, they slept on opposite edges of the bed. Then Carter said he wanted to sleep on the sofa until the next attempt. She agreed.

When the time came to try again, Carter asked whether she'd like to wait one more day.

"No," she said. "Do it now. The more…now…the less…"

Carter nodded.

Two days later, Megan made a stop on the way home from work at one of the few accessible sex shops that remained in the city. The neon lights and rotating displays bewildered her. She had little experience with such places. She realized that she had no idea what Carter might like.

"Can I help you, ma'am?" The word "ma'am" sounded funny coming from the scrawny young guy in a cap and denim shirt who had left the front counter to attend her.

He looked at her, at her neat brown ponytail, her bright fuzzy sweater, and her tailored blue pants.

She hesitated, but then explained that she was looking for a movie for a man she knew, a sort of gag gift that he would nevertheless enjoy.

"Do you plan to, um, enjoy it with him?"

No, she had no use for such things.

The young man went on to tell her that it was an established truth in the business that almost every dude's biggest fantasy was girl-on-girl action. He started to go into detail about a movie involving two girls in a sorority house, but Megan interrupted him.

"Thank you, I'll take it."

When she got home, Megan set the plain brown bag on the kitchen table, and tried to give her husband an affectionate smile. "I brought you something."

Carter was chopping tomatoes for a sauce. He set down the knife and walked over to the table. "Oh, really? Hmm. Funny things come in little brown paper bags." He took out the newly-purchased copy of *Sisterhood of Sin*. His face fell. "What the hell is this?"

Megan concentrated on keeping her smile. "I thought you might like it. I know…I know I don't really turn you on anymore."

Carter shook his head. "This is a trap, right? My wife wants me to watch porn. This *can't* be for real. Megan, *darling*, you're still pretty. The problem is me, not you. The problem is the situation. I don't need a porno movie. I just need you. Blah, blah, blah. Is that what you wanted to hear?"

Her smile faltered a little. "No need to get hostile," she said. "You're always telling me about the reality of our situation. Well, here's a reality: I'm not turning you on. We need you to be turned on. So maybe this will work. I'm not trying to insult you. I'm certainly not trying to offend your manhood." She glanced down at the crotch of Carter's jeans. "I think you've done remarkably well."

"But?"

Megan wasn't sure whether Carter was annoyed or amused. She didn't know which she wanted him to be. "But...the reality of our situation is that *Sisterhood of Sin* might make things a whole lot easier for you. I'm not playing mind games. I thought about suggesting that you go buy something like this for yourself, but *that* really would have been too much of a game. So I went to get it for you, to prove I'm sincere. I'll put it in the DVD player and press play if you want. But that's all I can do." She paused, looking at his face, and thought, *I'm not the one looking for reassurance here.*

Carter dropped the empty bag on the table and held up the movie. "Do you want to watch it now, or do you want to have dinner first?"

Megan thought about what Carter had said about forcing your will on the world, about bending the rules of the real. Carter's book and Carter himself both had such interesting ways of talking about the "phenomena of the will." Though their task, their ritual, might seem supernatural, Carter said it was really just another sort of nature, a reality with different rules, rules that you can often, but not always, make yourself. Carter and his book didn't use words like "witchcraft" and "magic." Too hokey, too unreal. The reality of the situation, however, was that the situation was unreal. It was hokey. It was *Sisterhood of Sin.*

The movie did what it was supposed to do.

Reality. A counselor at Caitlin's long-term care facility told them that, considering the nature of their daughter's illness, they should be ready for reality to intrude on what they might consider their parental ideals. Long hospital visits just didn't work in most people's busy daily schedules. They had to keep to as many of their routines as they could; letting Caitlin's illness take over and destroy their lives would decrease their ability to be there in the ways that their daughter really needed them. There was nothing wrong with visiting every day or as much as they could, but sometimes as much as they could might not *be* every day. It might help, the counselor said, to think of the hospital as sort of like summer camp. There are people around all the time to look after her and give her affection. It's hard to accept that you alone can't meet all of your child's needs, but in a case like Caitlin's, it's just something they would have to do.

Megan kept up her visiting routine. She tried to view the hospital and her chats with her drugged little girl as escapes. One night when Megan was looking at Caitlin, she thought about what she would have to do to save her daughter's life, and her face started to burn. Looking at her daughter made her want to scream, to hit something. The illness that was wasting her daughter's face would devour more lives than one. It would eat the life of the new baby. It would consume her own life and maybe Carter's, too. She left the hospital room quickly, not looking back at the quiet bed.

Megan told herself that, once she conceived, she would only have to keep her health and sanity for forty weeks. Then she could have a complete breakdown, run away, or die. She could do anything once her daughter was okay. Her objective was not to bring their family back together, not to make things like they used to be. It was to make sure Caitlin lived, nothing more. She didn't have to look at that wasted face, not now. As February waned, Megan stopped going to the hospital. She hated being with Carter, but that was the only thing she was obliged to do.

After another premature pregnancy test, Megan's period came again. Megan told Carter, and Carter took out the calendar they kept in their nightstand drawer. They planned their hiatus, and they planned the next attempt. No explanation needed: Carter slept on the sofa.

In late March, Megan started to feel something. She didn't tell Carter. It wasn't anything that involved evidence – there were no symptoms yet. She just felt different, and she knew. Carter watched the calendar as closely as she did, but he didn't ask any questions on the day she expected to get her period. He said something about how long couples have to try sometimes, about how lucky they would be if it had worked this time. Megan didn't take a test that day or the next. On the third day, she retrieved one of the tests from under the bathroom sink. She read the instructions even though she had memorized them. She followed them precisely, careful to observe the exact amount of time the instructions indicated. *Lucky*, Megan thought.

She hadn't been able to hide what she was doing from Carter. She came out to the living room where he sat upright on the sofa, his back stiff, his hands in his lap.

Their eyes met. Megan nodded, and Carter stood. He looked perplexed for a moment before he started walking toward her. She raised her hand to stop him. They stood in the center of the room, four feet apart.

"I'm pregnant," Megan said. "Never touch me again."

The Descent of Carter Anderson

Carter had met Megan at Harvard a decade earlier. She was sitting alone in the first-year dining hall. One hand held a fork that was picking at macaroni, and the other held open a book. Wisps of brown hair framed a face that was distant and dreaming, made ethereal by the nearby stained glass's brilliant illumination. Carter had spotted her in the printed face-book, and he had made a mental note about meeting her.

"Do you mind if I join you?" He held his tray of food close to him, showing her that he wouldn't dare set it down without her permission.

"Have we met?" she said. "You look familiar."

Carter gave her a disarming smile. "I go running by the river most mornings – have I seen you there?" He already knew the answer.

"I jog on mornings when it isn't too cold."

Smiling, he glanced at his tray and then gave her a questioning look.

"Oh, sorry," she said. "Have a seat." She closed her book and sat up straight in her chair.

They exchanged names and chatted about classes until Brian, Carter's roommate, began hovering near their table. Brian held his tray with obvious anxiety, apparently hoping for an invitation.

"Megan Penser," Carter said, "this gentleman is not a stalker but is, in fact, my roommate, Brian."

Brian shifted from one foot to the other, rattling the dishes on his tray. His eyes, dilated behind thick glasses, bounced between Carter and Megan. "I don't want to, um, hone in on your, uh, date here, Carter."

Megan laughed, blushing. "Actually, we just met. Join us if you want."

Carter let out a pained sigh. "Sit down already."

Brian joined them at the table, looking unusually preoccupied. He and Carter ate, and Megan continued to reconfigure her macaroni.

When Brian set down his fork, Megan turned to him. "What's up?"

Brian cleared his throat and looked at Carter, who nodded. "Well, I've been thinking about Kierkegaard. Trying to sort out issues about infinite resignation and faith."

"Hmm. I actually have heard of Kierkegaard, I think."

"Don't let Brian intimidate you with name-dropping," Carter said. "Books are his best friends. Well, books and me, I guess. He talks about Kant, Nietzsche, and Wittgenstein like some people talk about lovers. Brian has been a major force in my education."

Brian coughed.

Megan tucked a lock of hair behind an ear. "You know, I'm glad to hear that. I always expected to meet lots of guys like Brian around here, but I just haven't. I guess Brian's more Harvard than Harvard." She chuckled. Carter decided she was good-natured.

Brian reddened. "Megan Penser," he said. "Is that Penser like Susan Penser? Like the Penser Foundation?"

Megan's posture wilted. "Yeah," she said. "How'd you know?"

"Just a hunch," Brian said. "I always expected to meet people with familiar last names here. More Harvard than Harvard, like you said."

Carter glared at Brian. "Hey, no need to get hostile."

Carter explained that he didn't think they'd ever escape the kinds of assumptions people make about Harvard students. He led them through more pleasant topics, and when he reached an appropriate endpoint, he asked Megan for a date.

"Tonight," he said. "Just the two of us." He nudged his roommate with a snicker.

The date ended in the doorway to the dorm room that Megan shared with Jess, a girl whose affinities with Brian had been a staple of dinner conversation. Carter was not satisfied by their chaste kiss, but he knew better than to push. He went home feeling restless, hoping that a skirmish with Brian would provide some release.

Carter opened the door and saw his roommate, skinny in blue boxers and a white T-shirt, pacing between Carter's side of the room and his own. He held a red book with worn edges in one hand, and the other hand fluttered at his side as if he were carrying on a heated debate.

"Whoa there, partner, what seems to be the trouble?" Carter's words stopped Brian in his tracks.

"What? Yes, oh my God." Brian started pacing again.

"Cease!" Carter ordered, and his friend halted. "Brian, look at me!"

Brian tore his eyes from the book. His hand kept fluttering.

Carter closed the door behind him. "Take a deep breath. Count to ten. Do *something* before you spontaneously combust."

"Carter, you're not going to believe what I found in the stacks yesterday. It's the most amazing thing I ever read. Period." He clapped the red book shut and handed it over.

"Aren't you worried you'll lose your place?" Carter asked.

"No," Brian said. "This is my second time reading it already."

Carter looked at the cover. *The Alchemy of Will*, by Dr. Allen Fincher. "Alchemy is a little far from your usual interests, don't you think?"

"It's not about alchemy," Brian said. "Okay, it sort of *is* about alchemy, but not about alchemy in the way you think. It's like – okay, right, so the elixir of life and the philosopher's stone and all the stuff about turning lead into gold is in some ways about just that, but in other ways it's about discovering the mutability of matter, and not just of matter, but of space and time, and of life and of the way that all those things are connected. He seriously anticipates Einstein and totally kicks some Nietzsche ass."

"He," Carter said, considering. "You mean this Dr. Fincher guy?"

"Yes, Dr. Fincher. I can't believe I never heard of him before. He must have been, like, one of the most learned men of his time, a medical doctor, a physicist, an anthropologist, a historian – he taught here, you know, about a hundred years ago or something. Why haven't we heard of him?"

Carter laughed. "Maybe because he wrote books about alchemy. Alchemy already sort of rubbed people the wrong way *five* hundred years ago."

"You're probably right," Brian said. "But it doesn't matter. You have to read this book, Carter. You have to. I think...I think I want to try something."

"Slow down, Brian, and understand that I don't have the vaguest clue of what you're talking about."

"Carter, you and I have spent hours talking about how frustrating modern philosophy is because it imagines the human mind as something that is...well, stultifying in its limitations. *The Alchemy of Will* is our antidote. Dr. Fincher argues that all the world's major mythologies have a common interest in a power that enables people to alter the world just by *willing* the change. The

Christian habit of praying for God's favors is a latter-day manifestation of an ancient wisdom that would enable the self to give the self anything that it truly wants simply by asking for it, by willing it."

Brian talked like a textbook. Carter was used to it. "Isn't your new doctor friend just a little bit sillier than your usual company?" Carter asked.

Brian ignored the interruption and continued. "Dr. Fincher studied obscure cults all over the world. He observed rituals that accomplished the kinds of miracles that modern religions see as metaphors. He says it's all about sacrifice. The sacrifice for fulfilling smaller desires could involve bloodletting, starvation, whatever, anything that could bring the mind into what he calls a 'borderland' state of consciousness, where the rules of reality...sort of...bend. The bigger the bend, the bigger the sacrifice. Dr. Fincher once met a holy man who severed his own leg in a ritual to bring rain. That man sat tending his wound while his village celebrated the end of a drought."

Carter went to his side of the room and flopped down on his bed.

"Are you listening to me?" Brian asked.

"Of course." Carter waved a hand. "Lecture on."

"According to Dr. Fincher, a man's will is powerful but not all-powerful. When he wants to do something extreme, a man can turn to something called 'disembodied wills' for help. Dr. Fincher doesn't say what these things are. They might be from a higher order of being. They might be human wills that survived death." Brian's elevated language didn't keep him from sounding younger and younger as he spoke. "They might be coherent organizations of the untapped potential of the population, the products of what Dr. Fincher calls a 'communal sub-will.' He's like Jung, only smarter."

Carter's mind caught on the words "survived death." "Wait a minute," he said. "Are we talking about ghosts?"

"Dr. Fincher claims to have seen them in action," Brian said. "Only the most extreme sacrifices can interest disembodied wills enough to bring about the extreme results that the person performing the ritual, 'the seeker,' desires. Christians believe that even God had to sacrifice his only son to accomplish the extreme task of cleansing the sins of the world. The idea is the same."

Carter snorted. "Kierkegaard has gone to your head. Why the sudden interest in Our Lord and Savior?" Carter was an atheist. Brian was supposed to be, too.

"The Jesus issue is beside the point," Brian said. "Dr. Fincher watched a man commit ritual suicide to restore the life of his people's leader. He recorded another ritual where a man sacrificed his second child to cure his firstborn of a fatal disease. He says that it only seems to work when 'the seeker' uses the established methods, the right rituals, to get the disembodied wills' attention. Think of it as a kind of spell book, but philosophical."

"Uh-huh," Carter said. "Yeah, I see why Dr. Fincher's name hasn't made it into the annals of greatness. How could *you* be taken in by such pulp-fiction bullshit?"

"I know, I know, I know," Brian said. "It sounds more like H. P. Lovecraft than Nietzsche, but if you read the book, you'll be convinced."

Carter pulled off his shirt, slipped off his pants, and scuttled under his sheets. "I'm tired, dear. If you're going to keep pacing and reading, please do so in the dark. I'm meeting Megan for breakfast tomorrow before class. Maybe I'll look at your magic red book when I come home in the afternoon."

Brian looked crestfallen, but he didn't argue.

The next afternoon, Carter came home and picked up Brian's book, thinking that reading a few pages would provide good fodder for mockery. He stretched out on his bed and turned on his reading lamp. He read a few pages, and then decided he'd go ahead and read the next chapter. Just before midnight, he turned the last page. The language *was* compelling, and there was something in the section on "disembodied wills" that Brian had neglected to mention. The seeker who gains the aid of a disembodied will sometimes get something called "the suture of the seeker." Dr. Fincher had heard of one seeker who had enjoyed the three-hundredth anniversary of his ritualistic bargain. The ritual had "modified his essence." It had made him immortal. Immortality: kitschy, something the goth kids would whisper about, but who could resist it? Over breakfast the next day, Carter suggested that he and Brian try something from the book.

Brian's voice dropped to a conspiratorial hush. "Which one?" he asked.

"Well, it's premature to try sacrificing a virgin for a plentiful harvest, don't you think? Virgins are pretty hard to come by these days, even around here."

Brian nodded. "We'd better start small." He was serious, almost somber.

Carter leaned over the table and lowered his voice. "Actually, I do have one in mind."

"Which one?"

"The virility ritual," Carter whispered, grinning.

Brian shifted in his seat. "You mean the one with—"

"Yeah, that one," Carter said. The virility ritual was supposed to result in a day-long spell of superhuman strength and unparalleled sexual prowess. It sounded easy; it sounded fun. Dr. Fincher's writing had made the *what if* part of Carter's brain a little more powerful than usual. And if it didn't work, the process would involve another form of amusement.

Brian squirmed. "You mean you really want to, you know, um... You know, the ingredients."

"What ingredients?"

Brian stared down at his plate of untouched scrambled eggs. "The, um, stuff we need."

"Might you be referring to spooj, my friend? Jizzzzzz?"

Brian's face flushed red, and the rest of him moved as if his chair were giving him electric shocks.

"Calm down there, partner. I know some guys back home who jerk off into cups at a crappy little clinic for thirty-five bucks as often as they're allowed. Touching those stiff magazines didn't turn them gay or anything." Carter laughed. "But don't get the wrong idea. I'm not offering to pay you."

"You're not being serious, Carter. It won't work if you're not serious."

"I am *deadly* serious." Carter's eyelids fluttered.

They fasted for the rest of the day and began the process that evening. They wrote "Do Not Disturb" on their door's message board and bolted out would-be intruders. They changed into their pajamas and made an altar by stacking up textbooks and crowning them with a hotplate. They opened the windows a crack and took the battery out of the smoke alarm. Carter took a bowl they'd stolen from the dining hall into his private corner of the room first. Brian went to his own corner and did the deed second. Carter used a magazine. Brian said he'd be fine without one. Carter couldn't look at Brian as he handed him the bowl, and neither one of them volunteered to transfer the contents to the pan that was warming on the altar. Brian finally did it.

Getting the blood was more painful, but easier. Carter offered to go first again. Brian shook more than Carter did as he sliced open Carter's palm with a pocketknife. He held Carter's hand in place as blood dripped down to join the other fluid in the pan, and then he offered his own hand for cutting. Carter had winced at the pain. Brian didn't.

As Dr. Fincher recommended, Carter and Brian wrote short English phrases to use as mantras between recitations in an incomprehensible and extinct tribal tongue. Carter wanted to quit after the first hour. He looked at Brian, preparing to say that the joke was over. Brian's eyes were closed. He wasn't referring to the script anymore – the words were moving through him, changing him into a conduit. Brian was exhibiting self-discipline that Carter had so far lacked. Carter reapplied himself.

They chanted for ten hours.

Dawn light filtered through the windows and started to bring them back. Carter sensed that his skin was sticky with sweat. The hot plate was still on, but the contents of the pan had sizzled to nothing. He took a breath, and the rush of air ignited his nerve-endings. He had tried cocaine once at a party. This was better. *Everything* was better. He leapt – floated – to his feet.

Carter shook Brian into consciousness, and Brian rose to his feet with inhuman grace. They made eye contact, and Carter laughed a deep, breathy, lunatic laugh. Carter wanted to shake Brian's bandaged hand and congratulate him for Creation itself. They were magnificent.

Carter's hands drifted to his sides, arms, and chest. His body still felt like himself, but something was different. He pulled off his pajama top, popping buttons, and sought his reflection in the full-length mirror on the back of their door. Muscles stood out as if he had been lifting weights for hours – still himself but to the *maximum*. He held his fingers in front of his face and watched them dance before his eyes. He was fluid. He breathed tidal waves.

Brian was yelling. "Go, let's go – get out of here – get outside! Run – come running with me! Always wanted – never before – now!"

Carter didn't answer, but he unbolted the door. The hallway beyond was infinitesimal. When they reached the brick sidewalk, Carter noticed that Brian was still clad head to toe in plaid pajamas. He laughed. Brian laughed with him. The morning was cold, but the cold against Carter's chest felt good. Every hair follicle crackled with energy. The two, as one, cascaded through the gate to the quiet street. They bounded toward an intersection and crossed four lanes with three steps – moving, gliding toward the river. They ran along the bank until the campus disappeared behind them. The river widened. Benches on the other side looked tiny.

"Let's jump it," Carter said.

Brian's eyes widened. "We're not *that*...are we?"

"One way to find out," Carter said. He backed from the riverbank to the street and erupted with speed. Brian mimicked his movements and kept up with him. They leapt, and their splash was a towering column. The river was deep, and their toes touched bottom. A quick push torpedoed them to the surface and beyond, back into the air before they splashed down again. The polluted water was probably close to freezing, but they didn't care. They slapped gallons at one another, laughing and splashing and exulting in how insubstantial everything was. They looked back to the bank where they'd started. It was an impossible distance away. They hadn't made it across, but they had come close. Brian didn't say it, but Carter knew what he was thinking: they had become supermen. They laughed together.

"Let's see what else we can do," one of them said.

They swam back to the bank where they'd started and sprung from the water. Carter spotted a thick wooden bench and approached it. He lifted; it flew. Their heads turned toward the street. A silver Mercedes was parallel-parked on the road not far from where they stood.

"Shall we?" Carter asked.

"It's probably got an alarm," Brian said.

"Something tells me we'll be long gone before anyone can complain." Carter gestured for Brian to lead the way, and he did.

Carter took the front of the car, Brian the back. Carter counted, "One, two, three!" Carter saw veins and cords in his arms that he'd never seen before. He heard Brian grunting, knew that he felt the same. The world swam, and the partial-peace-sign hood ornament rocked like a pendulum in front of Carter's nose. They lifted.

They didn't keep it off the ground long enough to be sure of a measurement. Brian estimated six inches; Carter said ten.

When they dropped it, Carter noticed that a car alarm had been screaming since their hands had first made contact with metal. They heard a voice from a window above.

"Hey, you guys...that's..." The grey-bearded white guy peering out from between steel bars couldn't finish his indignant objection. He had seen them in action. Their greatness silenced him.

"Out of here?" Brian asked.

Carter imagined overwhelming an army of policemen like the Incredible Hulk on a bad day. He remembered that they had failed to cross the river, and he knew that they couldn't have tossed the car. There were limits.

"Sure," Carter said, "out of here." As they raced back to the dorm, Carter took a strong lead.

When they got home they weren't yet themselves, but they were calmer. Back in their room, Brian looked at Carter for a long time. When he finally looked away, he asked, "What do we do now?"

Carter stripped off his wet pajama bottoms and changed into regular clothes. He saw that he had reopened the cut on his hand while lifting the car, so he replaced the bloody bandage. He wasn't done yet. He had a day, a whole *day*. The rush of strength was diminishing, but the effects of their ritual still buzzed in Carter's veins. He remembered stories about panicked mothers lifting cars to save their pinned and bleeding children. Had he simply been running on adrenaline? Had a night of focused meditation simply pushed the go-button on a gland, creating effects that were unusual and marvelous but totally natural? Carter looked at his fragile, dripping roommate – the skinny bookmark of a boy who had managed to keep up with a seasoned runner – and had doubts.

Brian's eyes met Carter's. "What do we do now?" he repeated.

"I don't know what to do now, really. I feel like the hero in an eighties movie who's just finished the kick-ass training montage. I wish there were some bullies somewhere we had a score to settle with." Carter imagined all the boys from Brian's childhood that Brian might be glad to pummel.

"Maybe the football team is somewhere doing spring training," Brian suggested. He started to peel off wet plaid.

Carter shook his head. "It probably wouldn't be good to kick too much ass. People might ask questions. Our boy Fincher might be exposed."

Had Dr. Fincher really taught here a hundred years ago? Had he been laughed out of academe for his outrageous theories?

Brian was looking at him. His eyes were spacey. He still wore the wet cotton pants, and his bloody hand was starting to fidget. "I just...wish...there were something we could...do...with all this...energy."

"The day's started now. There'll be people in the Yard and on the street and by the river. Another jaunt like the last one would draw too much attention. I feel like I could go to the gym, but people would notice that all the free weights were being used by just two guys." Achilles had the Trojan army to pick on, and Superman had super- villains. They didn't have anything. Well, Carter did have one thing. He had another date with Megan that night.

Brian didn't say anything. He finished changing clothes. On an impulse, Carter dropped to the floor and did push-ups. Brian watched him.

"That's never been so easy before," he said, after a final push brought him to his feet. "I could get used to this."

Brian looked away. "Something tells me we're going to be in a whole lot of pain tomorrow," he said.

The next morning, Carter awoke in rigid agony. Hours later, he managed to find the strength to sit up when Megan rose beside him. The girl who had refused a real kiss had succumbed.

"Nobody's ever made me feel that way before," she said.

Stifling the laughter made him ache, but Carter managed.

Parallels

Six weeks into the new pregnancy, washing only two forks after dinner did not upset Megan. She was used to Caitlin's absence. When she dropped one of the forks on the kitchen floor, however, she started bawling.

As Megan's moods changed, Carter's habits changed. He switched from his usual breakfast of a bagel with jelly to more elaborate meals of bacon, eggs, and toast, heavy with butter. The scent of Carter's morning cooking triggered Megan's first episode of morning sickness. Afterwards, she had afternoon sickness, evening sickness, and night sickness. Carter started calling her Queen Vomit.

Even though she hadn't vomited since early in the afternoon, Megan didn't want to go to dinner at her friend Gina's apartment.

"We have to keep up appearances," Carter said. "Pretty soon we'll have to make our social calendar a total blank."

Pretty soon she'd be switching into her maternity wardrobe. Pretty soon she'd have to stay out of sight.

"Besides, Gina's a great cook. You need to eat. You need to eat, and you need to keep something down."

Megan put a hand on her forehead and found clammy heat. "Won't all the vomiting give people like Gina a clue?"

"Not necessarily," Carter said. "You can just say you think you've got a twenty-four hour bug or something. Sooner or later people at work will notice that it's lasting more than twenty-four hours, but you won't say anything at all. Eventually you'll have to quit. You'll have to say that you need to take some time off to deal with the stress of what's happening with Caitlin. They'll put the stress and the vomiting together on their own."

"But they'll ask questions," Megan said.

Carter shook his head. "No they won't. People don't want details. Everybody who's had to sit through descriptions of bedsores and radiation sickness stopped asking questions about Caitlin a long time ago."

He was right, of course. Carter was always right. Gina didn't even mention Caitlin anymore unless Megan brought her up. Carter never hesitated to point out Gina's tendency to avoid personal topics unless they held gossipy interest. Carter was right, but Gina remained Megan's closest friend. Gina saw through Carter as easily as Carter saw through her.

"I certainly shouldn't judge other people's taste in men," Gina once said, "but Megan, that man of yours gives me a funny feeling. You told me you feel like your mom is watching you all the time, even when she's not around. I think Carter's kind of the same way. Sweetie, I think you might have married your mother."

"That friend of yours could be a problem," Carter said, "*especially* if we cancel dinner again. If we don't go tonight, she really might start asking questions."

"Maybe we could tell her. The truth, I mean. Maybe she'd understand." Megan looked at her husband from the corner of her eye as she spoke.

Carter's expression was one of incredulity. "She's a third-grade teacher, for Christ's sake. You really think *Miss Hernandez* would let us get away with killing a baby?"

Carter only called it a "baby" when talking about the risks they were taking. The word gave their danger a special urgency.

Megan shook her head. "She knows how I feel about Caitlin. She knows all we've been through. She doesn't have any kids of her own, but she understands the lengths a person can go to for the sake of—"

"Quit fooling yourself, Megan. You know I'm right. You might be able to trust her with anything else, but not this."

Yes, he was right.

"Let me get you some drinks," Gina said, as Megan and Carter walked through her door for the dinner that Megan didn't want.

"Sure, I'll have a beer," Carter replied. He did not say that it would be his third one that evening.

"A martini for me, please," Megan said.

"Onion instead of olive, right, honey?"

Megan nodded. "You know it, babe."

"Do you really think that's a good idea, Megan?" Carter squeezed his eyebrows together – concern.

Worried about fetal alcohol syndrome?

"I think a drink is a marvelous idea, don't you?" Megan asked, raising her voice. Carter winced.

"What's that?" Gina yelled from the kitchen.

Megan stepped further into the living room, leaving Carter by the coat rack. "I said make it very dry."

"That's my girl."

Carter followed Megan to the couch. "Whatever you say, my Queen," he whispered.

Instead of sitting on the couch with Carter, Megan chose the rocking chair. The sound of a flushing toilet startled her.

"Ah, he returns," Gina said, setting the drinks on the coffee table. A tall man with a shaved head and a dark complexion appeared from the hallway.

"Megan and Carter, I want you to meet Stefan," Gina said. Megan remembered the name: Gina had identified him on the phone as the newest man that she had decided to consider. Gina "considered" a new man every month or two. She said she had two choices: serial monogamy or serial killing. Naturally, she chose the more pleasurable of the two evils.

"Gina has told me much about you," Stefan said. "It is a pleasure to meet you both." Stefan extended his hand in greeting. Carter stood up to shake it. Megan rocked forward and took a sip of her martini.

"If you're wondering about the accent," Gina said, "it's Trinidad. Sexy, yes?" Gina squeezed one of Stefan's significant biceps.

Megan nodded and smiled. The accent was faint, but it did have allure.

They all sat to eat. Gina asked Stefan to explain his work in investment banking. She mentioned that Stefan had a share of a place on Cape Cod. He planned to take her there once summer was in full bloom. As they finished dinner, the conversation turned.

"My family is Catholic, and I consider myself a Catholic," Stefan said.

"My family is Catholic," Gina said, "and I consider myself a raving-bitch atheist. Isn't that right, Megan?"

"That's right," Megan said, sipping her wine. "She does tend to rave."

"Fuck you, sweetie." Gina winked.

Carter finished his wine, dropped his fork on his empty plate, and asked if he might open another bottle. Gina told him to get another plate of pasta, too. Carter refused. He had already had two large servings.

"Don't get me wrong," Stefan said. "I'm not a conservative. I don't think many Catholics would approve of my views on things."

"And what views are those?" Carter asked, twisting the corkscrew.

Stefan glanced at Gina before continuing. "For one thing, there's all this controversy about gay marriage. I don't think that Catholics should allow gays to marry in their churches. I also don't think it's right for bishops to tell senators to pass laws about it. The time when the Church pulled the government's strings should be in the past."

"Here, here," Megan said, raising her glass.

"Another thing," Stefan said, "I don't think the church should influence the government to restrict women's rights. I don't think a Catholic woman should have an abortion, but I don't think my church has the right to tell non-Catholics what they can do with their bodies."

"Well, well, well," Gina said. "You get a passing grade so far."

"I mean, it's her body and her soul. Why should the government make her decisions for her?" Stefan cast his eyes first on Gina, who smiled, and then at Megan, who set down her glass and stared at her half-empty plate.

"It sounds like you're pro-choice," Carter said. "But are you pro-abortion?"

Stefan frowned. "I don't know what you mean."

Carter held his glass in one hand and his fork in the other. He let the fork tap quietly on his plate. "You said you don't think a Catholic woman should have an abortion, but do you think abortion is wrong?"

"I think," Stefan said, "that a woman can have very good reasons for making such a decision."

Carter let the tapping become more audible. "You're avoiding the question. Do you think abortion is wrong?" He looked up at the ceiling, collecting his words, and then he let out: "Do you think abortion is murder?"

Stefan shook his head. "I would not use the word murder."

Gina stood up and started gathering plates. She slid Carter's out from under his fork.

"Good choice," she said to Stefan. "Murder is a nasty word. It's also an irrelevant question. The question about whether or not abortion is murder is something people on the far right ask to distract us from what the real issue is." She turned back to Carter. "Like Stefan said, the real issue is a woman's right to govern her own body. As long as the baby is inside of her, it's not about the baby – it's about whether or not a woman wants to share her body.

The baby might be a life; it might be a tumor. It doesn't matter. She has the right to take it out."

At the word "tumor," Megan slowly slid back her chair. Gina cast her friend a worried look, but said nothing. She walked the four plates over to the sink.

"Okay, so what about the partial-birth abortion issue," Carter said. "What about a procedure that kills a baby that might otherwise survive?"

Megan traced the rim of her lips with the corner of her napkin. She held the white fabric over her mouth, obscuring much of her blood-drained face.

"The woman's life is the first consideration," Stefan said.

"Another good answer," said Gina as she reseated herself at the table. "You're acing this quiz."

"So the procedure is okay only if the woman's life is in danger?" Carter asked.

"Yes," said Stefan. "That is what I believe. An effort does have to be made to save the child, if the effort can be made without endangering the mother's life."

Gina poured more wine for Stefan and herself. When Gina brought the bottle toward Megan, Megan blocked her glass. An upward glance found Gina frowning. Megan lowered the napkin from her lips and smiled.

Carter finished his wine in three swallows. He rose to refill his glass.

"I believe in doing everything that can be done for the sake of the child," Gina said, "but I don't like putting limits on the law. If you only allow it to happen when there's a threat to the mother's life, suddenly doctors have this enormous power. What if the risk isn't life-or-death – what if it's a debilitating injury? Or even minor injury, or emotional damage? Are these things *okay*? Can a doctor choose to damage one person for the sake of another person, or a potential person, or whatever? It'd be like the government requiring people to donate blood or bone marrow or organs or whatever just because it could save someone's life. The woman should have the power to make that call, not the doctor."

"It is a very grey area," Stefan said.

Carter settled back into his chair. "So you're saying it's okay to kill the baby even if it's not a life-or-death situation?" He placed a hand on his wife's shoulder.

Gina looked flustered. "Again, that's missing the point. It isn't *about* the baby. I don't like to think about killing the baby. It's not *okay*. It's tragic and awful. But the woman has to have the *right*. Megan, are you okay?"

Megan had stood up from the table. The napkin was back at her mouth. She pressed it against her quivering lips and shook her head from side to side. "Excuse me," she whispered. She dashed for the bathroom, where she stayed for over an hour. When she emerged, Carter negotiated their swift exit with apologies and gratitude.

Once he and Megan found seats on the subway train, Carter reported what he had said to Gina.

"Megan was feeling sort of queasy earlier," he'd explained. "She says it's a twenty-four hour thing, but I'm not so sure. She hasn't been herself. I thought that drinking the way she did might have been pushing it."

Megan imagined the way he had said it: the confidential hush of his voice, the warmth in his eyes. Stefan, Gina, gin, wine, investment banking, and abortion became a nonsensical din in the back of Megan's thoughts. The din faded while Megan looked forward to the solitude of a private room.

Carter had given up the living room sofa and reclaimed the master bedroom, so Caitlin's abandoned bedroom had become Megan's new refuge. Leaving the din of the evening behind, Megan entered Caitlin's room, closed the door behind her, and sat down on the edge of the bed. In the pale yellow streetlight, she strained to make out the shapes of her fingers. Without thinking, she placed her fingertips on her neck. Her pulse slowed to soothing regularity.

Megan got up from her daughter's bed and started walking around the room. She looked at the row of dolls on the top shelf of Caitlin's bookcase. The dolls on display were the porcelain treasures Megan's mother had bought for her granddaughter. Susan Penser could rail against the injustice of Barbie's physical dimensions, but her feminism had nothing to say against the traditional practice of showering young girls with baby dolls.

"Darling," Susan said, "just because we're liberated doesn't mean we can't like pretty things anymore. Dolls are pretty things. My granddaughter should have pretty things."

Caitlin had never taken to these expensive porcelain dolls. Caitlin's favorite doll was one she had found when Megan had brought her on an errand to the drugstore, promising some sour candies as a treat. It was a cheap piece of plastic with dull eyes and coarse hair. Caitlin called it "Little Katy." She had recently learned to spell her own name, and she had asked if she could spell her dolly's name a different way. Megan had suggested the K. Little Katy was always at Caitlin's side. Little Katy shared Caitlin's hospital bed whenever Caitlin was lucid enough to ask for her.

When Megan was a girl, she called her own favorite doll Della. Della was a gift from Maria, Megan's nanny. One summer afternoon, Susan had come into seven-year-old Megan's bedroom and found her daughter hosting a tea party where Della was the principal invitee.

"Why didn't you invite Shirley to your party?" Susan had asked.

"Because Shirley isn't very nice," young Megan had answered.

"But she is nice. She's *very* nice. Don't you know that Shirley was your grandmother's dolly when she was a girl your age?"

Megan did know. The exquisite alabaster doll with the red hair had been in her bedroom as long as she could remember. When her glass eyes caught the sunlight at certain angles, she looked alive. Megan didn't like Shirley at all, even though she knew she was *supposed* to like her the best. "I know all about Shirley," Megan told her mother. "Shirley doesn't like Della."

"Maybe Shirley doesn't like Della because you play with Della all the time and never include Shirley. Maybe if you let Della and Shirley play together, they'd all get along." Susan's voice was conciliating but forceful.

Megan rose from her miniature tea set and walked to the shelf where Shirley slept. Alabaster in hand, Megan made a place for Shirley next to Della at the cardboard table and poured the new guest some invisible tea. She flashed a toothy grin at her mother.

"That's very nice, Meg," Susan said. "I think Shirley and Della are going to get along famously. Finish your tea soon, though, because Maria almost has lunch ready."

Susan was leaving for a week-long business trip the next day, so she gave Maria the afternoon off and spent the time with her daughter. Megan didn't go back to her bedroom to clean up the tea party. She and her mother went to the movies and then out for pizza. After her parents' divorce, Megan often asked to share her mother's king-sized bed, and Susan usually agreed. That night Susan showed no reluctance.

They awoke to the sound of shattering glass. "Damn it!" a man shouted.

Half-awake and already afraid, Megan said, "Mommy, what is it?"

"Stay there," said Susan, getting out of bed. She hurried to the bedroom door, closed it, and locked it. Rubbing her fingers together, Susan searched the room, found a chair she could barely lift, and propped it up against the door. "Be quiet, sweetie. Somebody's in the house. Be very quiet. Mommy's going to call the police, and everything will be all right."

Megan counted two distinct male voices, then three. Her mother was quiet and efficient on the phone, explaining their situation and giving their address. The radiance of her mother's strength kept Megan from screaming as the voices came closer. Susan hung up the phone and tiptoed toward her closet. She took out a long black umbrella with a metal tip, and then she fetched a pair of scissors from the bathroom. They glinted in the moonlight.

Susan stood near the door, ready to act. Megan cowered on the bed, listening. More glass broke, and men's voices cursed. Something heavy and wooden made a scraping noise in the room below them. Something toppled and smashed. Megan became lost in the wide dilation of time within terror. The intruders were not men but monsters, marauding vampires not looking for treasure but for the blood of a little girl. Alone on a bed as big and empty as a desert plain, Megan trembled.

"Everything's going to be all right. We just have to wait," Susan whispered. No part of Susan's body had budged from her post at the door. If the door opened, she would ram the umbrella through the vampire's heart, right up to the wooden hilt. She would sink the scissors into one eye and then another, crippling them, stopping them. Megan felt her mother's invincibility as keenly as she felt her own vulnerability.

Sounds of hushed cursing and objects breaking marked the men's progress through the house. The digital clock at the far edge of the bed counted out ten minutes of rustling and rumbling. Fifteen.

The central staircase creaked. Footsteps came up, two feet stomping, four, six. Megan clutched the sheet in her hands. She didn't usually sleep with her dolls, but she thought of the abandoned tea party and longed for Della.

There were voices outside the bedroom door, cautious, preparing.

The doorknob turned, rattled.

"It's locked," one of the men said. "Ms. Penser?"

Susan stayed in place, weapons ready.

"Ms. Penser, all we're after is your jewelry. We're not going to hurt you if you do what we want. Open the door."

"Other room's empty," said a second low voice.

The first voice resumed, "Do you have your little girl in there with you, Ms. Penser?" Megan made a whiny noise. "All your jewels and money aren't worth getting *her* hurt over, are they?"

The rattling of the doorknob became more insistent. A third voice spoke: "Open the door, bitch, or we'll break it down and you *will* get hurt. We'll hurt you bad."

Susan's voice was smooth and powerful: "Open the door, asshole, and I'll splatter your brains all over the fucking wall. I've got a gun, and I know how to use it." She shifted her feet, holding her scissors just a little bit higher. "And the police will be here any second. You'd better get the hell out of here while you still can."

The third voice answered her: "The phone downstairs is off the hook. You couldn't use it to call anybody. It's the first thing we did when we got here. You don't have a gun. You don't have a choice. If you don't open the door right now, I'm going to break it—"

"And I'm going to enjoy seeing your face right before I blow it off. Don't think I'll do it? Try me. Oh, and by the way, did you happen to notice that this house has *two* phone lines? Did any of you three geniuses happen to notice that?"

Low murmuring, fast, confused. Megan started to ease her grip on the twisted sheet. Her mother was winning.

"What's that I hear?" Susan said. "You hear that boys? That's the sound of life in prison." Megan stopped breathing and listened. She heard the sirens. They were close. They were turning into the long driveway.

"Oh, fuck, Ray, oh, fuck!"

"They'll be at the front door any second," Susan said. "Run while you still can."

Susan did not exaggerate: Megan heard the police at the front door. The three burglars murmured to one another for a few seconds before they started stomping in the direction of Megan's bedroom.

Another masculine voice called up from the foyer, "Are you okay, Mrs. Penser?"

"UPSTAIRS!!! THEY'RE UPSTAIRS!!!"

While the police searched the house, Susan sat with Megan on the giant bed, rocking her terrified child in her arms. The police found nothing but the ladder the burglars had set up at Megan's window as an escape route. The burglars were not vampires. They were merely human, but they had still managed to get away. Susan was furious, but all the police could do was apologize.

Susan cancelled her business trip and spent the next week at home. One morning, Megan awoke in her mother's bed and found herself alone. She was scared to get up at first, but eventually she did, and she walked to the top of the main stairs. Her mother's voice was saying, "The police have fingerprints. They have names. That's all you need. Find them. I don't want a messy situation. I don't want these men to affect another day of my daughter's life." That was all Megan heard. To the best of her knowledge, the burglars were never captured, but adult Megan had suspicions. Susan didn't purchase a gun until Megan was grown and out of the house, but she had other means of effecting her will.

After the police left that night, Susan brought young Megan into her own bedroom so they could look at what the burglars had done. The damage was less here than it was downstairs, but it was still significant. The tea party had been trampled. Della had survived; Shirley's alabaster face was a broken footprint.

Alone in her daughter's dim bedroom, adult Megan took a porcelain doll down from the high shelf. It wasn't Little Katy; it wasn't important enough to go to the hospital. It didn't even have a name. Megan brought it back to her daughter's bed and sat down with it in her lap. Tonight with Gina, that night with her mother. Megan searched her neck with calm fingers and again found a steady pulse. Then she started combing the nameless doll's corn-silk hair.

The Descent of Carter Anderson, Continued

When the painful aftermath of the car-lifting excursion subsided, Carter left Megan's bedroom for the one he shared with Brian. He found his roommate twisted and frozen in bed. Brian didn't raise a hand in greeting; he didn't speak. Carter didn't stay to nurse his roommate back to mobility. After a nap, he went back to Megan's bedroom and indulged new freedoms. Their second and third nights lacked the singular excellence of their first, but Megan seemed pleased nonetheless.

Routines returned with classes on Monday. The next time Carter saw him, Brian was sitting at his desk, slumped over a book in his usual way. Carter decided to let some time pass before bringing up Dr. Fincher again. On Thursday, Carter came home and found Brian sitting listlessly on the edge of his bed.

After Carter closed and locked the door behind him, Brian said, "So how's Megan?"

"She's doing great. She was smiling in her sleep when I left."

"You two are...progressing, I assume?"

Carter sat next to Brian. "What the hell does 'progressing' mean?" he asked. "Oh, wait. I get it. You want your roommate to kiss and tell."

Brian stood up and walked over to his desk. "Don't say anything if you don't want to. I'm just trying to start a conversation."

Carter traded his seat on the bed for a corner of Brian's desk. "It was *magnificent*," Carter said. "This girl is...well, she's kinetic. Forceful. I'd say I'm falling in love."

"Is that what you'd call it?" Brian asked.

"Hey, what's with you? You seem kind of down." Carter studied Brian's sour face and crumpled posture. "Jealous? I don't think she's your type." He laughed. "Her *roommate* on the other hand..."

Jess didn't have half the looks Megan did, but she was a sweet girl, kind of mousy – kind of Brian. "Maybe Megan and I could fix you up. Stranger things have happened."

"Yeah, stranger things," Brian said. "Don't do me any favors. I'm okay. Maybe I'm still just feeling drained."

Brian's allusion to his exhaustion was a first strike at the topic that Carter had been itching to broach.

"I know what you mean," Carter said. "I went running for the first time this morning and could hardly finish my usual route. I've never been so sore in my life. But it was worth it, wasn't it?"

Brian sighed. "I guess so, yeah."

"What do you mean you *guess so*? Hell, yes, it was worth it. We spend all this time talking about philosophy, about the meaning of existence and the limits of experience. All anybody does around here is talk. You and I, we *did* something."

"You're right, Carter. We did something. It's just that..."

Brian's chin sunk so low on his chest that Carter thought the boy's neck might snap. Carter set a hand on his roommate's shoulder. "Cheer up, partner," he said. "If you're not satisfied, we can always do something else."

Brian lifted his head slowly and met Carter's gaze. "What'd you have in mind?"

"Well, we'll have to consult a certain doctor I know. He's got a lot of prescriptions to cure the blues."

Brian looked away. "Not tonight, Carter. I'm tired."

Carter left the room and stayed with Megan until Saturday. On Saturday afternoon, Megan took a train to New York to meet her mother, who had come north on business. As Carter walked home, he tried to figure out how to work the idea of a second experiment into conversation.

"So, Brian, I was thinking about what you said about being unsatisfied with our little experiment. Do you still want to do something?"

"Do something?" Brian asked. "I've already *done* something."

Carter's eyes narrowed. "What did you *do*?"

"I made a pencil float. And a paperback novel. And our little TV." Brian stood up. He was smiling. "It's nothing for you to get upset about. It was...an exercise."

Carter's hands balled into fists. He wanted to smash Brian's smile in a spray of blood and teeth.

Brian hesitated. "Carter, you have to understand," he said. "I was so miserable after what we did, and you recovered so fast, and then you weren't around, I just...I just had to see if I could do something. On my own."

Carter shrugged and tried to look bored.

"Don't be that way," Brian said. "It was just practice. What I did was easier than what we did. Some chanting, some other stuff – it didn't take half as much time, and it wasn't nearly as tiring. We could do something else right now if you wanted to." He picked up Widener Library's copy – their copy – of *The Alchemy of Will* and held it up. "Just choose what you want to do."

Carter straddled his desk chair backward. He watched Brian wave the red book at him while his memory leafed through pages and found what it wanted. "You tried levitation. It involved some chanting and – was it tears?" He pondered. "Something about a symbolic link between sadness and gravity. Am I right?"

"Yes, Carter, you're right."

"You're a sad case, Brian, a really sad case. You should let me fix you up with Megan's roommate."

"Whatever you say."

Carter smiled. "That's what I wanted to hear." He paused, feigning reflection. "There's a party tonight at one of the upper-class houses," he said. "Dunster, maybe. I wasn't planning on going, but I think we should go and bring a little party favor. It's time to see if these little exercises could add up to real power. Power over other people."

"You mean mind control," Brian said.

"What else would I be talking about?"

Instead of splitting the scabs from the first ritual, they slashed new openings in their arms. They focused on a flask of their mingled blood and repeated the required text until eleven o'clock, when the party would just be starting.

"How do we know if it worked?" Brian asked.

Carter tucked the flask into his pocket. "We don't know anything," he said. "We're just taking a chance. If our little flask of liquid willpower doesn't do the trick, maybe the blood loss will mean we get drunk faster. Either way, we win."

Carter and Brian walked side by side to Dunster House, a dorm by the river. Somewhere inside, a junior was celebrating his twenty-first birthday. The loud music and stream of people guided them to the room. Crashing wouldn't be a problem: the crowd was thick, probably twice as large as the hosts had anticipated. They fought through the throng of other freshmen and found the inner sanctum. By the red light of a tinted lamp, Carter spied the table stacked high with plastic cups, liquor bottles, and mixers. The bottle of cranberry juice looked almost black in the red light. Carter pointed it out to Brian as they fetched beers. Huddling near the booze, they scanned the undulating crowd. Outdated dance music made the walls vibrate.

"What sort of person are we looking for?" Brian shouted.

"Whoever strikes our fancy and happens into range," Carter said.

The first prospect who tried to maneuver around them to access the vodka was a fellow freshman who rowed for an intramural crew team. He squeezed between Brian and Carter to get at the plastic cups, and Brian made eye contact with Carter behind the rower's broad back. Carter shook his head no.

A stream of solo men and accompanied women pushed by them, gradually widening the space between them and the bar. Brian opened his second beer; Carter finished his third. Brian asked if they should give up, and Carter said no.

"Excuse me, but can I help you with a drink?" Carter said when, at last, his eyes captured the attention of an unattached young woman.

"Okay," she said. She had shoulder-length black hair that curled under at the ends and Asian facial features, although she was definitely some sort of American blend. "Not too strong," she shouted, as Carter poured.

He set down the plastic cup. While one hand moved toward the cranberry juice, the other gestured across the room. "Do you think that guy in the blue baseball cap is finally going to put on some decent music?" he asked.

The girl looked away to search the crowd, and Carter brought out the flask. He poured some of the blood into the cup and hid it with juice. The concoction was finished by the time the girl looked back. "I don't see who you're talking about," she said.

Carter pretended to search. "I lost him. So much for hoping. My name's Carter by the way." He handed her the drink.

"I'm Julie." She sipped. "Ugh, this tastes awful!"

Carter looked hurt. "A bartender is only as good as his ingredients!"

She shrugged and took a larger gulp. "Beggars can't be choosers, right? Thanks, Arthur!" She started to edge back into the crowd.

"Wait a minute," he called out. "Do you want – would you like to dance with me?"

Julie's eyes mapped Carter's contours. "I'm not a very good dancer," she said.

"Neither am I," Carter said. With a nod to Brian, who nodded back, Carter took Julie by the hand and led her into the sweaty mass. They danced and sipped. Carter observed the liquid level in the plastic cup drop by two thirds. A song ended, and a slower one began. Carter tried to put his arm around her for a slow dance. She dodged it, saying she'd sit this one out.

With knitted brows, Carter crossed back to Brian, who had not moved. "What now?" he asked.

"She's over there by the wall," Brian said. "She's finishing her drink."

"Again I ask – what now?"

"Hey, I thought you were in charge," Brian said.

Carter shook his head. "Obviously not. At least not yet. What do you think?"

Brian looked at his shoes, considering. "I think we wait," he said, "and see what happens. I told you I hate parties, didn't I?"

Carter fetched himself another beer and led Brian to an inconspicuous corner. He gestured toward Julie. She had two other girls with her now, and they were leaning toward each other in a small circle. Carter whispered that they were probably talking about him, and he nodded when Julie searched the crowd and pointed him out.

An hour passed. Carter lost count of the beers, and Brian traded a half-empty beer for an untainted vodka-cranberry. They changed positions three times while maintaining surveillance. Carter's attention was fading, but an elbow to the ribs snapped him into focus. "Look," Brian said.

Julie and her two friends were walking toward the exit. "Now or never," Carter said, and he made his way toward her. Brian followed at a respectable distance. "Hey," Carter said, "you mind if I walk you home?"

Julie looked unwell. Her face was drawn, and her eyes were vacant. She said nothing. One of her friends answered for her, "No thanks, we'll take care of her."

Carter looked into Julie's eyes, thinking of cartoon mesmerism. "Let me walk you home."

Life sparked in her face. She turned to her friends and said, "It's okay, Arthur will walk me home."

The friend that had answered for her looked uncertain. "You sure? You don't look too good."

"She's sure," Carter said.

"I'm sure," Julie said. She looked reanimated, almost sober. Her friends didn't argue. They all exited the building together with Brian trailing behind. Once her friends had split off in another direction, Brian caught up to Carter and Julie. They guided Julie toward their room.

"Stop for a second," Brian said. Julie stopped instantly, and Carter's speed diminished. "Julie, let's jump up and down together," Brian said. In unison, Brian and Julie jumped up and down. Carter stopped walking. "I think it's working," Brian declared.

Carter glanced left and right at the other students stumbling home. "Great. No more public demonstrations, okay?"

They reached the room, and Brian bolted the door behind them. When Carter and Brian released Julie's arms, she stood still, smiling, waiting. "We've got her," Brian said. "Now what are we going to do with her?"

"I don't know," Carter said. "Julie, is there anything you want to do?"

Julie's face started to resume the drawn, drunken look it had had at the party.

"I guess she's not too good with questions," Brian said.

"I guess not." Carter's eyes ran over her body. She was thin, sort of sporty – a tennis player. She wore a red sleeveless top with narrow shoulder straps that, slightly askew, showed the bra straps beneath them. Her jeans hugged her hips and backside. Her eyes were dead.

"Okay," Brian said, "we use the imperative. Let's experiment. Julie, say your ABCs."

She said them; her voice defaulted to a childish rendering of the song.

"Julie," Carter said, "take off your top." Her fingers went to where the red top overlapped her jeans and started lifting. "Wait!" Carter said, and her arms froze, leaving her bare stomach exposed. "She's like a puppet," Carter said. "Tug, tug." He laughed.

Brian looked down at the floorboards and then back up at Carter. "What are you doing?"

"Like you said, I'm experimenting. Julie, do it slowly. Take off your top slowly." As red fabric slipped over translucent, skin-colored lace, Carter's pulse quickened.

Brian kept his eyes on Carter. "I didn't think we'd... isn't this...what if she remembers this tomorrow?"

"Then she remembers it," Carter said, walking up to her, grazing her bare shoulder with a fingertip. "What's she going to do? I'll stop as soon as she says no." Carter thought for a moment. "Julie, please say yes."

"Yes."

"You see?" He walked behind her, observing the place where her bra fastened between her shoulder blades. He adjusted the erection that was pushing against his pants.

"It's wrong," Brian said.

"Julie, take off your jeans. Do it slowly." He stayed behind her, his eyes following the denim sliding over supple thighs. Her panties didn't match her bra – they were generic cotton.

"Carter," Brian said, "I won't do it." He started pacing, moving his hands in the air as if searching for an argument. He turned to Julie, who stood like a mannequin, arms dangling at her sides. "Julie, tell me if you're okay with this."

Her eyes were dead.

"Julie," Carter said, "smile and tell him you're okay with this." She smiled. "I'm okay with this."

"I won't do it," Brian repeated.

"Then don't," Carter said. "Watch if you want to. Hide your head under a pillow if you have to." Carter took off his shirt.

"Julie," Brian said, "put your pants back on."

She reached down to follow his order. "Don't do that," Carter said, and she halted. "Don't listen to Brian anymore. I'm the one that you want." He pulled her toward him, pressing her bare back against his chest. As his hands moved over her shoulders, over the bra straps, down to her covered nipples, his breathing quickened.

"Julie, tell me it's okay to take off your underwear. Tell me you want me to."

"I want you to take off my underwear," she said.

Carter unfastened her bra. He stayed behind her, cupping her breasts in his hands, massaging her nipples with his thumbs. He kissed her shoulder and looked up at Brian.

Brian took a few steps backward, found his desk chair, pulled it closer to the center of the room, and sat facing them, his eyes wide.

Carter slid Julie's panties to the floor, and she stepped out of them. He unbuttoned his pants and let them join the pile of Julie's clothes. His erection was straining against the elastic of his boxer shorts. Pressed up against her, he circled to Julie's front. "Do you want me to fuck you?" he whispered in her ear.

She stood naked and still, saying nothing.

Brian sat motionless in his chair. Carter locked eyes with him, and then reached down between Julie's legs. He felt the soft hair, the skin – nothing to indicate arousal. He let a finger pry between the folds of skin, searched, tickled, got no response. "Want me," he said to her.

Julie did not respond.

Carter severed his gaze from Brian's. "I…I left the condoms in Megan's room," he said. "We don't want to take any chances." His mouth felt dry, but he made himself swallow. "I guess we'll have to do something else." He snickered. "Julie, how'd you feel about blowing me?"

No response.

"Let's see how much she *can* respond," Carter said. "We're supposed to be experimenting, right? Julie, do you know how to give a blowjob?"

"Yes," she said.

"Comprehension – check," Carter said. "Julie," he continued, "I'm going to sit in that chair, and you are going to blow me."

"Yes," she said.

He walked over to his own desk chair, which was directly opposite Brian's, and rotated it toward the center of the room. Julie stayed in position, waiting. He glanced right and left, looked at Brian, shrugged, slid his boxers to his ankles, and kicked them to the pile of clothes. His erection did not falter.

"Come here," Carter said, making contact with Julie's dead eyes. She walked to him. "Get on your knees." She complied. "Now do it."

Her lips encircled his penis and slid down. The bobbing of her head was mechanical, and the tension in her tongue and lips fluctuated with regularity. Carter closed his eyes and let his head drift back.

Brian shifted in his chair. Carter straightened his neck and opened his eyes. He looked at the clock. Julie had been working for several minutes, and he wasn't ready to come. Carter looked at Brian. Brian's eyes were fixed on Carter and the naked girl bobbing between Carter's legs.

"Enjoying the show?" Carter asked.

Brian did not respond.

Carter closed his eyes and tilted his head back again. It wasn't working. He was never going to come. His imagination summoned pictures of other experiences. Julie's lips became Megan's, and Carter became aware of the cold air against his chest. Even with his eyes closed, he could sense Brian's stare. Carter's imagination searched for other images, and he found a memory of the first girl who had gone down on him. He was a high school freshman, and she was a senior. Her lips had been thick and wet, and the movements of her mouth had been natural, pulsing with spasms of want. Carter stayed with the memory of her until it was over.

Julie coughed and spat in Carter's pubic hair. Her posture folded, and she rested her head against Carter's inner thigh. Brian's gaze lingered on them. Carter folded his arms across his chest, hiding gooseflesh. "Okay, Julie, nice work," he said. "Thank you." She didn't move. "You can stand up now." Her head stayed on his thigh, her chin drooping, her face empty. "Stand up," he said. She rose to her feet. "Bring me my clothes."

She did as he asked. While Carter was getting dressed, Brian got up from his chair and started rummaging through his desk.

"What are you doing?" Carter asked, as he zipped up his jeans.

"You'll see," Brian said. His voice was faint.

Carter buttoned his shirt and stared at Julie's breasts. He hadn't noticed before how small they were.

"Julie, get dressed," Brian said. He didn't turn to face her as he spoke; he just kept rummaging.

Julie did nothing. Carter remembered why. "Julie, it's okay to listen to Brian again. Put on your clothes."

She got dressed.

Carter watched as Brian took out the pocketknife they had used in the rituals. He opened the blade and held it out to Julie. "Hold this by the handle," he told her. She took the knife. "Now listen carefully. I want you to make a little cut on your left arm. Shallow, like a scratch. Will you do that?"

"Yes," she said.

"Then do it." Julie made a cut on her arm, and Brian leaned over to look at it. He dabbed the blood with his index finger and held up the red tip for Carter to see. "That's good, Julie, thank you," he said. "If I wanted you to – if I told you to – would you make a bigger cut?"

"Yes," Julie said.

"Would you slit your wrists if I told you to?" Brian asked.

"Yes," she said. Anticipating, she held the knife over a vein.

"Brian, no," Carter said. In the aftermath of orgasm, he felt sluggish.

Brian looked at Carter and shook his head. "Of course I wouldn't," he said. "I just wanted to see the extent of our control. I didn't have to *do* anything to test that. You already *did* more than enough." He turned back to Julie. "Thank you, Julie. Close the knife and hand it to me." She obeyed.

Once Julie had stepped away from him, Brian reopened the knife. He grabbed a tissue from the box on his desk and wiped the residue of Julie's blood from the blade. He glanced from the red splotch on the tissue to the scratch on Julie's arm, which had already clotted. He looked at the long sleeve that hid his own bandaged arm.

Carter's face burned. "Brian, why the hell did you—"

"Just making a point," Brian said, "just making a point." He looked at Julie while he spoke. "Julie, you're a good person," he said. "Feel good about yourself." Julie smiled. "If I tell you to forget all about tonight, will you?" he asked.

She did not respond.

Brian looked at Carter before glancing down at the knife. He then looked back at Julie. "Well, it's worth a shot." His voice became softer. "Julie, keep feeling good about yourself. In the morning, you won't remember what happened after you left the party. You'll think you must have been pretty drunk, but you won't feel bad about it." He stopped, thinking. "When I tell you to go, walk to the bathroom down the hall, and wash your face." He took a deep breath. "Wash your face and then walk directly home. When you get home, go directly to bed. Wake up in the morning after you've had a good night's sleep. When you wake up, feel good about yourself. Don't remember tonight. If you do remember, don't feel bad about it. Do you understand what I'm telling you?"

"Yes."

"Will you do what I say?"

"Yes."

"Now go." Julie left.

Seconds later, Carter heard the faint sound of running water from the bathroom down the hall. He looked at Brian. Brian didn't look back.

Intersection

Twenty-five weeks remained. Megan woke up feeling good. The nausea had abated, and she'd gotten through the night without having to pee every hour. Carter cooked breakfast, and she ate almost as much as he did. She nearly kissed Carter goodbye as he went out the door, but she caught herself in time. Megan took a deep breath and surveyed Carter-free space. Her own territory had expanded. When Carter hadn't been looking, she'd escaped Caitlin's room and had colonized the living room.

She wasn't working at the Penser Foundation anymore. She hadn't told her mother about quitting, but she was confident that Susan already knew. Sooner or later, there would be a confrontation, a collision. But not now. Now Megan felt safe. Daytime television would protect her. Talk shows, game shows, soap operas. An entire universe spun with frenzied activity during the hours when most people had to work.

During a foray into the master bedroom for a pair of socks, she glimpsed herself in the full-length mirror. The master bedroom was *his* territory, and she thought at first that he had somehow arranged this nasty little surprise. No – he had no part in the puffiness of her face and the flatness of her hair. Well, no *direct* part, anyway. She remembered this phase from the first pregnancy, this transition of bodily woes. She lifted up her T-shirt. Yes, her belly had swelled far beyond her usual waistline. Even her baggiest non-maternity clothes were tight now.

Megan took a deep breath and journeyed to the sofa. Her fingers settled on the remote control. They tickled the ON button. The morning was young. The best shows would air in the afternoon. ON, yes or no? She felt jittery. The good feelings of first waking had vanished, but their energy hadn't dissipated. She would do something. Yes, she would.

She was marching down the long flights of stairs before she even realized that she'd decided to go out. Somewhere around the third floor she stopped, trying to figure out what she was doing while she caught her breath. She saw the usual "Out of Order" sign on the elevator doors. The elevator hadn't been working for months. The lack of order probably violated a city ordinance, but no one ever did anything about it. The stairs would soon be much harder to take, but now, at least, she could handle them. The downward trek continued as the idea of shopping, which her mother considered to be an acceptable feminine indulgence, occurred to her. A warm summer breeze was pressing on her back before she noticed the direction she was taking. Her feet were not moving toward her favorite shops. They were leading her to the hospital.

Why now? Why was she going to visit Caitlin now that she was presenting symptoms a nurse might recognize at a distance? As she shuffled down another block, the answer came to her: she had to go now because the symptoms would only get worse. Her visits had become more infrequent, but she'd still been making them. Soon she'd take a long, long vacation from such duties. Megan made a mental note to tell Carter that he'd have to come up with an explanation for her absence at the hospital. Would they believe that a therapist had suggested she take the time away? Maybe. The hospital staff constantly warned about parental instability during the awesome stress of a child's long – and terminal – illness. They'd probably seen something like this before. They'd probably be *understanding*. Wasn't that their job? Didn't she deserve a little fucking sympathy?

Megan stopped at the corner to catch her breath and ponder her options. She could cut over a block for the subway, or she could hail a cab. Her arm rose. She got into the yellow vehicle and zoomed to the hospital. As she pulled open one of the glass front doors, she wondered if she had paid the cabbie. She must have; he'd left. The lobby was almost as congested as it would be on the weekend. Megan took the elevator to the pediatric oncology unit. Shouldn't the children's cancer ward have a nicer name, or at least a name that had a little bit of pizzazz? The suckling's sarcoma citadel! Infected infantry! Megan snickered aloud as she ascended, and her aged elevator companion seemed discomfited. Hey babe, once you're an old pro at this sort of thing, the rules of decorum no longer apply. Only rookies get bent out of shape by laughter in the antiseptic hallways of death.

Had Megan *really* stuck out her middle finger at the septuagenarian rookie as she'd gotten out of the elevator? Indeed she had! With uncharacteristic springiness of step, Megan sauntered past the nurses' station. They'd recognize her and sign her in without any interruption or ceremony. Her face said, "Don't talk to me." Keep your appropriate professional distance. Be *understanding*. And don't notice the fact that my body has already started to balloon with my skeletal daughter's *cure*.

Caitlin was awake in her bed, watching cartoons. "Hey, there, kiddo," Megan said.

"Hi, Mommy," Caitlin said. Her weary eyes moved from the screen to Megan and back to the screen again. The room's other occupants faded into the background, away from her perception. Megan was alone with her dying daughter. But was it really still fair to think of her as a "dying daughter?" Wasn't there going to be a dramatic rescue in about twenty-five weeks?

Caitlin said something about wanting to go home. Megan had a speech prepared for that one: Mommy wants you home, but Mommy wants you to get better even more. The speech had once comforted both of them. After the time Caitlin had replied, "I'm not going to get better," the speech had lost all efficacy for Megan. It probably meant nothing to Caitlin, too. The words of comfort were just filler, something to pass the time Megan spent with someone who sometimes seemed less like a patient and more like the disease itself.

The visit went downhill. The words "I miss you, Mommy" rang out like an air raid siren. Megan's brain manufactured machine-gun fire as she searched for a response. Her head throbbed as she said that Mommy hadn't been feeling so good. "Will you get better?" No, sweetie. Mommy's going to go completely insane. She's going to have not one but *two* phantom children, aching like severed limbs.

"You know Mommy loves you, right, kiddo? You know that even when I'm not here I think about you all the time and hope that you'll feel all better soon and come home to me." A lie. "I'll get better," another lie, "but I might not be around while I'm resting." Resting. Himalayan lie! She imagined how restful it would be: breathe, breathe, now push! Throb, throb, rat-a-tat-tat-tat-tat-tat-tat...

Come off it, bitch. You only wish you were going insane. It'd be a nice excuse, wouldn't it?

Incoming! Neeeeeeeeeeeeeeeeeoooooooooooooooooooooooooom, BAM!

Megan's heels clicked against the tiled hall floor as she hurried away from her daughter's room. It wasn't the first time she had fled that room with a smile and a kiss just before her face shattered into sobs. With chest heaving and vision blurred, she marched back past the nurses. Megan didn't hide her face. This wasn't a *comfort me* face. This was a *back the fuck off* face.

Out in the morning air again with oblivious city sounds all around her, Megan lost whatever thread she'd been following. Had she really just come out from a visit with her daughter? Had she gone in and turned around again, mistaking a daydream for an obligation fulfilled? Her puffy cheeks felt a bit soggy; that was evidence enough. She could go home. She could go…shopping.

The elastic on her shorts wouldn't suffice for long, but she couldn't buy maternity clothes. Carter said that buying maternity clothes would be like publishing a record of the pregnancy. He reminded her that many of the outfits from six years ago still hung crumpled in their overflow closet.

No, not clothes. Something else.

Something for *him*.

Later that afternoon, Megan sat on the sofa, getting her TV fix, and imagined what Carter's reaction to her purchase might be. He would squirm, and it would be lovely. The television was transmitting a shock-jock talk show about mothers who steal their daughters' boyfriends. Hey, I've got a topic for you – how about mothers who murder one child to save another? Drummer, hit the rim shot! Maybe it would make a better Lifetime Original Movie than a talk show topic. Maybe they could get Meryl Streep to play Megan. A woman with a choice. Ha-ha.

The afternoon passed, and sunset brought Carter through the front door. He set down the bag that held the laptop computer she'd bought him for Christmas two years ago, scratched his head and his expanding ass, and went to the bathroom for a piss. They had both been suffering from frequent urination: pregnancy her excuse, beer his.

"Hello, honey, how was your day?" Carter said. Megan imagined an alien bursting out of his stomach.

"Great, dear, how was yours?" She turned down the volume on the television but kept her eyes stuck to it.

Carter walked around the sofa and sat in his easy chair. "Starting with the sarcasm a little bit early tonight, are we?"

"I thought it started when you walked in the door. Since when do you call me *honey*?" Gotcha, you fat bastard.

Carter shook his head. "Look, I know this is hard for you. Don't I say that just about every day? I'm just trying to maintain an atmosphere of civility around here. What do you want me to say? I really do want to know how your day was."

Carter was a scorpion, or maybe a spider. "I went to see our daughter today," Megan said.

He scratched the back of his head again. "God, I haven't been in almost a week. How was she?"

"Awake and talking. Wondering where the hell we are. Dealing as well as an almost seven-year-old girl can with the prospect of her own demise. Pretty lucid, I guess. The doc says the treatment is showing some positive results." Yes, she had spoken to a doctor. She remembered that. Sort of. "Prognosis is the same, of course."

"Maybe I'll go tomorrow," Carter said.

Megan nodded. "Yeah, maybe you will. You need to start going more often, you know, since I won't be able to go anymore. Have you noticed? I'm showing."

"I hadn't really noticed," Carter said, "but I guess the time is right. How do you feel?"

"Let's skip that question."

"Okay," Carter said, leaning back, "next question then. What else did you do today?"

"I went *shopping*," she said.

"Really?" Carter said. "What did you buy?"

She got up from the sofa and went after the colorful bag she had deposited on Caitlin's bed. She walked back to Carter and suspended its content in front of him.

"What is *that*?" Carter asked.

"Don't you see?" Megan said, winding it up. "It's a mobile, you know, the kind you hang above a baby's crib." Red, yellow, and blue plastic flowers dangled from thin cords attached to rotating spokes. It played "Ring Around the Roses."

"Are you *high*?" Carter asked.

"High on life, *honey*, high on life." Megan smiled as the flowers went round and round. She mouthed the words – pocket full of posies, ashes, ashes—

Carter stood up and tried to remove the mobile from Megan's hand. She backed away from him. "Give it to me, Megan. Let's put it away."

"Don't you *like* it, Carter? Won't it be so *lovely* in the nursery?"

Carter shook his head. "What, are you trying to hurt me or something? There's not going to be a nursery. You know that."

"We all...fall...down," Megan said.

Carter folded his arms across his chest. "I see we've discovered melodrama," he said.

Megan looked at the spinning toy, and her conviction faltered. "You know, I hardly remember buying it," she said. "Really. I just thought...it was pretty. I just thought I needed something. You said I couldn't buy new maternity clothes because it would be like publishing a record."

"So you bought something for an infant? Smooth solution there, Meggie."

"You're right, it was a dumb thing to do," she said. "I think maybe I *was* trying to hurt you. I should know by now that that's impossible."

"You want me to hurt?" Carter said. "I hurt. I can't concentrate on a thing, so I end up at the bar down the street. I guess we express our hurt differently."

"You want me to feel *sorry* for you because you've started drinking too much? You're unbelievable." She tried to keep her edge, but the attempt only drained her conviction. She did feel sorry for him. His breath, his gut – they were disgusting, but they were signs of a man on a downward spiral. She might have hugged him if the thought of his touch didn't make her cringe.

"I don't want you to feel anything for me," Carter said. "It's my fault. All of it. If I hadn't done ... if it weren't for me, we wouldn't be facing this awful choice. We'd be stuck with watching our daughter die, but...we might be able to be happy some other way. So I don't want you to feel sorry for me. But we *do* have the choice, and since Caitlin is both my daughter and yours, it's my fault but it's *our* choice. I think it's killing us both, but I think neither one of us can turn back now. The decision is made."

Megan sighed. "Spare me, Carter, I've heard it all before."

"Then tell me what you want me to do."

The phone rang. Neither of them budged.

"Tell me," Carter said, as the phone continued to ring.

Megan wanted to produce an answer for him, but nothing came. "I just want you to answer the phone," she said.

Carter picked up the receiver. "Hello?" His eyes got wide. "Hello, Susan."

Megan imagined the squealing of tires, the sounds of a crash.

"Yes, Megan's here." She wanted to hit him. "You're what? Susan, I don't really know if this is... Of course you can visit your daughter whenever you want, but. Yes, she has quit work. Yes, she was going to talk to you about it. You know it's been a hard time for – you're what? Okay. We'll see you when you get here."

"Oh, God," Megan said, "she's in town?"

"Worse," Carter said. "Her car is dropping her at the door as we speak."

Megan crossed to the sofa and sat down, hard. The mobile's plastic flowers clattered against one another. Her throbbing eyes stared at all the reds, blues, and yellows. Megan's mother was a healthy woman. It wouldn't take her long to climb the stairs. The mobile, the mood, and the moment had to be packed up and swept under the nearest rug. Her nerves yelled out for her to hide everything, but she sat frozen like a deer in headlights, holding a practical joke and an impractical secret in her hands.

Carter snatched the toy from Megan's hand, dashed to the bag in Caitlin's room, dropped it in, and slammed the bedroom door as he left. Her arm still floating in the air where she had held the mobile, Megan watched her husband scan the room for other tell-tale signs.

They heard a light, firm knocking – pleasant but commanding.

"Just a minute!" Carter yelled. He came to Megan on the sofa, pushed her floating arm down to her side, and brought his face right up to hers. "You're going to be okay," he said. "You can handle this. Just…be…minimal." Megan straightened her posture but did not join her husband to meet her mother at the door.

"Susan, what a pleasant surprise!" Carter said.

Susan walked straight past him, toward the sofa where her daughter waited. "Carter, you're very cute, but you're a terrible liar." She stopped and half-turned toward him. "Actually, no, your lying is good, but it's terribly frequent. Something about those glasses of yours makes you convincing. I think I'll tell my favorite lawyer to get glasses. Damned fool has perfect eyesight."

Carter moved closer to Susan. She halted his approach by placing her long fingernails affectionately on his shoulder. "Don't worry," she said. "I still approve of your decision to study literature instead of law. I wouldn't trust my daughter in the hands of someone who lies professionally. I prefer recreational equivocation." She smiled her semi-flirtatious smile.

Megan heard Carter gulp, and suddenly noticed that she'd been grinding her own teeth.

"Meg, I'm very upset with you," Susan said.

Megan stood to greet her mother. Susan was in fine form. Her newly highlighted caramel-colored spiral curls were draped neatly around her face and shoulders. The flowing fabric and elaborate patterns of her dress evoked India and would remind all who saw her that even a woman of her means could bear the imprint of 1960s counterculture. "Hi, Mom," Megan said, offering her arms for a hug.

"You can sit back down. Hugs later. Serious talk first."

Megan sat on the sofa, and Susan sat right next to her. Carter took the chair.

"My spies tell me you quit work," Susan said.

"I'm sorry, Mom, I just...well, I made sure all of my projects were either completed or in good enough shape to be picked up by someone else." Eye contact with Susan was difficult but essential. Megan managed.

Susan shook her head. "I don't care about that." She paused. "Well, of course I care. You're my daughter and I expect nothing less of you than attention to details. But you've never disappointed me on that front. You are appropriately meticulous." Susan glanced at Carter, who nodded. "Because of your usual thoughtfulness, when I heard that you'd quit work without telling me, alarm bells went off in my head immediately. I booked the first flight I could."

Susan hadn't said "the first flight available." She'd probably heard twelve days ago, immediately after Megan told her boss she was leaving. The first flight *available* for Susan would have been twelve days ago. "The first flight I could" eased Megan's mind: her mother had not been upset enough to clear her calendar. "Mom, I was going to tell you. I just didn't want you to worry."

"My dear, your husband is a talented liar, but you, thankfully, are not." Susan smiled. "You knew I'd find out if you didn't tell me. You might even have known I'd worry *because* you didn't tell me."

The idea hadn't occurred to Megan, but Susan was right – it should have.

"So you see, I was confronted by a conundrum," Susan continued. "Why would my daughter do something that would worry me? It isn't like her. It's an almost *aggressive* cry for attention."

Megan thought of the mobile.

"Maybe that wasn't your intention," Susan said, "but it worked nonetheless. I'm here. I have descended like a whirlwind to shake you into telling me the truth. *What's wrong?*"

Before she could stop herself, Megan laughed. The question! The thought of *answering* it!

"Apparently your troubles amuse you," Susan said.

Carter leaned forward, about to speak, but Megan warned him off with a subtle gesture. "No, Mom, they don't amuse me. But you know the answer to your own question." She thought of adding, *how very like you*, but she didn't. "That's why I laughed. I laughed because the question really is very funny, considering. What's wrong? How do I answer that?"

Megan felt a calming surge of understanding. Carter had said that quitting work would basically explain itself in the light of Caitlin's condition. No one could possibly estimate the impact such an ordeal would have on Megan. No one, not even Susan, could possibly tell the difference between the stress of a dying daughter and the stress of a pregnancy – or the stress of planning a baby's murder. Beyond certain thresholds, all stresses bleed together. Megan felt confident now because she understood that, within limits, she could simply tell her mother the truth. She didn't even need to speak. She finished answering her mother by glaring at Caitlin's closed bedroom door.

"Has there been anything...new?" Susan asked.

"I went to see her today," Megan said. Tears welled up in her eyes. "She was awake, and...talking. She asked me again if she could come home. The truth is I don't think I want her to come home now. I couldn't deal with seeing her suffer every minute of every day, I just couldn't." The crying would explain the pregnant puffiness of her face.

"No one expects you to," Susan said. "What you're going through is unimaginable."

"So why do you come here like a fucking *whirlwind* and ask me what's wrong?"

Carter handed Megan a box of tissues. She blew her nose.

Susan straightened her back. "I always thought the office was a welcome distraction for you. I thought it gave you something else to fill up the hours. I thought that it kept you from spending every minute of every day thinking about Caitlin."

"It used to, Mom, but now it doesn't. I need some time. My work has been shit lately. I've been so stressed out that I've been throwing up, and people have started to notice. I can't deal with the way they look at me."

Susan reached over and began stroking her daughter's hair. "Have you been to a doctor?"

Megan looked at Carter, who gave her no signal. "I...I go to a hospital almost every day. I'm surrounded by doctors."

The stroking stopped. "What I mean is, have you talked to a doctor about your condition?"

The word *condition* hit Megan's stomach like a well-aimed shot-put. Could Susan possibly...? "There's a counselor at the hospital I talk to," Megan said. "She says that it's perfectly understandable stress. I...I haven't been sick since I quit work. Throwing up, I mean."

Susan squeezed her daughter's hand before standing up. She starting pacing around the room, looking back and forth at Carter and Megan. "I just get the feeling there's something more, something you're not telling me." She stopped in the center of the room and stared down at her fine leather pumps.

Megan seized the moment to show her mounting panic to Carter. Carter's lack of reaction did not bode well.

"Wha...what do you mean, Mom?" Megan said.

Susan's gaze lingered on Carter before she started pacing again. "I just think there has to be some catalyst for your leaving work. Something has changed. And you tell me it's your health, and I believe you – you don't look at all well, I have to say – but what is it that brought on this obviously very physical transformation?"

"I don't understand," Megan said. "I'm sorry I don't look attractive enough for you."

"Megan, that's not what I mean and you know it."

"No, Mom, I honestly don't. You already know everything." *How much?*

"I flew all the way up here because I felt it in my belly – something has changed. What is it?"

"I've already told you, nothing!"

"I don't believe you, Megan." Susan stopped pacing. "Tell me what it is."

"Mom!"

"It's me," Carter said, jumping up. "I...I've started drinking. Not...abusively, but I've started going to a bar because I can't get any work done. It's like it all finally started catching up to me."

"You're not the type to fold under pressure, Carter," Susan said.

"I know I'm not," he said. "I've spent the last year trying to be a pillar for Megan, and I think half the time she's really been supporting me. I buried myself in books and routines. But then one day I just realized that a book wasn't the solution anymore." He paused. Megan recognized his private joke. "A book alone wouldn't do it. So I had a beer, and I...I started staying out later even though I wasn't getting as much done...and I'm so sorry but it's made Megan worse and it's not fair but I don't think I can be the person you know me to be anymore, Susan. I'm just not holding it together."

Susan tucked a stray curl behind an ear and shook her head. "I must admit I'm surprised. I thought that if you were going to crack, you'd have cracked long before now." She approached him. "I feel for you, Carter, I do. But you have to understand that my daughter and granddaughter are my number one priority."

"Of course they are. Believe it or not, they're mine, too."

"I do believe it," Susan said, taking another step closer, "but I can also smell the beer on your breath. I should have smelt it before. I might not have played the inquisitor quite so harshly with my daughter. Or maybe I'd have been worse. Maybe I should be harsh with you now, Carter. I can't have you becoming a drunk. If I find out – and I've got ways of finding out – that you've become a raging alcoholic, I'll come and I'll take my girls away from here – away from this city. You know I'll do it."

"Yes," Carter said, "I believe you'd do that. What's more, I'd want you to. I can promise you that I won't become a drunk. I've been talking to the counselor, too. I just need some time. And Megan needs some time. *We* need some time for ourselves."

"Of course you do," Susan said.

Megan had known her mother was bluffing, and Carter had apparently known, too. Susan was powerful, but she had lied about having ways to discover Carter's habits.

Whether or not she believed Carter's explanation for Megan's sudden change, Susan made the rest of her short visit more pleasant. Unlike Gina and the rest of the world, Susan wanted details about Caitlin's condition, and Megan and Carter took turns providing them. She prodded, comforted, and sympathized. She tried to offer light-hearted insights.

"Megan was always a strong-willed child," Susan said, smiling. "I suspect that wanting something as badly as she wants Caitlin to get well might be terribly exhausting. You're both used to getting your way. I'm not being critical. I'm like that, too. I want Caitlin to get better, and not getting what I want really pisses me off. We all need some time to deal with the unpleasantness of the universe's failure to cooperate."

Susan ended up agreeing that Megan's decision to quit work had been a good idea. She suggested that Carter might also take time off – from the library as well as the bar. They needed time for themselves. "Get to know each other again," she said, right before leaving.

After Susan's exit, Megan and Carter stood still, staring at each other. Megan thought of the colorful bag with the mobile in it. The bag, the bedroom with the pink curtains, the hospital, Caitlin, the baby inside her – they all seemed so infinitely far away.

She heard a car pull up to the curb. She crossed to the window and saw her mother open the door and step inside. The car eased away and rolled down the street.

The distance of everything became a swirling shaft of vertigo. The room spun, and Megan grabbed the windowsill. She could feel Carter standing behind her, watching as Susan disappeared. He had no idea. None.

She didn't hear it herself until Carter made a move to stop it. She was screaming – shrill, horrible cries. Her head felt light, her body was wobbling, and the force of her own voice almost knocked her over. The sound came full and fast, tapering off when she ran out of breath, only to start again with a fresh gulp of air. Carter was gone from behind her for a moment, but then he was back again. He steadied her with one arm. His other hand carried one of the sofa's feather-stuffed pillows. He forced it over Megan's face and held it there until she stopped screaming. Then he carried her, barely conscious, to the bed they had once shared.

The Descent of Carter Anderson, Continued

Carter knocked on the door. He knew that Megan wouldn't be home and hoped that Jess would. Like Brian, Jess seemed happiest when buried in her books, but unlike Brian, she usually read in the library. According to Megan, Jess found Carter "distracting," so she gave him and Megan their space whenever possible. Megan said that Jess got "giggly" whenever the subject arose. Carter was skeptical: giggling didn't seem to fit within Jess's range of abilities.

The door swung open halfway, and Jess stood there, staring down at the book she held open in one hand. After a few seconds, she glanced up. "Carter, I didn't know you still knocked," she said. Her gaze dropped once more to the book. Her reddish-brown hair was pinned back, but some strands fell down around her eyes, hovering above the pages. She stepped away from the door, leaving Carter room for entry.

"I can't help it," Carter said. "I'm a gentleman."

Jess clapped the book shut. "Of course you are," she said. "You know, Megan isn't here." She set the book on her desk and sat in her chair, looking at Carter from across the room.

"Darn," he said. "I guess you'll just have to entertain me for awhile."

Jess pushed her glasses up the bridge of her nose and laughed. "I don't know when she'll be back, and to be honest, I'm not much of an entertainer."

Carter sat on the side of the futon closest to Jess. "Well, you and I never get to talk anyway. Megan says we've got things in common – we both wear glasses and we're both here on the college's dime, which is something that really impresses the hell out of Princess Penser." His attempt at bonding didn't even cause the girl to crack a smile. Carter continued anyway. "I sort of suspect you've got even more in common with my roommate. Have you met Brian?" He winced at the awkward segue.

"No," Jess said. "I've seen him, though, and I know where this is going. Megan said you've been having delusions of Emma Woodhouse." Jess sniffled as she adjusted her glasses again.

Carter had convinced Megan that Brian and Jess would help each other out of their asexual shells. Brian didn't know what Carter was doing. Their conversations had been minimal since the experiment with Julie. "Am I really that delusional?" Carter asked, fluttering his eyelashes. "By yourselves, both of you are adorable. Together, you'd just be monstrously cute."

Jess leaned forward in her chair. "Monstrously, huh?"

Carter maintained the patter for ten minutes before Jess pronounced with certainty that the union would never occur. Three minutes later, she said she'd have dinner with Brian in the dining hall, just to meet him, if Carter and Megan came along.

"Everything's in place," Carter said to Brian as he walked into their room.

Brian was stretched out on the bed in his corner, reading. He sat up and rubbed his eyes. "What did you say?"

"Everything's in place, so it's time to do the ritual."

"What ritual are you talking about?" Brian closed his book. "I'm not doing any more rituals."

"So are you a liar now? You said you'd let me fix you up with Jess, Megan's roommate."

"I said no such thing. And besides, what does that have to do with any rituals? Have you forgotten what happened last time? About what you – about what we – did?"

Carter crossed the room and sat on the edge of Brian's bed, facing him. "Look, I'm sorry about that. It was...it was a stupid thing to do. And because of you, I don't think anybody really got hurt, so I'm grateful. I know I've been selfish with all this stuff. That's why I think we should make Dr. Fincher's magic work just for you this time. You know what I'm talking about. The binding ritual. You deserve to have someone fall madly in love with you." Carter gave Brian a sly grin.

"I get what you're saying, but I think it's stupid," Brian said with a shake of his head. He was blushing. "I thought you were only interested in real power. Playing Cupid seems beneath you."

"I appreciate your appeal to my vanity, but I think you're missing the real point. This *is* about power. Think about it – what does, like, the entire history of literature say is the strongest human emotion?" Carter paused. "It's love. You can shame me with your chivalry, if you like, but I just want to see you happy."

Brian went through variations of the word "no" for an hour before he finally agreed.

Carter got the sample of Jess's menstrual blood from the trashcan in Megan and Jess's bathroom. Brian's blood came from a cut on his chest, just above his heart.

After the four of them had dinner together, Megan mentioned that she had never seen Jess so animated. "Oh, Brian, philosophy is such a cool major," she mimicked. "Oh, Brian, I think Nietzsche was misunderstood, too." Megan shook her head. "I thought Jess only regressed into girly adolescence with me!"

"I'll regress with you if you want," Carter said. "Wanna have a slumber party?"

The phone rang at midnight. "Hey there, I just wanted to say goodnight." Carter recognized Jess's voice and gave the phone to Brian, who mumbled a quick goodnight and hung up.

The next day, the flowers arrived. "I loaned her the money," Megan explained. "She's smitten. She just goes on and on. If Brian doesn't fall for her, this girl is going to be shattered."

The following day, there were chocolates. Brian tossed the box on Carter's desk. "I think we've got to do the unbinding ritual," Brian said. "This is ridiculous."

"Come on," Carter said. "Give her a chance."

Brian stopped answering the phone, and Carter stopped making excuses. It rang once an hour, then once every half hour. Neighbors complained. "Chill out," Carter said, watching Brian pace. "We don't even have a bunny for her to boil. Besides, the good Dr. Fincher warns that the unbinding ritual can backfire."

When the photographs arrived, Carter agreed to help Brian with the unbinding. Jess had perched on the steps of Widener Library and had snapped a series of shots – all of Brian simply walking across the Yard. Each candid photo had a caption about "beauty in motion."

The unbinding called for Jess's hair and Brian's skin. "Don't let Jess see you messing with her brush," Megan said to Carter when she found him searching Jess's things. He hid the stolen sample in his palm. "She'll think that Brian asked for a memento." Carter laughed.

"It's not funny," Megan said. "The girl is seriously out of her mind."

The morning after the ritual, Carter sat in a lecture hall, doodling, while a professor rambled about leeches, cupping, and other wonders of medicine from the "all too recent past." Carter ignored the first tap on his shoulder. The second tap became a swat, so he turned around.

Brian was pale, almost green. He held something in his trembling hand, but Carter couldn't see it. Brian motioned for Carter to follow him. Carter stared at the carpet as he went out, feeling all eyes in the class boring into his back.

When they reached the sidewalk, Carter tried to sound angry. "What the hell is going on? Why the hell would you pull me out of class like that?"

Brian sat down on the grass and closed his eyes. "I think I'm going to be sick," he said.

Carter looked down at Brian's hand. It held an envelope. Carter thought about flowers and candy. He thought about photographs. "What did she send you now?" He chuckled. "I'm guessing the unbinding ritual didn't work, huh?"

Brian's upper body convulsed. He covered his mouth with his free hand for a minute before regaining control. Then he offered the envelope to Carter.

Carter spoke in a hushed voice. *"What is it?"*

Brian shook his head. He wouldn't say.

Carter took the envelope from Brian's hand and noticed a tremor in his own fingers. Flowers, candy, photographs – what came next? The envelope was brown and thick, large enough for a book. As Carter lifted it for closer examination, he noticed the maroon splotches along the bottom edge.

The envelope was open. Carter looked in, but saw nothing. Whatever it contained was small, lodged at the bottom where the stains were. Carter reached in and felt something dry, soft, and solid – a bent cylinder with knobs.

"I told her she had nice hands," Brian said. "She asked if I thought she was ugly, and I said no, and she asked what part of her was pretty, and I had to say something, and I thought of her hands. Oh." He covered his mouth again.

Carter pulled a severed pinky finger out of the envelope. He recognized the lavender shade of the nail polish and thought that Jess must have borrowed it from Megan. The nail polish clashed with the dried blood. He shoved the finger back into the envelope. His head swiveled from side to side, searching. No one was watching them.

"Where is she?" Carter asked.

"I don't know," Brian murmured into his lap. "I told her. Her hands...."

"*Where is she?*"

"I did this! I did!"

"Shut up, Brian. You didn't do it." Carter took a deep breath. "I did it. I'm responsible. But I don't even know what I'm responsible for. We have to find her. So think. Where is she?"

Brian stared at the envelope. "Did you see the note?" he asked.

"What note?"

"The note." Brian's voice cracked. Carter saw that he was crying. "When I first... got it out, it was wrapped in a piece of paper that was stiff with...but I could still read it, and I read what it said before I saw what...."

Carter reached back into the envelope. He felt around, letting a finger press against Jess's severed digit as he scratched, trying to find the note. "It's not here," he said. His heart hammered in his chest. "If it's not here, it's – Brian, where did you open this?"

"It said, 'I don't need it anymore.' Don't...need...."

"Fuck you, Brian. Shut up! Shut up and stop thinking about that right now." But Carter was thinking hard. *Don't need it?* Was this how unbinding worked? Or was this how it backfired? "I'm sorry, Brian. Listen – it's not your fault. It's my fault. It's my fault and I need to know where you opened the envelope because I need to find it...I need to see it. Tell me, Brian."

"The mailroom. The envelope was just there. It was taped to the front of my mailbox. She must have taped it – even though she was hurt – she must have."

Carter left Brian sitting on the grass and ran to the mailroom in the basement of the Science Center. He didn't remember Brian's mailbox number, but he knew its row, and as he ran around the corner, he saw the brownish paper lying on the floor. Someone had stepped on it, creating a smear on the tile. A girl stood near it, opening her mailbox. Carter would have to get close to the girl to pick it up. "Excuse me," he said, "but that's...that's mine." She stepped away. Carter knelt, grabbed the blood-soaked paper from the floor, and rubbed at the smeared tile with his bare hand, cleaning it. He kept his head down. He didn't want the girl at her mailbox to get a clear view of his face while he rubbed his hand in dried blood. He slipped the note back into the envelope and bolted.

There was still an impression on the grass where Brian had sat, but Brian was gone. Carter looked around, scanning the clusters of students emerging from dorms and classroom buildings as a clock struck the hour. Brian knew, and Brian was unstable. Carter had to find him.

Carter saw that the door to their dorm room was open, and he heard Brian talking inside. "Answer, answer, answer," Brian said. He sat at his desk with the phone tucked between his ear and shoulder. His fingers scratched at the sides of his legs.

"Hang up," Carter said. "We can handle this ourselves."

Brian didn't look at Carter. "I'm calling Jess," he said. "Jess and Megan's room. I didn't know I knew the number until I dialed. I guess hearing it on the answering machine all those times—"

"Megan's in class," Carter said. "How many times has it rung?"

"I don't know," Brian said. "Twenty. Thirty. I don't know."

"She's not there. You were right to call, but she's not there. We have to find her. Where would she go?"

Brian slammed down the phone and jumped from his seat. "Why are you asking me? I don't even KNOW the girl! This was your idea! You thought you knew everything! You should know where she is! You should...you should—"

"Shut up," Carter said. "I think I know how to find her. Megan's got classes all morning. She's probably heading into her art history class right now. We can catch her. Follow me."

They ran together. For the second time, Brian managed to keep up with Carter.

By the time they got Megan into the hall, she was sharing their panic. "You guys look awful. What is it? Tell me!"

"Not here," Carter said. There were still students loitering nearby. "Let's go outside."

They huddled near a bike rack and whispered. "We have to find Jess," Carter said.

"Jess? Oh, my," Megan said, letting out a sigh. She smiled. "Is that all? What's she doing now? Not compromising pictures of herself, I hope, because she'll be embarrassed for the rest of her—" She stopped when she saw the envelope in Carter's hand. "What is it? More photos?"

"We think she might have hurt herself," Carter said.

Her gaze fell on the maroon splotches. "You *think*? What's in the envelope? A note?"

Carter tucked the envelope under his arm and grasped Megan's shoulders. "Nevermind. Just tell me. Where do you think she is right now?"

"I don't know," Megan said. "The library, maybe. If you don't tell me what's going on—"

"Megan, be quiet, just—"

She snatched the envelope and opened it before Carter could react. She turned it upside down, and the finger fell into her hand. She looked at it for a moment, puzzled, and then yanked her hand out from under it, letting it fall to the sidewalk. She buried her face in Carter's chest for a second before shoving him away. "What is this – a joke? Is it...*real?*"

"Carter," Brian said, "we should tell her."

"It's not...real, is it Carter? If this is your idea of a joke I'm totally breaking up with you."

"Tell her, Carter."

Carter picked the finger up from the sidewalk, pulled the envelope from Megan's hand, and dropped it back inside. Megan followed his movements, studying the object he was trying to conceal. She looked down at her hands. "That looks like my nail polish," she said, her voice shaking. "Yesterday afternoon, while she babbled on and on about Brian, I painted her nails and – this isn't real. This can't be Jess's finger." She sucked in air. Tears trickled down her face. "She's crazy. She's really crazy."

"Megan," Brian said, "we did something to Jess. This isn't her fault. We did something and we've got to find her because this might not be the end of it. Because—"

"*You* did this?" Megan asked.

Brian stepped back. "Me? No. I mean, we didn't *do* this – to her hand, I mean, but we—"

"Brian, goddamn you," Carter said, "I'll tell her."

"Yes, tell me," Megan said. "Give me an explanation." She wiped her eyes. "Don't I deserve one? Doesn't *she?*"

"First, tell me where to go. Tell me where Jess might be," Carter said, "and I'll explain on the way."

"We should start in our room," Megan said. "I'll be able to guess where she is based on which books she took with her."

As they walked, Carter told Megan about Dr. Fincher's theories and about the first experiment. "The running, the jumping, and lifting the car – it was impossible, but I still didn't believe, you know, that it wasn't just some adrenaline thing or something. And when I thought of doing the binding, it was almost like a joke, almost—"

Megan slid her ID card into the door of the dormitory and opened it. "So wait a minute," she said, stopping. "You're telling me my roommate went crazy because you and your roommate cast a love spell on her. Is that it?"

Carter shrugged. "More or less."

"You're absurd," she said, "and I'm calling the police when we get to my room."

"Go," Carter said. "Keep walking. When we get there, you can do that if you want." They started moving again, climbing the stairs. "You can do that, but I'm going to keep looking for her. I'm absurd, but the situation is real. We've already wasted enough time. Do you really think the cops are going to be any help?"

They got to her door. She pulled her keys from her purse and struggled with the lock. "What are you worried about, Carter? Even if you tell them your crazy story, they won't believe you any more than I do. I don't know what to think, but I certainly don't think—"

The door swung open, and Megan screamed.

Most of Jess was sitting on the futon. Part of her was on her desk. Tatters of skin checkered the rug. Pushing Megan in front and pulling Brian behind, Carter got them into the room and slammed the door. There was blood on the back of it.

A rag of some sort was wrapped around Jess's left hand, binding the wound where her finger had been. The bound hand held the knife. The other hand was gone. Blood still ran from the wrist. She hadn't bandaged it. The rag around her left hand was the only binding she wore.

"aaa...nnnn...."

She was still alive.

Megan let out another scream. Carter could only stand there staring.

Brian crossed the room, stepping on a shred of skin, and grabbed the phone. "Police? We need help."

"aaaaaaaa...yyyyy...iiiiii...nnnnn...."

Jess couldn't form a B or an R without lips.

"ayyyyyyyy...nnnnnnnn...."

Her head drooped. The hand with the knife took off another slice.

Brian dropped the receiver. Carter could hear a voice on the other end asking for the nature of their emergency. Without taking his eyes off the futon, Carter started walking toward the phone.

Megan's screaming had become mere babbling. "How could she...what is she... how could this be real...all this blood...can't be...it can't be...."

"She should be dead," Brian said. "No one could do that to themselves and live." He bent over and vomited.

Carter picked up the receiver. "Hello?" he said. The voice on the other end of the line said something.

Megan was catching her breath. "Help her! For God's sake, somebody help her!"

"Hello? Yes, this is Carter Anderson."

Carter saw that the door had opened. He had slammed it shut but not locked it. People had heard Megan screaming, and they had come to see what was causing the commotion. Two girls filled the doorway. One of them gawked. The other started crying. The crowd behind pushed for a view, but the girls in the doorway did not move.

"Carter Anderson, yes," he said. "Send an ambulance. I did this. This is my fault."

Megan had grabbed some clothes off the bedroom floor and was wrapping them around the parts of Jess that were bleeding. She searched for more.

"ayyyyyyyy...."

Brian's knees landed in his own vomit. "I didn't know her. I didn't even know her," he said. "Her hands."

"I did this. This is my fault," Carter whispered.

Jess was silent by the time the ambulance arrived. The paramedics pronounced her dead. The police did not believe Carter's story. They could not explain how she had survived the trauma for as long as she had, but they did not believe his story. They said Jess was crazy. They said it was suicide. They pitied Carter and the others. There would be free counseling.

Later that night, at the end of all the questioning, Megan told Carter she believed him. His story had to be true because what had happened didn't seem real, yet she had seen it with her own eyes.

Continuity

Ten weeks remained.

Several of Megan's books about pregnancy suggested that dreams about the unborn represent a kind of psychic umbilical cord, through which mother and baby share anxieties and joys. Megan dreamt once about giving birth not to a baby but to her own vital organs. In another dream, Caitlin was healthy and at Megan's bedside during labor. The baby arrived, and Carter gave it a bath. Shiny and soft, the baby rested on Megan's chest. Caitlin asked if she could hold her tiny brother. She took the infant in her child arms and twisted its screaming head around, giggling at the snapping of newborn vertebrae.

Megan and Carter were sharing the same bed again, and Megan knew that Carter was having trouble sleeping, too. He didn't have the backaches, or the constipation, or the swollen feet. He didn't have to worry about stumbling over his own feet every time he went to the refrigerator. He did have insomnia, and that comforted her.

The move back into the master bedroom had happened without discussion. The night after her mother's unexpected visit had been the first, and every night since had drawn her back. She didn't understand how Carter had reclaimed all her territory. All she knew was that after the first night in the master bedroom, nothing in the apartment was hers.

In Megan's dreams, the baby was a boy. She couldn't get an ultrasound, so she asked Carter for a stethoscope. She wanted to hear the baby's heartbeat. His. Hers. Its. Carter said he didn't think that would be "psychologically sound." She said she needed to hear the heartbeat because it would help her know that the thing trapped inside of her actually lived. Like the baby, Megan was trapped, and Megan was doomed. She hadn't left the apartment in months. When she thought about the steep stairs, she wondered if she *could* leave.

She waddled from the bedroom to the living room, turned on the television, and took a pill. Carter had made tranquilizers part of her routine. She didn't know how he acquired them, and she didn't care. Carter had his ways. She had her pills.

Carter was reading at the kitchen table, but he might as well have been sitting on her shoulder. He rarely left the apartment. "I want to be here for you," he said. "There's no reason for you to suffer alone." Bullshit. He wanted to be there to make sure she didn't try to leave.

"Carter, would you bring me a drink?"

"Sure," he said. "What can I get you?"

"A double shot of whiskey with a sprinkle of arsenic." Had she said that aloud?

"How about some lemonade? The sugar might perk up your spirits some."

"Whatever."

Her face didn't turn away from the television, but her ears followed Carter's progress through the kitchen. Thudding footfalls crossed tiles: the sounds told her which tile each foot hit. She listened to the whir as the refrigerator swung open, the clinking as condiment jars shook. Other chilled items shifted when the lemonade jug's weight disappeared. Liquid tinkled into a tall glass. Carter stopped, got the rag from the sink, and wiped up the yellow spots he had dribbled on the counter. He strode into the living room, stood in front of the sofa, and handed her the glass. "How are you feeling today?"

"Super," Megan said. "I feel like going for a long walk."

Carter smiled. "Is there anything else I can get you?"

"How about a taxi? I could look at all the fallen leaves they haven't cleaned up at the park yet. A plane ticket? I could go someplace warm."

"Have you taken a pill yet today?" he asked.

"Just did."

"Good. You'll feel better soon."

"No I won't. I'm really not going to feel better, Carter. Not ever."

"Why do you say that?"

Megan turned toward him. "You used to be so goddamned *smart*."

Carter sighed. "It's like you're not even trying anymore," he said. "We have to keep trying. It's not about us. It's about—"

"Oh, good! Let's try!" Megan attempted to jump up from the sofa, but her knees buckled, and Carter helped her to her feet. "Let's you and me try going for a walk! Come on, you used to be creative. We could go in *disguise.* I know! I'll put on a shower curtain, and you can go naked, with a bar of soap in one hand and a rubber duckie in the other! I think Caitlin's duckie is still in the cabinet under the bathroom sink!"

"Megan, *honey,* you're raving. Sit down." Carter nudged her back towards the sofa.

She stepped up to him; their noses almost touched. "I WILL NOT SIT DOWN!!!"

Carter grabbed her shoulders and forced her down onto the sofa. His strength surprised her. Her knees couldn't resist. "I told you to sit. Now sit."

"Arf! Arf! Arf!" Megan let her tongue roll out of her mouth and panted.

Carter took a step back. "You're pathetic," he said. "Do us both a favor and shut the fuck up."

"Tell me to shut up again, and I'll scream so loud they'll hear it in the next building."

"They'll hear, but they won't do a damned thing about it. And I'll tie a gag around your mouth to keep you from doing it again. I have a headache, Megan, and I'm not in a very good mood."

Carter's face wore an expression that was far from normal. His cheeks looked like ghostly putty, and his eyes were completely devoid of warmth.

Megan stood up, faster this time. "Arf! Arf! Arf!"

"Shut up," Carter said.

"Don't tempt me," Megan said, and she dropped her jaw in a silent scream.

Carter's grin was unpleasant. "Don't tempt *me,*" he said.

Megan's left knee wavered, and she almost sat despite herself. "Poor Carter has a headache," she whimpered. "Poor boy. You want Mommy to kiss it better?"

Carter leaned over and grabbed the TV remote from the coffee table. He turned up the volume. "I highly recommend sitting down and shutting up," he said.

"*Or what?*"

He stepped forward, grabbed her shoulders, and pushed her back onto the sofa again. "Isn't it obvious?" he said. She had to strain to hear him. "One way or another, you'll do what I tell you."

She stood again, and her knees were strong. She splashed the glass of lemonade on his face, soaking the top of his shirt.

One of his hands rose to his wet cheek and swiped at the liquid. He licked a fingertip. A feeling of intense satisfaction distracted

Megan for a moment, and she didn't see his response coming. He slapped her so hard that she found herself sitting again. He had never hit her before.

"Big man," she said. "Beating up the pregnant lady. You're low, Carter. Low."

He gave her a predatory stare. "You have no idea how low I am. You don't know what I'm capable of."

"I think I do," Megan whispered.

"What? Speak up!"

Megan shook her head.

"Good." He looked from Megan to the kitchen. "The lemonade tastes good. I think I want some." On his way to the refrigerator, he stripped off his wet shirt and dropped it on the floor.

Annoyed by the hot tear that trickled down her stinging cheek, Megan reached for the TV remote and hit the OFF button. She heard the sounds again – clinking condiments, flowing liquid. She imagined Carter breaking the tall glass he was filling, the glass that matched her own, and slicing his throat with a shard.

Megan stood up again, took a deep breath. She had to stop and think. She was on the verge of something. "Carter," she called.

"What?" He was walking back from the kitchen, toward his chair.

"Carter, I can't."

"You can't what? Sit down and shut up? It's easy." In demonstration, Carter dropped into his chair and took a sip of his lemonade. "Aaaah. If you want some more, you'll have to get it yourself."

"No, Carter. Forget about all that for a moment." Her hand touched her red cheek. "Forget about what just happened, about all this petty squabbling."

"Done," he said.

"Be serious! I'm serious! I can't do it, Carter! I can't go through with it!"

"*Go through with what?*"

Her fists hammered the air in frustration. "All of it! The – the murder. The baby. All of it. I can't kill my baby. You don't know what it's like, having it inside you. It. Him! Her! It's not an it or a cure or anything, it's a—"

"Whatever happened to sitting down and shutting up? It was such a *good* idea." He leaned forward and set his glass on the coffee table, then got out of his chair. "There. Now we're both standing."

"Carter, please," Megan said. More tears. She knew better than to think they might help her. "Please, Carter, you're not listening."

"I'm listening, but I'm just not hearing anything new, Megan. As you're so fond of saying, we've had this conversation a million times. You have doubts about what we're doing. 'It's a life, not a means to an end, wah, wah, wah!' Okay, so we're not going to have that conversation. I'm not going to remind you that you've got Caitlin's life in your hands – or in your belly – and I'm not going to go on and on about how hard the decision is, and how I regret this or that, and how I know it's harder for you, and all that shit. Let's just say *insert conversation here*. Cut the crap, right? Isn't sitting down and shutting the fuck up just SO much better than going through all that again and again every fucking time your hormones tell you you've got to throw another fit? Isn't that BETTER, Megan?"

Megan tried to steady her trembling hands. "Carter, what's with you? I don't think I know who you are anymore."

He rolled his eyes. "Spare me the melodramatic bullshit, please! 'I don't know who you are anymore.' Can't your first-rate education provide you with a line better than *that*? Your retorts aren't worthy of an Anderson or a Penser."

She did know who he was. He had always been this man. They had had the other conversation – the one in which he said all the right things – before, but this time, he was saying what he had always meant. "So," Megan said, gathering nerve, "it's not a choice anymore. It never was, was it?"

Carter nodded. "There's my Megan. *Now* you're being clever, trying to push responsibility away from yourself because now you can see me as a great big monster, right? Well, if that works for you, then by all means. I'm a monster. Grr. Argh."

Megan took a few steps away from the sofa and from Carter. "I'm not *trying* to evade responsibility. I've been responsible up to this point because I've gone along with it. Because I've believed that I was actually involved in what's happening in my life. That's over. I don't believe anymore. This isn't me. I'm not responsible anymore. I'm no longer your accomplice. I'm your prisoner."

The hand he had used to slap her now massaged his forehead. "You're not a prisoner, Megan. The door's right over there. It always has been. You should look at yourself while you're grabbing at these excuses. It's pathetic."

She looked down at her gargantuan middle. She was wearing the pajamas she wore every day. Frumpy, bloated, unkempt – she hadn't even showered today. Carter was right. She was pathetic. Carter was right, but she didn't care. *Move, move now!* She couldn't run, but she shuffled quickly toward the door.

She managed to get the door open a crack before Carter loomed over her and slammed it shut. The unfastened chain clattered against the vibrating doorframe. Inserting his body between her and the door, Carter forced Megan back while he turned the lock and fastened the chain. "Well, then," he said, "this is a new development, isn't it?"

"No," Megan said. "It's just the proof of what I should have known all along."

"We never use the deadbolt," Carter said, "but I think it's about time we started. The city isn't a safe place. We have to be careful. If I remember correctly, there are only two keys to the bolt. I think I know where they are..."

Megan started backing away from Carter and the door, toward the kitchen. "So all I do is try to leave, and the charade ends like that, huh? Say it, Carter. Say you won't *let* me leave. I want to hear it."

Carter moved toward the sofa, staying in range to beat Megan in a race for the door. Megan maintained eye contact with her husband while she took tiny sideways steps toward the kitchen. "Megan, you're not being rational," Carter said. "Maybe you should get back in bed until you're feeling better."

"Maybe? *Maybe?* You can do better than that! Show your strength! 'Maybe' is not the word of a man who hits pregnant women. Or are you trying to make me forget you did that?"

"I didn't hit you. I slapped you when you were being hysterical. You'd know if I hit you. Don't go trying to play the abused wife here. That strategy of evading your own responsibility is shallower than the last."

Megan turned away from him, toward the table where he had been reading. She started stacking papers, rearranging things that didn't need rearranging. "You're right, Carter. Of course you're right." She paused. "I think I *do* want some lemonade, and I'll get it myself." She walked into the kitchen and approached the drawers by the refrigerator.

She heard the creak of boards as Carter sat on the sofa. Unless he turned at just the right angle, he wouldn't be able to see her from where he was sitting. She opened the refrigerator, whir and clink. While one hand slid cool objects around on the shelf, the other pulled the top drawer open slowly – almost silently.

Now all she had to do was find what she wanted. *Move your eyes directly to the drawer. Don't let them drift to Carter. He'll know.* He had turned the TV back on. The volume was low.

Megan focused on her target: the chef's knife – long, sharp, part of the set Susan had sent as a housewarming gift. Megan reached into the knife drawer, trying to keep the metal blades from clanking against each other. She had what she wanted. She couldn't outrun him, and she couldn't outfight him, but there were other ways of evening the odds.

Grasping the handle, she stood up straight and looked toward the living room. Carter actually seemed to be watching the TV. Was it possible he had been so careless, had accepted her shift from plans for escape to plans for lemonade? It seemed unlikely, but she had to proceed. As she took soft steps back into the living room, she realized she'd left the refrigerator door open. The television volume was low enough for her to hear the refrigerator's whir from the living room, which meant Carter could hear it, too. That meant he'd soon notice...

"Taking the knife for a walk, huh, Megan?" Carter said, without turning to look at her. Megan could hear the amusement in his voice.

She stopped behind the sofa, halfway between the kitchen and the front door. "I'm leaving, Carter. It's over. All of this...is over. I'm going to knock on doors, I'm going to call the police, I'm going to make sure there's no way we can go through with it. Part of you wants that, Carter. I know it. You feel remorse. I know you do."

He stood, facing her across the sofa, and talked fast. "You're right. Part of me wants this to end as much as you do. But we're so *close* now. Two more months. Two more months, and in one day, it'll be over. We'll have our daughter back. We probably won't have much of a marriage left to salvage...but we'll have Caitlin back. I'll give her to you. No shared custody, no contest in the divorce. It'll be enough for me to know that because of me she'll have a chance to grow up, go to the prom, graduate, choose a college...in two more months, we can give her everything. I hate this. I hate what we've become. You don't know what I've learned...about myself...about...what I'm capable of. You don't know everything I've done."

Megan looked at Carter. He was bare from the waist up. The lemonade made his chest hairs stick together. His new belly made him look vulnerable. "Stop it, Carter," she said. "And keep your confessions to yourself. I'm going out that door. I don't advise coming anywhere close to me while I do."

He took a step toward the door. "Going to race me? You know I'll win."

"I'm not afraid of you, Carter."

"Yes, you are. That's why you grabbed the knife in the first place. You're more terrified than I ever knew. I never wanted you to be afraid of me, but if you need fear to get through the next two months, then I'll give you good reason to feel it. I can be a scary, scary guy."

He laughed, and Megan's spine stiffened. She could not move as he circled around the sofa and claimed the space between her and the door once again.

"Put down the knife and go to bed, Megan. I'll clean up everything. You'll let me know whatever you need. I'll be here, at your side, for the next two months. I'll be your personal servant. And I'll have to sleep sometime, which means you'll have plenty of opportunities to cut my throat if you want to. Now's not the time. Go to bed. Let the pill kick in. Calm down. All this stress isn't good for you."

"It's not good for the baby, either," she said.

Carter shook his head. "You're hurting yourself, thinking like that. It's too late, I guess, to change the way you think of it. Do you think I want to see myself as plotting to murder my own child? People sell their children, drown them, abandon them in public trashcans – do you think I want to be one of them? You'll be able to spend the rest of your life blaming me. I'll just blame myself. If you hate me as much as you think you do, and you really want to hurt me, you'll put down that knife and let me follow my own path to Hell."

"Now who's being melodramatic?" Megan asked.

He took a step toward her. "Who's the one holding the knife?"

"I am." She looked at the shiny blade. "It's not melodramatic. It's practical."

Another step. "You think you can do it? You think you can drive that thing into me? And then...what? Run through the door, screaming and hollering about how I was holding you prisoner in order to sacrifice your baby in some Satanic ritual? They'll come and find my body and no evidence of abuse, and they'll either put you in prison or in a madhouse, and then I'm gone and our children are gone, too. Caitlin dies, and the new one, if it lives at all, grows up a virtual orphan, knowing Mommy went crazy and killed Daddy. Is that what you want?"

Another step. "Stab me, Megan. Go on. Do it. Then it's not my fault anymore. I get to be the good guy. Do it. Make it easy for me. I want out. God, I really do. Jam the blade in my chest or my stomach or wherever you want as long as it *kills*. Are you a killer, Megan? Are you? Can you kill your husband and daughter both?"

She knew it was bullshit, so why was the knife handle trembling in her grip, why were more fresh tears streaming down her cheeks? *Damn it, no!*

"Don't come any closer! I'll do it! You don't believe me, but I will!"

Another step. She could slash him from here if she wanted.

"Megan was always a strong-willed child," Carter said in his best imitation of Susan. "So used to getting her way. She'd do *anything*, wouldn't she? Would she?"

He took another step. So close now, too close.

Megan stepped backward and raised the knife. "I'm warning you," she said.

"I know." Another step. "So, is she a killer?"

He was in grabbing range. She stepped back again and looked over her shoulder. He could back her up as far as the kitchen wall, and then there'd be nowhere to go. Step, step, back. Step, step, back. Her feet were getting closer to the tiles. She tightened her grip on the trembling handle.

"Is she a killer?" Carter hissed. "Is she?"

"Stop it," she said, letting out a sob. "Stop it, Carter."

They were on the tiled floor now. The wall was getting closer.

"Did I marry a killer? Did I?"

Megan raised the knife higher, bracing herself for a plunge. She had to move to the side to avoid backing into the table.

He kept moving forward. The wall was right behind her. Another step back, and she'd have to lower the knife.

"Nowhere else to go, is there?" Carter said. "It's now or never." He paused. "I don't think she's a killer. I think she'd better put down the knife and go to bed. It's easier that way. Go back to bed. Sleep through all of it."

She raised the knife as high as she could. "I'm warning you!"

"I'm waiting," he said. He tapped his foot on the tile.

The tapping snapped her. Megan's arm descended. She aimed the blade at Carter's chest. He caught her arm mid-arc and twisted it, hard. Her hand opened and dropped the blade. It clattered on the tiles.

"Maybe she is after all," Carter said. He yanked her toward him and pushed her further into the kitchen, away from the knife. She lost her balance and smashed her bottom on the floor. The pain rocked through her, and she felt movement in her belly. She yowled.

Carter leaned over and picked up the knife. Megan sat exposed. "You okay?" he said. "Didn't break anything, did you? Want a lift up?"

The baby inside her awoke and protested the wrenching violence of the fall. Megan squeezed her eyes shut, waiting for a contraction, waiting for some indication of early and fatal labor. The pain passed.

"Megan, are you okay?"

"Help me up," she said. He offered her one hand while the other held the knife at a distance. Together, they got her to her feet. Standing close, she took her husband's free hand and pressed it against her chest. "Now push me down again. Hard. As many times as you want. Kill me. Kill the baby. Kill Caitlin. Finish it all right now."

"No, Megan," he said with a shake of his head. "You're the killer, remember?" He carved circles in the air with the knife. "Remember? If I hadn't disarmed you, I would've been the one on the floor, bleeding all over the tiles. That's what you wanted, right? Another memory of a bloody room?"

He stood, brought the knife closer, and examined the blade. "I'll tell you what I'll do. I'll give you another chance." He extended the knife-handle in her direction. "Take it. I want you to."

Megan reached out. Hesitant, slow, she took the handle and yanked the knife closer to her body, into the sphere of her control. She stepped backward, to striking distance. Carter clasped his hands behind his back. His bare chest protruded, vulnerable. He tilted back his head, exposing his throat. "Come on, what are you waiting for?" he said. "Do it."

She dropped the knife, stepped over it, and shuffled to the living room. She heard Carter lift the blade, open the drawer, and set it back in place. "So you're not a killer after all," he said.

She was walking alongside the sofa, and the door was in front of her again, calling out as if it had just emerged from hiding. Carter was still in the kitchen. She kept walking, and the door got closer. She stood in front of it, and Carter hadn't arrived to stop her. With her last burst of energy, she reached up, unfastened the chain, unlocked the knob, and threw the door open. It was banging against the wall when she heard Carter rushing in her direction. She was out in the fluorescent lights of the hall before he could stop her. She waited at the top of the stairs she hadn't climbed in so long. There were two other apartments on this floor, three on the floor below that, three below that, and so on, all the way down. "SOMEBODY!" she yelled. The echoes exploded all around her.

"Megan," Carter said as he stepped into the hall.

"ANYBODY!"

"Remember," said Carter, coming closer, "that if you want help in the city, you yell FIRE. Nobody comes if you say help, or rape, or anything else that isn't their business. Come on, yell FIRE."

"Fire," Megan said. The word echoed, became distorted. She hadn't been loud enough to be convincing.

"Yell it, and somebody will come. Somebody's got to be home." A fluorescent light above Carter's head flickered. "Remember this, though: I'll be gone before you have time to explain what's happening. Maybe somebody will believe you, and maybe not. It depends on how creative you are with the crazier parts of the truth."

He lowered his voice. A neighbor with an ear to a door wouldn't have been able to hear him. "It doesn't matter because I won't be here anymore as soon as you stop yelling. I'll go to the hospital. Yell FIRE, and you doom Caitlin to death. I don't much care about myself. All I know is that I can't keep watching her die. I don't know if that's more or less selfish than you wanting your part of this to be over, but it's how I feel. You yell FIRE, and I'll go to the hospital and finish it. FIRE, Megan. Say it. Scream it."

Megan didn't speak or move.

"You're not a killer," Carter said, "but I am." He took a deep breath. "I am." He looked around the hallway in the flickering light. "Come on, Megan. Let's go back inside. It won't be long now."

Ten weeks. She went back inside.

The Descent of Carter Anderson, Continued

She believed Carter and Brian had caused Jess's death, but Megan didn't blame them. Carter and Brian had set events in motion that had culminated in a horrible accident. It shouldn't have been possible. They couldn't have known. She told Carter these things. She offered him comfort.

She said she needed to understand the details, so Carter told her everything about the ritual. He loaned her *The Alchemy of Will*. She gave it back and said that she hadn't read it all, but she had read enough to see why he and Brian had been curious. Dr. Fincher was eloquent. The prospects were tantalizing.

She didn't blame him, but she broke up with him. Carter said he understood. When she left school early, he offered her the number of the place he'd be during the summer. "In case you need to talk."

Her first call came in July. "I can't sleep," she said.

"Me neither," Carter answered. They described the dreams that kept them up and the way the images of Jess were most vivid at night.

When the fall semester arrived, Megan returned to school, took exams to make up for the ones she had missed, and relied on Carter as a friend. She could talk to him because he knew what had really happened – he was the only one who really knew. After that semester, they never talked about Jess again. Carter saw Megan through two bad relationships, and she saw him through a series of flings.

A careless night led to Caitlin. They discussed their options. Megan said she didn't want an abortion, and Carter said he would support any decision she made. Carter pointed out that they both seemed to have developed a chronic phobia of relationships, and Megan suggested that, in the absence of any other cure for their persistent incompatibility with humankind, they might as well get married.

After her opposition to the marriage faded, Susan admitted that she thought the mixture of genes would have good results. In Carter's presence, Susan said to Megan, "Carter is the first significant rebellion in your life, and I applaud you for it. As rebellions go, though, this one is not particularly impressive. You've decided to have the baby, and that's fine. You're not due until after graduation, so you can finish college. A June wedding is trite but not disagreeable. You could wait to get married until after the baby comes, if you want. No one really cares about legitimacy anymore anyway."

Carter thought that Susan would have preferred the wedding to be after the delivery, but Megan perversely preferred tradition. He sensed Susan's disappointment: she thought her daughter conventional, perhaps even boring. She saw hope for redemption in her granddaughter.

During the days following Jess's death, Carter and Brian had many long conversations in which they took turns blaming themselves and blaming each other. As Brian became more disconsolate, Carter started to favor Megan's "accident" theory. "Things went wrong," Carter said. "They wouldn't necessarily go wrong if we tried something again."

"You're insane," Brian said. "Nothing you could say would be more persuasive than the guilt I feel. I will never, never do anything like that again. Ever."

"You know I can't do it without you," Carter said. "I've tried."

"Then for God's sake, Carter, don't do it! Was everything you said about your own guilt and responsibility just bullshit? You're not stupid, Carter. *Learn.*"

They said brief goodbyes when they were moving out of the dorm. Over the next three years, Carter saw Brian around campus, but they didn't acknowledge each other. Carter heard about Brian's academic troubles from the sort of people who said, "Hey, weren't you and that guy Brian Mowbray involved in that girl's suicide somehow? Mowbray was supposed to be some kind of genius or something, but now..." On commencement day, Carter saw Brian's name on the long, impersonal list of those graduating without honors.

Soon after he started graduate school, Carter discovered that Brian owned a bookstore in the city. Carter didn't make contact until the decision to save Caitlin's life gave him a reason. A few days after Megan confirmed that she was pregnant, Carter took the train to the address downtown that he had already memorized. He pulled open the narrow glass door and surveyed the labyrinth of high bookcases. He rubbed his hands together and unzipped his coat.

Brian sat behind the cash register. His hair had thinned, and Carter could see lines around his eyes. His boyish skinniness had turned into the soft angularity of an adult. As the cowbell tied to the door handle settled, Brian didn't look up from his reading.

"Let me know if you need help finding something," he said. "If you want something from a high shelf, I'll get a ladder. Don't try to climb the bookcases." He turned a page.

"Hello, Brian," Carter said.

Without looking up, Brian reached for a bookmark, slid it into place, and closed the book in front of him. Staring at the book's blank cover, he said, "I remember the voice. Funny how something so long ago can seem so immediate." He sighed, and looked up. "Hello, Carter. You're looking well." He did not stand.

"I didn't think you'd be happy to see me," Carter said, "but you don't seem surprised."

"I *am* surprised that you came to see me today. I guess I'd be surprised on any given day. But am I surprised to see you again? Not really."

"Why's that?"

"Because I know you never returned the book to the library," Brian said. "I paid the fine. And I knew you wouldn't burn it like I asked you to."

Carter looked around. "Shouldn't someone in your line of work be morally opposed to book-burning?"

"I am."

Carter looked around again. "I wouldn't be surprised if at some point you came across another copy."

"Am I wrong?" Brian asked. "Are you here because you're looking for a copy, not because you already have one?"

"Would you find me a copy if I wanted it?"

"No," Brian said, "I wouldn't. But the question is moot. You already have a copy. You're here because you want me to do something you know I don't want to do."

Carter nodded.

"Leave, Carter. Get out of my life."

Carter moved closer. "I've always wondered – at exactly what point did you decide that everything was my fault? You used to be ambivalent."

"I never said anything was your fault. My life might have been easier if I thought everything was your fault, but I don't."

"What do you mean, exactly?"

Brian took off his glasses and stared at Carter. Carter thought he saw a spark of the admiration he had once taken for granted. "I don't care to discuss my thoughts with you," he said.

Carter shrugged. "Okay. But I want to discuss something with you. Will you hear me out?"

"Are you still married to Megan Penser?"

"Megan Penser Anderson," Carter said. "Yes."

"Humph. Surprised her mother let her change the name."

"It was a sore point."

Brian shook his head. "I'm sure you managed it. You always managed everything."

"You know, even after ten years of not speaking to each other, I still never thought we'd get down to accusations so quickly."

Brian stiffened. "If you feel accused, check your conscience. All I'm saying is that I was impressed when I heard you managed to win Megan over again. I wonder if you could have done the same with me if you'd tried."

"I'm flattered," Carter said.

"Don't be," Brian said. "I was putting myself down, not flattering you."

Carter shook his head. "I'm flattered that you think I have a conscience."

"Look, Carter, while I can't say that I've been around men who are better at it than you, I can say I've played mind games with some who might compete. In order for that particular pity-ploy to work, you need to have some kind of rapport to draw on. You don't have that with me."

Carter took a step closer. "Don't I?"

Brian blinked. "I'm not a kid anymore, Carter. Do me a favor and cut to the chase."

"Thank you," Carter said. "All I want is for you to listen."

Carter sketched a history of Caitlin's illness. The expression in Brian's eyes showed the emotional impact of this tragic news. When Carter finished, Brian said, "Well, I guess pity works even without any rapport. I'm sorry for you, Carter, I really am."

"So you know what comes next, don't you?" Carter asked.

Brian's face became darker. "I'd rather not guess."

"Megan is pregnant again."

Standing, Brian said, "You're not thinking of—"

"I am." Carter glanced at the floor. "I don't feel like I have a choice, knowing it can be done." He smiled. "You were awfully quick to get it. I think you *have* looked at the *Alchemy* again, haven't you?"

"I prefer Dr. Fincher's *Six Theses on Global Anthropology*," he said. "It's less esoteric. It's what made his reputation, you know. The *Alchemy* ruined him. Yes, I read it again."

"So you know exactly what I'm going to do."

"I think I do."

"So you understand why I need your help?"

"Yes," Brian said, "and you understand that there's no way in hell that I'm going to help you, right? If I do anything, I'm going to try my best to talk you out of it."

Carter grinned. "You really think you can talk me out of it?"

Brian did not return the smile. "That you can be so flippant about it disgusts me. Let's get this out on the table: you're planning on murdering your own child, right?"

"Murder is an ugly word. Sacrifice is uglier. I'm harvesting an unwanted fetus in order to save the life of my daughter. All the moral issues surrounding stem cell research and abortion apply here, but the issues surrounding murder do not."

Brian shook his head. "You know, there's something else I've always wondered. Do you believe your own rationalizations? For example, do you actually believe now that you and I were not directly responsible for that girl's death?"

"We were not blameless," Carter said, "but it *was* an accident. Even if you could convince a jury that the facts of the case were real, there could be no verdict worse than manslaughter. Involuntary manslaughter. Maybe reckless endangerment. I don't know. I don't study law."

"And what would a jury say about what you're planning on doing when your wife gives birth?"

"Touché. I don't think the law is equipped to handle my special circumstances."

"Oh, I think the law is perfectly well-equipped. You'd be found guilty of murder, and you know why? Because that's precisely what you'd be guilty of. People have had babies so they could use their organs to help sick older children before, you know. And come on, do you think you're the first person to think of sacrificing a child in exchange for eternal life?"

Brian waited while Carter soaked in his knowledge of the truth. "That's what this is really about, isn't it? It's not a new idea, Carter. People would get the whole story just from the headlines that label you as a satanic baby-killer. If you didn't get the death penalty, someone righteous would probably finish you off in prison."

Carter glared. "Thanks for the hypotheticals," he said. "I really didn't expect this kind of moral majority shit from you. You sound so fucking *smug*. How can you be so certain? What would you do in my position, watching someone you love die a slow and terrible death, knowing you have the power to stop it? Wouldn't you at least be tempted?"

Carter looked at Brian's bare fingers. "Or maybe you can't understand. Not married, right? No kids, right? You probably don't know anything about the kind of love that can drive a person to do desperate things. She's my *daughter*, Brian. I don't feel like I have much of a choice."

The cowbell on the door rang. A woman stepped through the narrow glass doorway, holding a tiny pad of paper in front of her beady librarian eyes. "Excuse me," she said, "but I've been combing the city for a few out-of-print titles, and I'm wondering if you might be able to help me."

Brian excused himself and led the woman back into the bookcase labyrinth. Carter heard him telling her that he didn't have a catalogue of every title on his shelves, so she'd have to do some searching. Some of the titles on her list were familiar; she might just get lucky. He came back to Carter and spoke softly: "I'm not married, and I don't have kids, but your assumption that you have some kind of superior understanding of love because you have a wife and a child is as offensive as it is stupid."

Carter's jaw tensed, and he clenched his fists. "Okay," he said, "so maybe you do know something about love. So answer my question – wouldn't you be tempted?"

"Probably," Brian said. "Definitely. But I wouldn't go through with it. I couldn't. Come on, Carter. Can you really imagine yourself looking down at your newborn baby, lifting up a knife, and—"

"Shhhh," Carter said. "Our lady librarian over there might have superhuman hearing. No need to be careless."

"If you're so worried about getting caught," Brian said, "you shouldn't have come here and told me your plan. Did you really think I'd help you?"

"Was that a threat?" Carter loosened his fists and took a deep breath. "Yes, I thought you might help me. I thought you might be in a unique position to sympathize with the choice I've made. Someday you might be in a similar situation – knowing you have the power to save someone you love…knowing the price is terrible. I'm under no delusion that I'll come out of this feeling good about myself. I might not even survive it at—"

"Bullshit, Carter. You are capable of an amazing amount of bullshit. I suppose you want me to think you're not at all interested in the main side-effect of this particular ritual, right? Like I said, I have read and reread the *Alchemy* in the last ten years. This plan of yours is all about survival. *Your* survival, Carter, not your daughter's. Immortality. 'The suture of the seeker,' Fincher calls it. It's what you're after."

"Yes, Brian, I don't want to die," Carter said. "If I get to live forever and save my daughter's life in the bargain, what's so wrong with that?"

"*That's* what you're willing to kill for. Yourself, not your daughter. Tell me – would you kill both your children if that's what it took?"

"Oh, you hurt me, Brian, you really do." Carter laughed, and then his eyes flared. "Come on, partner, it's the ultimate Faust trip – infinite life, which means infinite knowledge, for a one-time-only fee. If you did it with me, we'd both get the benefits. The Brian I used to know wouldn't be able to resist this."

"He certainly could," Brian said. "I don't hate myself enough to agree with you on that. I can't even imagine doing it, and it wouldn't even be my own child. How could you, Carter? How *could* you?"

Carter leaned over, brought his face close to Brian's, and whispered. "Because, like you, I hated myself after what happened with Jess, so I resigned myself to living a normal life. I tried it. I got the wife, I got the kid, I got into a good graduate school and was ready to be a good fucking husband, father, and citizen. Then suddenly the kid was diagnosed with a horrible disease, and every day of my life was about *death*. Hospitals and soiled sheets and hair falling out and obligation after obligation and the same goddamned shit every motherfucking day – I want more – I deserve more. You know about that, don't you Brian? You've lost enough over one mistake, haven't you? You want *more*, and I can give it to you."

Brian backed away. "I used to want more," he said. "But I've got my store. I've got a decent enough life, even though I still wonder if I deserve it. I don't want to live forever if it means living with *that*. And whether you realize it or not, you don't, either."

The shopper emerged from the bookcases and asked Brian about the price of an unmarked first edition. When Brian went to answer her, Carter left without a word.

He came back after Megan quit her job at the Penser Foundation. While Megan was still working, Carter had secretly spent days at home, working with Dr. Fincher. He performed Brian's levitation trick. He performed enough of the lesser rituals to feel confident that he didn't need Brian after all.

Carter arrived at the narrow glass door to Brian's shop just as he was closing. Brian was jangling his keys in the doorway when Carter knocked on the glass. He let Carter in. "Carter, I never thought I'd say this, but I'm glad to see you again."

Carter wiped his feet on the doormat and stepped away so that Brian could finish locking the door. "Oh, really," Carter said. "Why's that?" He had been drinking. He felt fine.

Brian didn't make eye contact. "I looked up your number and your address. I kept meaning to call or stop by to talk to you more about...about what you came here to talk to me about. You left so suddenly, I never got a chance—"

"To what? Tell me more about how stupid I am? Make more threats about how far you might go to stop me?"

Brian grabbed a stack of books and started walking into the bookcase labyrinth. Only half of the lights were still on. He didn't motion for Carter to follow him, but Carter did, looking down each crooked aisle of books that they passed. Some of them connected to one another, and some were dead ends. They were all uninhabited.

Brian turned down an aisle and spoke with his back to Carter. "More or less," he said. "I don't want to insult you or threaten you. I don't know why I still care, but I kind of think I want to save you. Is that stupid?"

"Save me from what?" Carter asked.

Brian found places on a shelf for two of the books in his arms. His shoulder brushed against Carter as he made his way around to another aisle. "Trite as it sounds, I want to save you from yourself," Brian said. "I know you, or knew you, and I can't believe you've changed that much. When we were younger, you were...intrepid...but you were never without some inhibitions, without some sense of right and wrong. Hell, ethics used to be one of your favorite topics of debate." He shelved more books, turning his back to Carter again.

Carter clinched his fists. "You want to save me from myself. I never asked you for that kind of help, Brian."

"Of course you didn't," Brian said. He had reduced the stack in his arms to two volumes. Following Brian back into the center aisle, Carter looked behind them. The glass front door seemed distant, almost invisible. Books and posters covered most of the other windows. Brian turned into another crooked aisle. Carter followed. From here, the front door would be totally invisible.

Carter looked at Brian's back, his narrow shoulders, his thin neck. "Stopping you is the only kind of help I can give you," Brian said. "Even if you think you could live with what you're going to do, I know you couldn't."

"News-flash, Brian," Carter said. "You never really knew me at all."

Brian slid the final book onto a shelf. "Maybe I didn't know you," Brian said. "But if I can't save you, I can at least save Megan from what you want to do. However you've managed to draw her into this, she can't want it, not really."

"You think you know an awful lot about my wife," Carter said.

"If I can't save her," Brian said, "I want to save the baby. It's...what I have to do."

"Ah-ha!" Carter cried. "Now we have the truth! You come off all noble, talking about how I say I want to save my daughter but I really want to save myself, but you're just as selfish as I am, aren't you? This isn't about me or my wife or the thing she's carrying in her womb. This is about *you*, about your guilt over some questionable things you did ten years ago. You're after redemption, right? You want to save yourself, right? You and I are the same, Brian. Admit it."

"We are *not* the same. You might be right about my motives, but if you can't see the difference, I'm not going to bother trying to show it to you. I'm going to stop you, Carter."

Carter laughed. "So now we get back to the threats. Tell me, are you going to go to the police right now? Get yourself locked up as some kind of lunatic? Hmmmm?"

Brian raised his chin. "I rather thought that threatening to go to the police *afterward* might be enough to stop you. You want to live forever, but are you willing to do it in prison?"

"So you're blackmailing me. Blackmail. Is that the best you've got?"

"It's enough, isn't it?"

Carter's hands were at his sides, balled into tight fists. When he spoke again, he curled his lip so Brian could see his teeth. "You're the one who's stupid, Brian. I used to have such respect for you. Think about it. If, as you say, I'm willing to murder my own child to get what I want, why wouldn't I just do the same to you?"

Brian's faced registered the words. He shifted his weight from foot to foot.

"Nothing to say to that, huh? How do you like feeling *threatened?*"

Brian rolled his shoulders back. "You don't scare me, Carter." Taking quick steps down the crooked, crowded aisle, Brian moved toward Carter. He stayed close to the shelves on the side away from where Carter was standing. When he started to pass, Carter grabbed him by the shirt and pushed him back. Brian stumbled but didn't fall. Carter backed him up to the aisle's dead end. Brian's shoulders pressed against shelves, and his eyes darted from side to side. "Carter, be reasonable," he said.

"I *am* being reasonable," Carter said. "For someone who's not scared of me, you look awfully unsettled. Is there something you want to say?"

When Carter moved closer, Brian leaned forward, giving himself room to throw a punch.

"Carter, we were friends once," he said. "You might be able to rationalize what we did to Jess as an accident, and you might be able to rationalize killing a newborn, but you can't rationalize murdering me in cold blood. You can't. Don't even try."

"Funny, that sounds kind of like begging for your life," Carter said. "After all that posturing, now you're only thinking of yourself. Selfish to the last."

Carter lunged, and Brian sidestepped. Before Carter could get new bearings, Brian swung, and his fist connected with Carter's chest. The hit stunned Carter long enough for Brian to find an opening. He pushed around Carter and dashed toward the center aisle.

Carter was faster: he closed the ground between them in a second and grabbed Brian from behind. He ripped Brian's shirt as he yanked it and swung him back into the crooked aisle, away from the sightlines of the glass door. Carter charged, forcing Brian against the shelves along the wall.

As Carter closed in on him, Brian raised his forearms to his face, creating a barrier. Carter wrapped his hands around Brian's wrists and yanked him to one side, slamming his shoulder against a bookcase. Brian cried out in pain, but he recovered and pushed away from the bookcase before Carter could make another move. Carter felt shelves hitting hard against his back.

Carter leaned over and plowed into Brian again, smashing him against a bookcase. The collision tipped it over, and the sound of tumbling books gave way to crash after crash of toppling bookcases, falling like dominoes as the labyrinth collapsed. Brian sprawled, held up at an angle by a bookcase. Dazed, he tried to push himself back to his feet. Carter descended on him, pinning Brian's legs with his knees. Carter's fingers wrapped around Brian's neck.

As Carter started to squeeze, Brian's hands grasped his wrists. Carter could feel Brian's whole frame straining to pry himself loose, but he wasn't strong enough. The hues of his face changed from red to purple. Carter saw veins standing out where they weren't supposed to be, and he started pushing against Brian's throat rhythmically, throttling him, crushing his larynx.

Carter's mind wandered. He thought about how Megan didn't seem to care that he sometimes came home late with beer on his breath. He thought he might stop off for another drink before going home.

He didn't notice when Brian ceased struggling. When he finally released Brian's neck, he saw that he'd probably been dead for awhile. Remembering the sounds of the collapsing bookcases, Carter dashed down the aisle and peered around the corner. He saw no one through the distant glass door. The street outside looked empty.

He found some flammable cleansers in a closet at the back of the store. He paused for a moment, wondering whether a copy of *The Alchemy of Will* might be somewhere in one of the fallen bookcases. If so, he would be fulfilling the request Brian had made a decade ago.

He emptied the cash register on the way out and dumped its contents in the river the next day. The fire in the bookstore didn't make big news. Some of the local stations reported on it, mostly to praise the fire department's efficient response. Investigators only found one body amidst the ashes of books, and forensics determined that the man had been dead before he had burned. Arson, robbery, murder – case unsolved. The bruise on Carter's chest where Brian had hit him faded in a couple of days.

Downward

Today. Laundry day.

Doing the laundry required the only significant excursion away from the apartment: Carter had to journey all the way to the basement to use the machines. Otherwise, the grocery store delivered, and Carter only had to walk down the hall to use the garbage chute. The front door was always bolted, and Carter kept the two deadbolt keys with him at all times. He usually carried the cell phone in the same pocket as the keys. He had disconnected the landline, and Internet access had gone with it. Carter and Megan ate together, slept together, and watched TV together. Megan got to bathe alone, but sometimes she thought she could feel Carter listening to each splash of water.

Megan had resigned herself to imprisonment. Her resignation weakened her sense of her own innocence – when Carter was asleep beside her, she knew she had options – but the locked door and severed lines of communication brought her far enough away from culpability. She could take pills, watch TV, and wait for the day when she'd lose her husband, drop the baggage around her middle, and regain her daughter.

She loved laundry days. They could come as little as three days or as much as two weeks apart. Since Megan and Carter never went anywhere or did anything, Carter reasoned that they could wear clothes more than once. The stench of Megan's pajamas provided the best indication of when Carter's next trip downstairs would have to be, but her tendency to stumble and spill things introduced pleasant randomness. Laundry day meant Carter's absence, time when Megan could pretend that the apartment was her territory again.

The baby had dropped a week ago, signaling the fast-approaching end of the pregnancy, and this was Carter's first trip out since. He offered to come back up between laundry loads, reducing his absences to little more than fifteen minutes. Megan refused. "Even if labor starts right when you're putting in the first load, it won't end until long after you're finished. I've got the instructions and lots of codeine. I won't miss you."

When the cramping started, Megan didn't think much of it. Between Braxton-Hicks contractions and unpredictable bowel movements, she had become used to odd troubles in her lower regions. Her back hurt, but her back always hurt. The cramps led to a panicked rush to the bathroom for diarrhea. Looking down from her seat on the toilet, she noticed new pink spots on her underwear, and she started to connect the symptoms.

On her way back to the sofa, the pain almost knocked her over. Yes, she had been having contractions, *real* ones, for some time. They were becoming regular, and the pain was getting more intense. Labor had begun.

She sat down and turned up the volume on the TV. It was going to take awhile, she knew, so she channel-surfed to find something that might distract her. With each channel flip, a nasty voice in her head chanted louder: *this is it, this is it, this is it.*

Detach, Megan. It's a bad dream, and when you wake up, it'll be like these last nine months never happened. It's just pain, meaningless pain. Do not think of what you are about to lose.

The delivery itself would be beyond her control, and she would have no part in what would come after. She would do nothing criminal. She turned up the volume some more and thought about how mild and brief the most recent contraction had been. How far had she dilated? Too soon to think about that. This wasn't it, not yet.

This is it, this is it, this is it.

Bright colors lit up the screen — a cartoon that Megan didn't recognize. Caitlin would probably know what it was. Caitlin spent much of her waking time watching television. Megan remembered Caitlin's toddler fascination with the TV screen, with DVDs Megan had once picked up of purple dinosaurs and incoherent bouncy characters who had once managed to stir political controversy. Megan couldn't comprehend the attraction of these things, but she enjoyed watching the pleasure that lit up her daughter's face each time a colorful character repeated a familiar song.

Waiting. When would the next contraction be? Thirty minutes, twenty, ten?

Megan knew she should change the channel again, but the colors hypnotized her. Her mind became stuck on the idea of childhood. Everything mattered. The color of the wallpaper in the nursery, the songs she chose to sing, everything. Megan remembered the primary colors of the mobile she had bought. "Ring around the Roses" was a good enough song for children who didn't know what it was about. It had a bouncing melody. It might evoke memories of the shaking, sheltering womb.

The mobile. What had Carter done with it? He had told her where he had put it, but Megan couldn't remember. In other circumstances, it would be in the baby's room. The baby would have a room of its own. They would be living in a bigger place, an apartment closer to ground level, or at least a building with an elevator that actually worked. If they couldn't afford such a place in a good part of town, Susan would make up the difference. Susan would say that it was important for each child to have her, or his, own room.

Its own room. A cure doesn't need a room. It needs a hypodermic needle, something to focus and maximize its utility. Shut up, Megan, just shut up. Stop thinking.

This is it, this is it, this is it.

Was that new pain or a memory of the old pain? A contraction or just a spasm of muscles, an earthquake of anxiety?

She had refused to know exactly how Carter would do it. He wouldn't just kill the baby; he'd kill it in a special way. She knew. She had read enough to know.

This is it.

Time passed, another contraction came, and then another. Pain. Trouble concentrating on the television. Megan managed to break away from the cartoons. The news channel nauseated her for a moment before she clicked and found reruns of black and white sitcoms, portals to another era. Women stayed at home because there was nowhere else to go, and men always seemed to have deep comforting voices. The men were strong and handsome, domineering but capable of infinite care. They'd never think of slaughtering a newborn. They'd never think of their children at all. Men worked; women reared. Black and white, stark, sickly, repulsive and attractive and – OWWWW!

Black and white fantasies about children who were obedient. About children who wouldn't have the audacity to get sick and spend years in the process of dying.

The TV blipped off. Megan stood and made her way to the stereo. She was rolling through rock stations when Carter came through the door, arms struggling with an overflowing basket of clean clothes and linens. Megan said nothing. She settled on a station while Carter set the basket on their bed. A sudden weakness in her legs forced her to sit in Carter's recliner. When Carter came back to the living room, he saw his pregnant wife collapsed in his chair and asked, "How are you?"

"Having contractions. How are you?"

Megan enjoyed watching the color drain out of Carter's face. In his head, there'd now be a voice saying *this is it, this is it, this is it.*

Would the blood he was about to spill make him suffer or salivate? Expectant fathers by the bedside, no longer able to demonstrate the way to breathe because their own tears and ecstasy had overwhelmed them. Expectant fathers, pacing in waiting rooms, jumping every time a door opened with news for someone else. Expectant fathers, sitting at home, not letting their anticipation of a phone call distract them from the work they had to do. Not Carter. He was *involved.*

"What can I do?" Carter said. "Can I get you anything? Do you want me to help you into the bedroom?"

"Nothing. They're getting close, but they're still more than ten minutes apart. I'm afraid my water broke while I was sitting on the sofa."

"Don't worry about that. Don't worry about anything. Just try to...relax. And let me know if I can do anything, anything at all."

"Bring me one of the codeine tablets. That last contraction hurt like crazy." It hadn't.

"You know you can't take more than two or three of those—"

"Bring it *now.*"

Carter obeyed. "Do you want water or something else to drink?"

"Water. Not too much of it. I don't want to piss all over the bed."

He smiled at her with manufactured warmth in his eyes. "If it happens, it happens. I don't want you to worry about anything at all."

"You keep saying that." Don't worry about the way you're going to kill it. Don't worry about its screams or all the blood. Don't worry about whether or not, after this is all over, it will all have been for nothing. What if Caitlin dies anyway? What if she recovers from her cancer and gets hit by a bus a week later? Nothing will erase this. Nothing. "I *am* worried, Carter." He handed her the glass of water and sat down on a clean part of the sofa. "What if something goes wrong? What if it's a breech, or I need a Caesarian, or—"

"We've gone over this," Carter said. "If that happens, then I'll call an ambulance. But it's not going to happen."

If it happens, then all the agony of the last nine months will have been for nothing, and yet...and yet the baby would live...but Caitlin would die...but the baby would live, and there wouldn't be this feeling, this horrible, aching feeling like termites gnawing through her chest. *Let it happen. Let it happen.*

"Don't *worry*," Carter said. "It won't happen."

And if it does happen, you probably wouldn't call for an ambulance. You'd just cut me open, get what you want, and let both of us die.

"Talk to me, Carter. Take me away from the things I'm thinking."

"What are you thinking?"

"Goddamn it! I said take me the fuck away!"

"All right, all right." He smiled radiantly, like nuclear fallout. "What do you want to talk about?"

"Anything that's far from now, from us, from the baby...."

Carter leapt to a default: literature. He talked about surrealism, about his latest thoughts on how early twentieth-century formal experimentation in fiction was just a battle over who could best claim the title of *real*. Ridiculous words describing the real brought Megan a comforting sense of unreality. Carter managed to maintain a steady drone of academic nonsense while timing contractions, which got closer and closer. Megan didn't listen to him. He wasn't really saying anything anyway. The tone of his voice was all she needed. She closed her eyes to obliterate his face. Not an image, not a meaning, just senseless sound, a cushion. An invitation to dream.

Eventually, she started to drift, not into sleep but into a distortion akin to sleep. Wild locks of hair looked like horns on Carter's head, and she laughed. "Prince of lies, destroyer of innocence," she mumbled.

The words halted his droning and brought Carter to attention. "What did you say?"

"Destroyer of innocence!" Her pronouncement sounded comical. "What?"

"My little, little baby, coming soon now. Bring me another pill, Carter. The destroyer. Ha-ha! How did we make it this far? How did we?"

He fetched the pill. "You know, I wonder if you're just pretending to be as out of it as you're acting."

"I am!" she said. "Pretending! Pretending I'm a real woman, and you're a real man, and this isn't a nightmare! Make-believe time! Caitlin loved make-believe. The new baby would love it, too. You, destroyer—"

"Of innocence, yeah, I heard. That's the problem, you know. People would keep life-saving research from being done because there's this idea that baby bodies, even dead fetuses, are somehow the most sacred and valuable things in the world. It's because of that thing you say I want to destroy. Innocence. It's a lie, Megan. Children aren't innocent.

"I've got an uncle who used to live down the street from this nice little family of four, a professional middle-aged couple and two beautiful boys. One of those precious little innocent boys slaughtered four of his neighbors and God knows what else. Bloody and horrible, young and innocent. Maybe the Christians have one thing right. Maybe we're all just born bad. Why are people who aren't born yet so much more important than people who are alive? Me, I value the living. My daughter is alive, and I want to keep her that way. There's no such thing as innocence, Megan. It's something a bunch of poets made up to fight child labor laws. It's a lie we tell ourselves so we can sleep at night."

"Sleep! Yes, I want to sleep!" In the background, faded but persistent: *this is it, this is it, this is it*, like a waltz. "I can't hear you, Carter. Don't you know I'm not listening to you?" She heard every word, but they floated around her like soap bubbles. They popped and left their slime all over her skin.

"Excuse me," he said. "I'll be back in a minute."

The hours were whizzing by, and with Carter out of the room, the waltz could get louder. The triple rhythm of *this-is-it* pulled against the complex counterpoint of two heartbeats, Megan's and the baby's. She couldn't hear them, but she could feel them both, her heart and his, hers, its. Thump-thump, thump-thump, this is it!

"Carter!" she yelled. "Carter!"

He scooted back into the room. "What is it?"

"Why did you leave? I need your voice in here. Keep talking. Distract me from the music in my head."

"Christ, Megan. I guess I have to indulge your melodramatic fantasies now, huh? I'll be right back. I was just getting the bed ready. I think it's time to move you."

Oh, you move me, Carter, you do. The first time we had sex was a revelation. I think that's when you infected me, planted the seed that grew into the gnarled hand that covered my eyes when I said *yes*, yes I want you to marry me, yes I'll believe you're not only a human being but also a decent one, yes, yes, yes. Thump-thump.

"Come on, let me help you stand." His arms were around her, touching her, making her skin crawl. She tried to pull away from him but almost lost her balance. She had no choice. She had to let him lead her into the bedroom. Their bedroom, where there was still a special calendar in a nightstand drawer. Their bedroom, where once they had made love and meant it. This is it!

"AHHH!" She buckled with the pain, intense and lasting, and Carter grabbed her beneath the armpits, steadying her rubber legs. Together, they stumbled the rest of the way to the bed, where Carter had piled several layers of old blankets and towels. A chair near the bed would prop up her legs when she scooted her bottom all the way to the bed's edge. *Not yet.*

Before getting her on the bed, they stripped off her pajama pants. "It's better now," she said, resting her head against the soft pillow. "Better." And quieter, too. Softer thumps. All in her head, of course. She knew that. Like Carter said, she was entitled to *indulge* now. This was her moment, her last moment of humanity.

Twilight dimmed the bedroom window. It was winter again, and the days were short. People would be coming up all those flights of stairs soon, getting home from work, preparing to kick up their feet for a quiet evening. They were people who had jobs to go to and husbands and wives and children to come home to. For them, the world was too big. It dwarfed them, made them feel like they didn't have any say in the rhythm of their days. Megan and Carter lived in a tiny twilight world where they *could* have a say, where rhythms thumped according to their wills. They had the power to get what they wanted, but they had to pay a price. One living child for the price of a dead one. They didn't have the power to change the way the universe balanced things out, but they got to choose who got which side of the teetering scales. Megan didn't want a say: she wanted the world big. "I want it," she said.

"What do you want?" Carter asked. "I'll get it for you," he said.

"I want both. I want my daughter and my baby. Can we make that happen? Can we will that to happen? Is there a formula for that in your book? Will you let me have both, Carter? Will you?"

"I can't," he said. His voice cracked. "I know what you mean. I want both, too. I want everything."

In the fading light, Megan could see tears in her husband's eyes. "We can have it, Carter. Take the choice away. We can have both. Caitlin will go when she goes, but she'll get to meet her baby brother or sister. Can you see that, Carter? Can you see the look on her face when she sees the brother or sister she gets to call her very own?"

Megan thought of Katy, Caitlin's worn out plastic doll, buried beneath the sheets of the hospital bed. Children often feared that new siblings would replace them. Caitlin would be an exception: unlike most older siblings, she'd *know* that the new baby would replace her. Megan imagined her precocious daughter, squeezing her doll under one arm, saying, "I'm glad you and Daddy will have a new baby when I'm gone. I know I'd be lonely without my baby."

"I want both, Carter. Please. Please don't kill my baby." She wondered how long Carter had been holding her hand. She wondered how long she had been sobbing.

"Megan, I can't take the choice away. We've already made it."

His words brought the music back: THUMP-THUMP! THIS IS IT!!

"Please, please, please, please, please!" She had seen the tears in his eyes. They had to be genuine. Her husband's eyes could manufacture all kinds of things, but she had never seen them fake tears. "Please," she gasped through a sob.

"Shhhh, Megan. Shhhh." He stroked her hair. This time his touch didn't repulse her.

She squeezed his hand and tried to smile at him. This was the man she had married, the man she had been happy with, the man she had suffered with. When they had heard Caitlin's prognosis, they had cried together. They were crying together now.

A contraction hit her, caught her by surprise and stayed there, seconds, a minute, countless frantic thumps. A sob became a scream. "I'm going to go turn up the stereo," Carter said.

Megan had to concentrate on breathing. When Carter came back into the room, heavy sounds of classic rock followed him, but they only brushed against the surface of Megan's ears. She had moved beyond sound and sight. The sun had finished setting. Even though Carter switched on a lamp by the bed, the darkness remained.

Shapes filled the darkness. At first they were geometric and strange, but eventually they became familiar. Bassinette, changing table, funny little animals on the wallpaper, a mobile: at first it was the nursery she had imagined for the new baby, but then she realized it was Caitlin's room, the one she *had* been able to decorate. Those sleepless nights, those long gazes into a tiny soft face filled with promise, the long daydreams about the future. All in that room. Right over there.

"Carter, I'm so tired," Megan said. When she blinked, the bed and her husband came back to her. She blinked again and brought back the mutating geometries of the dark.

"You'll get to rest soon," he said. "Just a little bit longer. It's so close. Keep breathing. Don't push yet."

A kite! Megan saw a kite! In the early days, after the diagnosis but while Caitlin still had the strength and desires of a normal child, they'd spent a whole day in the park teaching Caitlin to fly a kite. It was the sort of scene every childhood needed. It was an archetype that Carter and Megan had decided Caitlin should have in her life, however short her life might end up being. All three of them, laughing on a windy day. Three of them.

Another contraction. Hardly any time had passed at all.

The kite transformed into a bird, a black one that descended on Megan's head and started plucking at her closed eyes. She knew it wasn't real, but she still tried to free her hand from Carter's to shoo it away. It morphed into darkness. Megan turned her head from side to side and found Caitlin.

For a moment, she became aware of her own closed eyelids, their blankness.

She found Caitlin, and Carter was standing there with her. This was the real Carter, not the Carter who had gained so much weight and was about to kill her baby, but the real one, lean and beautiful and passionate. He loved his daughter. He did. Something of that love had gotten lost somehow, had been eaten by the cancer, but it had been real. How he stood there next to her, beaming down at her – there was no way that the look on his face wasn't real love. The real Carter who had that kind of love could never go through with the murder. He would hear Megan begging for her child's life and melt. There were two Carters, one of them holding her hand, and the other standing with their daughter in the dark.

Caitlin and Carter approached the bed. Caitlin got on the bed and crawled toward Megan, treading heavily with hands and feet like she did when she pretended to be a bear. Megan felt her daughter on one side and her husband on the other. The second Carter had somehow managed to overlap the first; the two men occupied the same space.

A contraction jolted her away from the waking dream, back to Caitlin's absence and the singular Carter. She crunched his hand in her own, and he bore with her through the pain. "They're really close now," he said. "Pretty soon you'll be able to start pushing."

She was aware of the desire to push, but her awareness was vague. She hadn't taken enough pills to make her this way. This vagueness, this thinning of perception – she had done this herself. It was a marvel. She was a marvel. He was a marvel. The whole great big tiny little world was a marvel.

"Everything's going to be all right, Megan." Her mother's voice, from the night of the vampire thieves.

Please don't. Please don't kill my baby.

THIS IS IT THIS IS IT THIS IS IT!!!!!!

Caitlin was beside her again. She was giggling and bouncing on the bed. The bounces made the whole room jiggle up and down, and Megan felt seasick. Caitlin bounced higher, giggled louder. "Stop it," Megan said. "Please don't."

"There's no stopping it now," Carter said. "Do you feel ready?"

"I can't stop it," Megan said. It was as if the idea had never occurred to her – if she just didn't *push*, the baby would never be born, and if the baby were never born, it would never die. It could stay inside her forever.

"Mommy, Mommy!" Caitlin cried, bouncing higher and higher.

She had to push. She couldn't resist it now. She nodded in answer to Carter's question. He helped her get into the final position, feet on the chair. He put himself in place to catch the baby with the hands that would kill it...him...her.

"Mommy, Mommy!"

"*What*, Caitlin? Can't you just give me a minute?"

The real Carter looked confused. "Megan, are you okay? Is something going wrong?"

THIS IS IT, the voice reminded her. "I'm pushing," she said.

"Mommy, Mommy!"

One high bounce, and Caitlin landed on top of her, right on top of her belly. Megan looked at her daughter's back as the girl's head dropped down out of sight. Caitlin was leaning down between Megan's legs, reaching, pulling, tearing the baby out, one piece a time. When Caitlin twisted around to giggle at her mother, her face was smeared with blood, and she held a tiny leg in one hand.

Megan screamed.

"I see the head!"

"Sleep, sleep, sleep, dear God let me sleep!"

"Soon, Megan, soon! It's almost here!"

"I don't want this! No, no, please God, don't let him do it! Please God, let me sleep!"

Megan's entire lower body was tingling, burning. Something was slithering out of her. Caitlin was gone now, and so was the other Carter. She was alone with the only other occupant of her tiny world, and he was about to catch a cure in his arms. A cure full of blood and organs and covered with delicate baby skin. It would have a face that looked like Megan's, or a face that looked like Carter's. It would have features that would mark it as their very own. It. Him. Her.

"Sleep, let me sleep. Please don't, Carter. I want to sleep."

THIS IS IT. THIS. IS. IT.

"I've got it!"

For a second, everything stopped: the thumping, the sound of her own breathing. And then – crying. A baby's crying.

"I want to hold it, please let me hold it." Megan's vision was blurry. She could see that Carter had something in his arms, but it wasn't clear. "Please, Carter, don't do it. Please let me hold it."

"Don't look at it, Megan. Don't look at it or think about it. It's over. Sleep now."

Chills wracked her body. She was shivering, vibrating, conducting a million violent spasms of freezing cold electricity from her toes to her brain. The field of her vision contracted, and all the sounds – the stereo, the crying, her own lonely heartbeat – diminished. She heard Carter saying she needed to push again, and she complied. She blinked her eyes, fighting against the spasms of cold, trying to get a glimpse of the thing he had set on the bed while he waited for the afterbirth.

Megan caught a glimpse. *It* was a girl.

Megan slept.

The Descent of Carter Anderson, Continued

Brian was a disappointment. Megan, with all her screaming about wanting to abandon the plan at the very moment when it was finally on its way – she was a disappointment, too. The people he had once claimed to care for had all disappointed him. Carter would not disappoint himself.

Megan was sleeping.

"Hesitation is the enemy," Carter said. The sound of his own voice surprised him. It wavered. "My will is law," he said, and then laughed. "Jesus, Carter, you sound like a motivational speaker hawking a pyramid scheme."

His voice hadn't roused Megan. She had escaped. Carter was glad.

Megan had begged not to know how he would perform the sacrifice. He had steered conversations in that direction on several occasions, trying to make a discussion of the details seem natural. Each time, she had cut him off. He did not force her to listen because there was no reason to. Carter was not cruel. He was simply a man who got the things he had good reason to want. *The Alchemy of Will* stated that reason is the backbone of the will. Dr. Fincher was very clear: whoever has reason has power.

Reason was the bridge between the idea of killing and killing itself. Brian had threatened Carter. He had told Carter no. Caitlin was dying. Carter would die someday. These were reasons. Will turned them into power.

All of Dr. Fincher's rituals, no matter how arcane or involved, were reasonable. The chanting blocked out any mental static that might interfere with the task at hand. The sacrifice promoted discipline, and infinite discipline created omnipotent thought. Carter interpreted the "disembodied will" that Dr. Fincher named as part of the coming sacrifice as little more than an excarnate expression of himself, a means to harness the unused energies of those who had no idea about what the mind could accomplish. The chanting, the sacrifice, the disembodied will, and the *Alchemy* itself were tools: Carter reasoned that the power to use them was his own.

He had bought a dagger and followed the book's directions for consecrating it a week before the birth. Without Megan noticing, he had hidden it in their bedroom. It was waiting under the bed throughout the delivery. He used the blade to cut the umbilical cord, introducing the consecrated blade to blood according to the *Alchemy*'s instructions.

He carried the shrieking baby and the dagger into the living room and shut the bedroom door behind him. The closed door and the stereo, he reasoned, could be – should be – enough to keep the baby-sounds from disturbing Megan and the neighbors.

Carter retrieved the small coffin from the back of the closet where he had hidden it under old coats. The *Alchemy* stressed that the details of this ritual had to be observed, so he had risked the visit to the funeral home. The funeral director had agreed that the coffin would be a perfect set piece for a play about vampires. Carrying the coffin up the stairs to his apartment by himself had been difficult, but Carter had managed. If Megan had ever noticed the mass in the coat closet, she had said nothing.

The closed coffin had to be draped with a white cloth. Glass jars of varying volumes had to line the edges. The baby had to lie in the center on top of the coffin. It had to be naked and unfettered, and Carter had to be careful not to let the wriggling, shivering thing knock over any of the jars.

The ritual called for a "representation" of the person the sacrifice would save; the "seeker" had to see and focus on the representation throughout the procedure. Carter used the most recent photograph of Caitlin that he could find. In it, she wore a blue bandana on her head and showed off crooked teeth in her smile. It was one of the few pictures he and Megan had taken at the hospital. They preferred not to bring their camera on most visits.

Naked and kneeling before the coffin, Carter brought the dagger's blade to his chest and began to cut. The diagonal line stretched from shoulder to ribs, crossing his heart. With his own blood on his fingers, he drew a line from the baby's forehead to its legs.

He started chanting. The tiny shrieking made concentration difficult. The urge to check the bedroom door, to see if Megan were bursting out to come to her baby's rescue, interfered as well. The chant continued, beating back the static of wife and daughter.

Megan battling to protect her young would be fierce. Carter understood that. He was not without protective feelings of his own, and he had seen the tension rippling through his wife's body as she had stood by Caitlin's bedside. The strength that had been useless for Caitlin could save this one. If she woke, if she could stand, if she could fight, she would. Carter had a dagger, but she had months of agony to unleash. He didn't know if he could disarm her a second time.

Chanting, concentrating, focusing. The only light in the room came from a lamp by the sofa and the window overlooking a night filled with headlights, streetlamps, and stars. There was no moon. The lighting was soft and pleasant, and the shadows were still. The only movements were the wriggling of the baby and the unsteadiness of the dagger in Carter's hands.

He looked at the sacrifice, the photograph, the dagger, and the door. Was Megan asleep? Was she listening? Was she waiting?

Concentrate! Focus!

After more chanting, Carter began to lose track of the door and the wriggling and the still shadows. He stopped feeling the dagger's handle in his palms, and he stopped hearing the music and screams. He was alone with the words he had to speak.

Detecting the right moment with a sense he had first developed ten years before, he halted the chanting, opened his eyes, and raised the dagger. He decided to plunge the blade into the baby's chest from a height. Since he didn't know how difficult penetrating the breastbone would be, he wanted to be sure he would have the force to do it in one thrust. He could not hesitate.

He thought about Megan throwing the door open and lunging at him. The blade was ready. He didn't want to kill Megan. He had never really *wanted* to kill anyone. Want was subordinate to reason. If Megan attacked, there would be more than one dead body in their apartment tonight. Carter would spill more blood than could fit into the jars that lined the coffin's edges.

The door. The jars. The coffin. The dagger. The screaming thing. The picture of Caitlin. The next step. The animus – Carter's will, a single stroke, a single act...

He lowered the dagger. The idea of plunging it in had been ridiculous. The force of the blow would cause too much damage. Baby bones would be soft. He wanted a quick end, but want was subordinate.

A song ended. The stereo was silent for a half-second, and the baby's screams seemed louder. They reached a new pitch as the blade bit into butter-soft skin. Sharp metal slid through bone as a new song began. When blood welled up through the incision, Carter had to use touch instead of sight to guide the blade. The screams had stopped by the time he slipped his fingers in and pried the tiny chest apart. Carter strained to identify the things he needed. Each jar required particular contents. When he finished, the baby's blood smeared his hands, arms, chest, stomach, and legs. It made his body hairs stick together.

Carter looked over at the bedroom door, which hadn't moved. He stood up. The room spun around him, and he vomited. When the nausea receded, he tracked blood from the altar to the stereo. Smearing the power button with red, he created a lasting silence. The air in the room was cold on his wet, naked skin.

He waited. If the ritual had worked, he expected that it would make him feel different. He expected to feel both his immortality and his ability to heal Caitlin in the same way he had felt strong when he and Brian had run by the river. When he knew he had succeeded, he would go to the hospital to perform the ritual's final phase. When he had the power, he would make his daughter, his only daughter, healthy again.

The *Alchemy* offered no advice about what to do after completing the sacrifice. Carter considered burning the contents of the jars as an offering and shook his head. An offering to what? Himself? He thought about putting all the jars inside the coffin. Somehow the ritual needed a final push, some sort of closure that would bring on the effects of the "disembodied will," the power to heal and "the suture of the seeker." He had done everything he was supposed to do, but nothing was happening. Carter's mind clouded over with doubt, and he shivered.

His knees buckled as his tired brain replayed his actions. The cutting – guiding the blade through...a baby – his baby – his daughter. *It*, he had called her. Always it. He had called her *it* for Megan's sake. He hadn't needed such delusions. He had known what had to be done, for Caitlin, for himself—

Doubt. Shivering. Cold blood on naked skin.

The carcass on the altar tugged at his attention. Something had to happen soon. Something was coming. Something had to come after what he had done. The thing could be power, or it could be...something else. But that was absurd.

He decided to shower. As he stepped into the stall and adjusted the water, he concentrated on practicality. He planned what to pack in his suitcase. He thought about getting on a bus to the airport. He wondered if he would be able to get a ticket and get out of the city before Megan could call the police, before the police could alert all the travel depots. Would Megan even call? She would have all the evidence she would need to name him as the sole culprit. Would she realize that?

Practical things, practical things. He had to get the blood out from under his fingernails. He had to scrub it out of the hairs on his chest.

Where would he go?

He turned off the shower when the water swirling down the drain ran clear. He was leaning out to grab his towel when his knees buckled a second time. His feet slipped on the shower floor, and his face almost crashed into porcelain. Recovering, he thought of falling, breaking his legs, and waiting until someone came and took him away. To a hospital, or to prison. He would go, and it would all be for nothing. He had spent a decade of his life planning, and a slip in the shower could end it. He laughed as he dried himself.

He was putting the towel on its rack when his legs collapsed. The hard tiles of the bathroom floor smashed against him, igniting his body with pain. He looked at his legs. They hurt. He could feel the pain, but he could feel nothing else. When he tried to move his legs, his thighs flexed, but nothing else responded.

He couldn't move his legs, but he didn't think he was paralyzed. When he pinched his calves, they hurt. Clenching every muscle that would respond, he tried to bend a knee. Nothing. He had sensation but no control.

His heart pounded, and his breathing quickened. "Megan!" he called. He had turned off the stereo. She should have been able to hear him through both the bathroom and the bedroom doors. "Megan!" he yelled again. "Megan, help!"

A second attempt to move, to flex even his quadriceps and hamstrings, resulted in failure. He slapped his thighs and felt the sting of his hands. "MEGAN!!" he screamed.

He reached up, using the muscles in his stomach and back to get his hand high enough to turn the bathroom doorknob. With one less door between them, he called to Megan again. "HELP ME, PLEASE!" Maybe if Megan didn't wake up and hear, some neighbor would. He remembered what he had said to Megan about getting help in the city. "FIRE!" he yelled. "FIRE! FIRE! PLEASE GOD, FIRE!"

No pounding on the front door. No wife rushing to help him. He was alone. Alone with a coffin, stripped bones, and jars full of gore. Unable to stand. Unable to run. Unable to do anything.

Maybe this was it. Maybe this was how his powers began to manifest themselves. He told himself to stop screaming. The last thing he needed was for some stranger to burst into the apartment and find the mess. This was just how it happened. He needed to wait through this part before he got what he wanted. After all, he had never done anything so extreme before. He should have expected extreme results.

He managed to roll onto his side, and he started pulling himself into the living room. The bathroom tiles were cold; if he had to lie naked and helpless, he wanted to do it somewhere other than on a bare floor. He reached the living room and rolled over, facing the ceiling. He had lost control of his abdomen and lower back. He pulled himself further into the room. Toward the sofa and the television. And the altar.

He got to the altar before he realized it was his destination. As he felt his chest fading from his control, he let his arms flail. A few of the stuffed jars fell to the floor but didn't smash. Since they weren't lidded, some of their contents spilled, and Carter had a new mess on his face and in his hair. A piece of something – something he had taken from inside the tiny body – fell between his nose and lips. He could smell it.

When his arms dropped, limp, at his sides, he could still smell it. He was still breathing. He couldn't control how deep a breath he took, but his body continued to pump air in and out. Air and smells.

He tried to open his mouth so he could blow the smelly thing away from his lip. He could sense the splatter on his cheeks, but he couldn't move his jaw. He could hear his own breathing. He could smell, feel, and hear. His mouth was closed, so he couldn't check taste. He thought of his eyes and felt a sudden terror of blinking. If he blinked at the wrong moment, he might not be able to reopen his eyes, and he'd be trapped in darkness. He looked down the length of his body, at the mass of parts he could no longer control. Straining to keep his eyes open, he felt cool air on corneas.

He had to give in. He had to blink. His eyes were becoming dry, painful.

His eyelids refused to respond. No blinking, no movement at all.

The pain in his legs from when he had fallen hadn't faded. It had gotten worse. The sensation was crawling upward just as the loss of mobility had. Pain eased past his thighs, burrowed through his groin, and filled up his stomach. It reached his chest, and all of his senses burst in agony.

Layer upon layer of pain flowed from his toes to his forehead. He had never felt anything like it before, and the only thought he could manage was that this much pain shouldn't have been possible. It should have killed him. He wanted it to. His mind screamed. He wanted to move, massage himself, scratch himself, get help, jump out a window, something, anything to end this agony, this massive weight of agony pushing down all over his body. Pain, pain, pain, pain.

Something was happening. His eyes were poised to see the movement of his skin. Starting at his feet and working its way upward, his flesh started to pulse. Ripples of skin rose and fell where pain had flowed before. The flesh was becoming loose, detaching itself. It was bubbling. The pain before had been inchoate, a diffuse and impossible pressure bearing down, but now it was hot. He was boiling. Bubbles of heat rose all over his body, swelled, exploded. Layers of skin started to peel and slide onto the floor.

He wanted to scream, and he thought: *I'm not allowed.* Instead, he watched as his body melted. The pounds gained in recent months fell away. He could smell burning fat, his own body cooking, reducing itself. Skin was gone, and he could see beneath it. His organs twisted, convulsed, and he thought they would burst or melt like the rest of him had, but instead they swelled and hardened. His muscles also rebuilt themselves, swelling and hardening, and a film started to spread over them, a new skin, shining in new blood.

With the new skin came a new kind of pain. It wasn't heat or pressure but a penetration of thought, like nails driven through synapses. What he was seeing was no longer his body. It had been, but now it was something else.

A coherent, skewered thought presented itself: the suture of the seeker.

Carter thought he was laughing, but there was no smile-sensation in his cheeks, no convulsion in his chest. The insane glee of realization was confined, not in his head – the object on the rebuilt shoulders was no longer his – but in his mind, which was somewhere else.

His vision started to blur, to narrow. Later, he would remember what happened next as the moment he blipped out, like an old television screen reduced to a single glowing point. When the point vanished, he died.

Book Two

Run

Rise

Megan woke up gasping. Her hand went to her chest and rubbed at her racing heart and sore breasts. Every part of her felt sore, tenderized, wasted. She felt as if she'd spent months treading water, teetering on the edge of drowning, waiting to be rescued. No rescue had come: she had simply washed up on the shore. Here, her bed. But not her bed. Funny blankets and towels covered her usual bedding.

Something…blood…spackled everything. On one corner of the bed, she could make out a small heap of something fleshy. The afterbirth.

She tried to scream, but what came out was merely a groan.

Megan had to rise, to get up on her legs despite the way they seemed to float detached from her body, despite her total exhaustion. How long had it been? Her head turned toward the nightstand, the digital clock. After midnight. Hours had passed since… since she'd…since…oh, God. Had he? Where was he?

"CARTER!!!" she yelled.

Sliding across the bloody extra bedding, Megan swiveled until her feet found the floor. The throbbing pain between her legs was incredible. It felt wrong, but since she had had an epidural with Caitlin, she didn't know how she was supposed to feel. Images, stereotypes, fantasies of native women crouching in fields to give birth before carrying on with their tasks, thoughts she'd once found laughable, occurred to her now as a lifeline: you *will* get up. You have no excuse. She stood.

The room tilted from side to side and threatened to spin. A strange lightness inflated her head. Megan remembered she hadn't eaten since the contractions had begun. Now there was no time to eat. She had to open the bedroom door, had to see…

"CARTER!!!"

No answer.

Lurching forward, she reached the door. The metal knob felt cold in her hand. A new sensation, which she recognized as fear, seized her as the metal twisted in her grip. The door swung open.

A wave of odor almost knocked her down. Her eyes found a coffin-shaped thing covered with a cloth that, judging from a few unsaturated specks, had once been white. On it and near it were jars of...she didn't know...and in the center...

A dry-heave and then steadiness. No, she would not fall apart now, not crumple beneath the weight of what she saw. It was only what she expected. It was the remains of what she had helped to plan, the unused portion of what she had prepared inside of her. It needed to be blocked out. She would see it later. She would grieve later. Now, there was something more pressing. What was it?

"CARTER!!!" The emptiness that resounded after her echo drained from the apartment told her that he wasn't there. Blood streaked the carpet, the furniture, everything. Calm reason suggested that only part of the blood could have come from something as small as...what had ended up as the remains she saw on the red-and-white cloth. The rest hadn't come from the delivery, either. Some of this had to be....

"Carter," she said. He had to be injured pretty severely to have bled this much. A man so wounded could not have gotten far. He, or his body, had to be around here somewhere.

Wounded? What could have wounded him? Where the hell would he have gone?

Shreds of paper caught Megan's eye. She stooped to examine them and recognized the whole from the fragments. It was the picture they had taken of Caitlin on one of the good days at the hospital. Megan saw parts of her daughter's covered head and parts of her toothy smile. Why would Carter tear up a picture of her little girl?

The ritual. It wouldn't have called for shredding a picture of the person it was supposed to help, would it? The ritual was about making Caitlin whole, not...

Megan noticed the stripped carcass on the cloth again. What if something had gone wrong? To complete the ritual, Carter would have to have some kind of contact with Caitlin. She was its purpose, after all. So maybe he had gone to the hospital. But if he were wounded, how could he possibly make it there? And if something had gone wrong?

Two possibilities. One, Carter went to the hospital to cure their daughter. Two, Carter went to the hospital to do something else. He had threatened to kill Caitlin if Megan refused to go through with the plan. If the ritual had failed, if something had gone wrong, would he make good on his threat?

Megan had no alternative. She had to get to the hospital.

Wounded or not, Carter had a strong lead. Megan was poised at the front door, which was damaged and ajar, when she looked down and saw her naked legs. Gaining speed, she went to the bedroom and lined black underwear with pads for her own bleeding. She searched for clothes that would fit her still-bloated body and found tan pants, black sneakers, and a grey sweater. She grabbed her purse, which she hadn't touched in months. Her skin was caked with bloody grime, and she probably smelled, but she couldn't do anything about that now. She had no time. She had to go. Dead babies and evil husbands and guilt would all wait. Caitlin was all the mattered.

A trail of red led up to and beyond the front door. Megan followed it to the top of the stairs. The long, long way down – flight after flight of steep stairs – taunted her weakened legs. Light in the hallway flickered, showed her the red trail going down in sickening strobes. The strength and speed she had found faltered, leaving room for the ache of her middle to announce itself. Could she really make it down the stairs?

She extended her foot and took a step down. She'd grasp the handrail with all her might and move down as steadily as she could, fast but not so fast that her feet would slip out from beneath her. Caitlin would get no help if Megan ended up unconscious. On the second step she realized how slippery the blood had made the stairs. She squeezed the handrail until the bones in her hand felt like they'd crack in protest. Down, down, another step, then another. Down to floor six. Floor five.

The scene at the fifth-floor landing stopped her, knocked her backward, connected her backside with a slippery step. She recognized the man, plump and middle-aged, as someone who had lived in the building longer than they had. Quite a few times he had helped her lug groceries, and once or twice she had returned the favor. His hair was shoulder-length, usually tied back in a ponytail. He had once said that his job involved computer programming. She couldn't remember his name. He was lying near the door to his apartment.

Something had torn off most of his face and split him down the middle. The gashes on his tattered chest and stomach looked like claw-marks. A five-fingered claw.

Carter? Impossible. But…

No time, no time! Keep going! Wrapping her fingers around the handrail again, she pulled herself up. She'd step over him. It was what she had to do. She couldn't help him now. He had bled out all over the floor. The pieces of face still attached were grey, death-colored. She had never seen anything like it, and she didn't need to start seeing it now. The man couldn't be helped. Only Caitlin mattered.

Megan extended a wobbly leg over the body and brought a sneaker down into the puddle that encircled it. She had to let go of the handrail to bring her other foot over. She'd have to do it with her eyes closed because, if she saw the remains without something to hold on to, she'd fall. She'd fall because the images wouldn't be able to wait anymore; they'd rush in and catch her, topple her, destroy her. Closing her eyes meant she'd be risking a blind step into a slippery puddle on unsteady legs, but that risk seemed less than the risk of letting the visions of carnage triumph.

She reopened her eyes, her arms swinging at her sides to maintain balance. She had made it. The trail of blood continued to the next staircase, and so would she. A handrail again, merciful and firm. Faster steps, down and down and down. Her sneakers left red prints, spreading the trail. She imagined a detective with a magnifying glass sleuthing his way in her wake. Wishful thinking – she needed that kind of help, finally wanted it, and she wouldn't get it. But maybe she didn't need it. She would get to Caitlin on her own. She would.

Floor four. Floor three. She was almost managing the pace of someone whose body hadn't been pushed wide open mere hours ago.

The red trail didn't thin. How much of it was Carter, how much of it the neighbor, how much of it the – it? The smear marks all over the floor and stairs looked like something out of a homemade house of horrors designed for a scary Halloween bash. Megan found comfort in the idea. That's all this was. Stage decorations. An obstacle course of horrors. She'd make it through and get the reward on the other side. Not candy. Her daughter. Her daughter, alive and safe and *well*.

She reached the main floor and launched from the handrail to the door, hurling it open with her weight, careening toward the sidewalk. Cold night air bit into her cheeks. She was glad she had grabbed the sweater, but it wouldn't be enough. She walked into a frigid city night of ice-slicked sidewalks and relentless wind. The streetlamps made everything in every direction a brownish-grey.

She started down the block, trudging into the grid of interlocking streets. Buildings towered on either side of her, smudged bricks, grimy ledges.

A glance both ways at the next intersection found no taxis. The walk signal lit up, and with arms folded across her chest in defiance of the cold, she forged into the wind. Eyes on asphalt, she navigated around frozen puddles, wondering if the street would scrape off the red that remained on the bottoms of her shoes.

She went two more blocks before she saw not one but two cabs. The first sped by her, carrying drunk college kids. The second slowed and pulled up to the curb. Megan's shivering body collapsed in the backseat. She gave the driver directions to the hospital.

For once, she welcomed the nausea of a taxi-ride, the way the driver insisted on weaving around the few cars that were out in the night and on flooring the gas pedal at each green light only to brake abruptly at the following red. Megan watched the driver's eyes switch back and forth from the road to the rearview mirror. After one "You okay lady?" got answered with "Just drive," he didn't voice his concern again. Megan didn't know how she looked, but she could guess. Her reflection in the mirror seemed to make the cabbie drive faster. He only slowed when they reached the hospital's block. A noisy crowd stood around the entrance and in the street, blocking the way.

"I'll get out here," Megan said. She was halfway out the door before she remembered to pay the cabbie. A too-large bill was the first she found in her purse. She shoved it through the opening in the glass partition and said, "Keep it all." She slammed the door behind her. The taxi sped off.

Megan's exposed skin registered the human warmth of the crowd. People were standing in clusters, shouting, crying, looking panicked and helpless and afraid. At first Megan saw them as an irrelevant impediment, something separate from her mission. Then she saw that the group closest to the hospital's glass main doors formed a barrier that pushed back the occasional man or woman who seemed desperate to get inside.

"What's going on?" she said, but her voice got lost in the crowd's cacophony. Instead of asking questions, Megan realized that she should listen. Someone was saying something about being deaf from the gunshots. Someone else said something about Miguel – had Miguel made it out? There was talk of evacuating the patients, and there was talk about how the patients shouldn't be outside on a night like this one. Megan saw the uniforms of doctors, nurses, and orderlies; she saw people in plain clothes. Several men and women in hospital gowns huddled together, shivering. They were skinny and pale and sick.

Megan scanned the crowd and saw no children.

She pushed deeper into the throng, listening for new information. Someone said something about terrorists, and someone said something about someone being high on PCP. Someone had read something about a shooting in a hospital in Boston. Did someone get shot? There had been gunshots, lots of them. People were dead, dying, they needed help! There were doctors everywhere, for Christ's sake! Someone should go back in there and help them! No one's going inside that building who isn't heavily armed. You'd need a fucking SWAT team. You'd need machine guns and bazookas.

How many of them were there? Ten? Five? One? How could there only be one? Was he wearing body armor? How many guns did he have? What do you mean he wasn't even *armed*? You must have been seeing things.

Oh, God! His head! It just came off! The thing, that thing...it just...oh, God!

Somebody has to go in and check on Jill! She was hit in the crossfire. She looked bad, but she was going to make it. She got to shelter, but she was bleeding. Who shot her? No, not...it was one of the security guards...someone's got to train these people not to just start shooting every-fucking-where at the first sign of trouble.

I counted six at least. Six terrorists? Six people dead. Lives gone, just like that.

When are these guys going to leave our city alone? Haven't we suffered enough?

I swear to God, man, the guy wasn't even human!

In the distance, Megan heard sirens. Whatever had happened here had happened recently. Carter's lead must not have been that big after all. Carter's lead? *Carter?* What could he have to do with any of this? She had to get inside. She had to get to her daughter. There were no children in the crowd. "Where are all the children?" she yelled, trying to make an impression in the din. The sound was lost.

A nurse with blood on her uniform was yowling, and a doctor at her side was trying to hold her arm still enough to examine the wound. More people talked about needing to go back in there, and more people said that was a really stupid idea. Wait for the police. Wait for the fucking army. They'll be here any minute.

It wasn't terrorists. Good God, will everyone please calm down? It wasn't terrorists. I saw it. Him. The guy, the one guy. They shot him, but he just kept going. He moved so fucking *fast*. He must have been wearing some kind of bulletproof vest, but I could have sworn that he wasn't wearing more than a shirt.

As Megan was pushing forward, a man vomited on the sidewalk near her shoes. Further down the street, she saw that a woman had fallen, and a few people were trying to keep others from trampling her. More people than were standing in all the confusion seemed to be fleeing it. Men and women screamed for taxis, flocked toward the nearest stairway down to the subway, and ran away in every direction.

A voice in the crowd popped out: "Jason's lost it, man. He keeps talking about seeing death itself. Some kind of monster."

Megan had to stop listening. The voices were a net entangling her, paralyzing her, keeping her from her goal. The longer she stayed here, the closer those images would get – the thing on the coffin, the neighbor who used to help her with groceries. She had to think about a way to get to the glass doors, a way past the human barrier that was keeping people from entering. Shoving and screaming, Megan made her way toward the door. She poked one of the large men who were deflecting people and yelled, "Excuse me, I have to get inside!"

"Nobody goes back in, lady. Not until we figure out what's going on and know it's safe."

Megan grabbed the lapels of his white coat. "Please, listen to me! I have to get inside! My daughter's in there!"

"A lot of people's daughters and sons are in there. You hear those sirens? Help will be here any minute. Your daughter'll be okay, ma'am, just wait for the police to come."

"WHAT THE HELL IS GOING ON! LET ME SEE MY DAUGHTER!"

"I don't know what's going on, ma'am. Try not to be hysterical. Just step back from the..." He kept talking, but either the volume of the crowd increased, erasing his voice, or Megan tuned him out. She released his coat and stepped back, weaving into the crowd until his eyes weren't following her anymore. There were doors on the other side of the building. She could go there, or...

Or she could exploit a weak link in the chain. Most of the people guarding the doors were men, large men, two of them dressed like doctors, two like orderlies, one like a nurse. One woman in plain clothes was helping them. She was about Megan's size. There were two sets of glass double doors that opened onto the hospital's main lobby, and the plainly dressed woman alone blocked the door on Megan's far left.

For a moment, Megan paused and marveled at her own clarity. This was the first time she had even been outside in months. She had just given birth. She had just discovered two dead bodies, one of them...unthinkable. And here she was, plotting a strategy to get inside a building surrounded by people intent on keeping her out. People were gibbering like the tenants of a madhouse about monsters and terrorists and gunshots and death, death, death. But Megan was used to death. She had lived with it every day for two years. Her experience in these matters set her apart from this throng of frantic, aimless people. She would get inside and get to her daughter.

Ramming speed! The sound of her own laughter, staccato and mirthless, rose to her ears despite the churning screams of the crowd. It pushed her on. She slammed against the woman on the far left, shoving her toward the men, drawing their attention from the doors to their fallen comrade. The men in range to grab Megan were too busy bending over to see if the woman she had hit was okay. They couldn't keep Megan from slipping by, opening the door, and running inside.

She didn't stop until she had put some distance between her and the door. When her legs lost her latest burst of urgency, her shoes squeaked with the suddenness of the halt. The glare of lights and the barrier of people had kept her from seeing through the doors into the lobby. The sight was familiar now, but it still shocked her. Splashes of red spread out before her, covering the path between Megan and the elevators. The trail didn't lead to the elevator doors but to the stairwell opposite.

Between Megan and the ways up to Caitlin lay bodies. Uniforms marked the two directly in her path as security guards. One of them looked whole, sprawling face-down in a pool of red. Another lay in two different places, the head separated from the body. In her periphery, Megan thought she could detect more people awash with red. Faint whimpering told her that at least one person was still alive. She wouldn't listen, couldn't help. Getting past the two dead guards was her only objective.

Megan neared the severed head as she made her way towards the elevator and the stairs. She didn't recognize the face. Its strangeness reminded her that she wouldn't know the hospital staff who'd be on duty at this hour. It was nighttime, or the wee hours of morning. She had never visited Caitlin at this hour before.

The elevator or the stairs? Something had tracked blood up the stairs. Whatever had caused this chaos had gone that way. Should she take the elevator then? What if it wasn't working? Should she take the stairs and risk encountering whatever it was that had caused all this? What if Carter slipped past on the stairs while she was enclosed by the elevator? Carter? Could he even *be* here?

No, no, no! This is madness! Carter spends his days in a library! People would never mistake him for an army of terrorists!

Megan longed for laughter, even the mirthless kind. The lobby was quiet, filled only by whimpering and the buzzing of fluorescent lights overhead. She stood still, no longer contemplating which route of ascent to take. Blood, mauled bodies, a severed head, her baby, her husband: they threatened to come in and remove all reason and hope of continuing. She was weak, goddamn it, too weak! She had spent the last few months cowering in tight quarters, so how was she supposed to face this? She couldn't face anything. She was a useless bitch who had plotted murder and then sat paralyzed for forty weeks. Weakness defined her.

And that's why, Megan. Forget yourself. As long as she could stand she *would* keep going. She didn't matter anymore. Only Caitlin.

More flights of stairs would destroy her. She pushed the button for the elevator, trying to blank her mind while she waited.

The light, the bell, the doors sliding open and then closing her in. The silver walls of the elevator chamber dimly reflected her, a distorted shadow. In one of the high corners, she found a real mirror, probably a cover for the security camera. The convex surface showed her what the cabbie had seen: wild hair, stringy and matted, deep black circles under her eyes, and flecks of reddish-brown on her skin. Her pants had blood on them. Was it her own, or had she picked it up in the apartment, on the stairs, in the crowd, the lobby... her reflection smiled at the list of bloody places. A comforting sense of absurdity warmed her cheeks.

Waiting. This was one of the elevators for visitors. Surely the larger ones designed for gurneys and emergency transports moved faster than this. Death due to slow elevator would mean major malpractice suits. Doctors thought about these things. They had to: insurance companies and HMOs made such considerations a greater priority than patients.

Good, Megan, good. Distract yourself with pettiness.

The strategy failed as soon as her mind articulated it. As the elevator climbed up to the ward where Caitlin waited, the images threatened to catch her again. What the hell had he done with all those *jars*? Years before, Megan had read something about cutting...but how was she supposed to remember something from so long ago? The thing on the coffin, the *altar* – it was a death more personal than the corpses that had been surrounding her since she had followed a blood trail into a cold winter night. All for Caitlin. If Carter had something to do with the chaos at the hospital, then Caitlin was the root of that as well.

Save her, Megan. Was that irony?

The bell rang again when the elevator came to a stop at Caitlin's floor, jolting Megan back into her mission. Her mind gave her legs the order to run, but they merely walked into the white antiseptic hallway. A nurse with a clipboard still clutched in one arm lay on the floor where the stairwell met the hall. Her uniform looked clean. The absence of blood might have suggested that she was only sleeping if her neck hadn't been twisted at an impossible angle. Something had snapped her, broken her.

Further down the hall, another security guard had been gutted.

Megan's legs failed; she sat to keep from sprawling. The distance was short – just one long hallway between her and Caitlin's room. She couldn't stop now. She had to go, had to save her daughter – but what was she going to do? She had been running from everything she had seen, everything she had done, racing against *something*, maybe Carter, maybe something else, to get to her daughter. The bodies in this final hallway said one thing: whatever had come here had beat Megan to the goal. If Carter had come to kill Caitlin, there wasn't a thing Megan could do to prevent it. There never had been. The end result of the ritual, of all the planning, had already come to pass. If Caitlin's body was the last she'd find on the trail she'd been following, she wouldn't be able to do a damned thing about it. She'd see her daughter's body, and all the rest of the corpses would come pounding around her, blaming and demanding revenge.

Stand up! Face it! Get what you deserve!

But Caitlin didn't deserve it. She didn't deserve any of this.

Megan felt the full measure of her exhaustion. She remembered begging for something at the last moment – not her baby's life, but sleep. She had begged for sleep. She had had some, and she wanted more. In her mind she saw herself stretching out and closing her eyes right where she sat. The authorities must be here by now. The cavalry must be storming up the stairs or maybe catching the elevator car that had brought her up. They'd take care of everything. They'd find her, call it shock, call it trauma. They'd tell her what happened to Caitlin, and she wouldn't have to *see*.

Her legs stretched out, not to recline but to push her once more to her feet. A head rush swayed her, almost knocked her down. If she couldn't stand, she'd get to her daughter's room by crawling. She had failed a million times, but she would *not* fail at this. She'd see what was waiting for her. She'd get what she deserved. After that, everything else would move with the momentum she had generated.

She passed the broken nurse. She passed the gutted security guard. Her eyes did not close or avoid them: these images would be her first confrontation with what she had caused. She and Carter. *Of course* this had everything to do with them. The coincidence was too great — the trail of blood was leading her through the consequences of their dark acts. Whether Carter was dead or alive didn't matter: whatever she'd find in Caitlin's room would be his. And hers. No more displacement of guilt. This madness was undeniably hers.

Megan turned a corner and looked into the room that kept her daughter. Several children cowered in one corner. They had seen something and were terrified. Megan scanned the group and did not find Caitlin.

Her heart didn't beat again until she heard her daughter's voice.

"Mommy, is that you?"

Caitlin was standing away from the other children, near an enormous broken window. Megan felt a pang of panic when she saw stray shards so dangerously close to her daughter's socked feet, but the feeling gave way immediately to something else: elation! Caitlin was *standing*! Her body and face and scalp still conveyed the ravages of disease, but the way she stood seemed vital, vigorous, animated. Invigorating brightness poured from Caitlin's eyes as Megan heard her daughter address her again.

"Mommy, was that Daddy?"

The Descent of Carter Anderson, Continued

Carter didn't know how much time had passed since he had finished dying. The eyes that had been his opened, and he saw the ceiling far above him. His body – or the body that had been his – lay on the ground where he had left it. Turns of his head from side to side showed him the altar where he had killed his second-born. He saw the bloodstained carpet. While his eyes took in the surroundings, his thoughts tried to focus on lifting an arm or a leg. Nothing. He tried to close his eyelids but kept seeing the room rocking back and forth as his head swiveled.

Attempts to move produced no sense of strain. He couldn't strain. His arms and legs had no connection to his thoughts. He felt as if he had forgotten how to move; he thought he might be paralyzed. Intuition told him otherwise. He *was* thought and feeling. His body gave him sensation, and it housed his thoughts, but it was no longer him. It was something else.

He was moving. He was standing up and running his hands along his body. His fingers stumbled along a rough, unfamiliar surface. They detected strange bumps, firm muscles, hard ribs. The volume of his flesh had diminished, and its quality had changed. It produced uncanny sensations, an awareness of touch without the possibility of pain. Carter concentrated on detecting the parts of his body that his hands were not exploring. His feet felt strangest: they only made contact with the carpet at the sharp ends of inhumanly high arches.

His eyes allowed him to see what his hands had been feeling. The skin was blue-grey and purple, a twisted mesh of what looked like bruises and scar tissue beneath a crimson sheen. Carter detected no traces of the body hair that had been matted with the baby's blood. The crimson on the smooth skin was blood, but he couldn't tell whether the plasma was still oozing from his pores. Carter took in the new thinness and angularity of his legs and torso. Even in his thinner college days, he had never looked like this. He tried to comprehend his posture, the way he stood with knees bent and back stooped. His body, a human body, was not supposed to be this way.

Carter had no genitals. Between his legs was a Ken-doll vacancy, a lump of scar.

The images that his eyes delivered assaulted his sanity, but Carter's breathing did not quicken, and his heart did not respond with hectic palpitations. His body felt calm. His consciousness produced something he recognized as terror, but the terror was weak compared to his thoughts' insistence on what he *should* have been feeling. Carter was still capable of emotion, but feeling itself had altered. Fear and panic had become disembodied. Unable to process sensation in his customary way, Carter's thoughts grew silent and waited for more data.

His legs began to walk, and he felt his revised body's first breath. The chest cavity expanded with extraordinary slowness, and the air rushing into his inflating lungs carried the smell and taste of rot. His first thought was to glance at the altar to see if the remains had started to decay, but the thought passed as he realized that his head was not going to turn in that direction. Instead, he was going into the bedroom, where Megan still slept.

The smell followed him. He reasoned that the baby's body could not yet have started decaying. He imagined that the putrid smell came from him, from the process through which he had lost the excess of flesh and parts.

For a moment, he gazed at the rising and falling of Megan's chest. Her sleep seemed genuine and untroubled. Why am I looking at her? Am I going to *do* something to her? His eyes traveled up and down her body as if they were assessing something.

He didn't touch her. Instead, he went to his closet and started sifting through clothes. His body went directly to *his* closet: whatever was controlling his movements knew which closet was which. The experience of dressing was odd. Without a cue from him, one leg found its way into the proper pants hole while the other kept him standing. The pants felt soft, and the skin of his legs communicated the friction of the fabric as it slid into place. He put on the baggy shirt his hands had selected. His elbows bent, and his fingers manipulated buttons. What had once been simple, habitual acts now seemed complex as Carter sensed them with his new skin. Without Carter contributing even a routine impulse, his body performed myriad subtle tricks of balance and direction.

Dressed now, his legs carried him toward the full-length mirror. He saw undeniable traces of himself in the thing that appeared in the glass. Beneath the twists of tissue where a human face should have been, Carter found the outline of his cheeks, and within darkened sockets he recognized his own eyes. His vision had improved: this face would never wear glasses. The head, like the rest of the body, had lost all its hair. The bare, withered crown suggested age. The rest of the body seemed young, vital, and charged. He remembered the way he had thought of his reflection after the first ritual with Brian: still himself but *maximum*. This image went beyond maximum; it was too great to be himself. The first ritual had given Carter the power to lift a car. What could *this* body do?

Carter thought of Henry Jekyll's fascination with his transmogrified reflection, and he expected such fascination to register on his face. It did not. Whatever had steered him to the mirror showed no signs of interest in what it saw. Carter wondered if this viewing were for his own sake. The thing controlling his body might have been choosing its sensory data with Carter, its captive audience, in mind.

As if in response to Carter's suspicion, the thing in the mirror smiled. Thin blue lips pulled back from sharp, grey teeth. They were the same teeth that Carter was accustomed to brushing, but now they were sharper, as if filed to points. Carter wondered if the thing controlling his body might have a sense of humor. Maybe it sensed the distress of its captive and was amused. Carter's puppeteer might have been taunting him.

Carter's attention shifted from the smile on his face to the clothes on his body. The black slacks he had selected were from his regular wardrobe, but the lavender and yellow striped shirt was an unused gift from a tasteless relative. The contrast of the bright colors with his body's dull complexion emphasized the skin's horridness. For an instant, the smile on Carter's face was in accord with his feelings.

The self-survey completed, he walked back into the living room. His bare feet tracked blood everywhere they stepped. He tracked over toward the altar, paused, and lifted the picture he had used to focus his will on Caitlin. One hand held the picture while the other unfurled fingers as if to caress his daughter's face. As the fingers approached the image, Carter noticed what had happened to them. They had gotten longer and skinnier, and the film of scar that covered them almost made them indistinguishable from bare bone.

Like the teeth, the fingertips looked as if they had been filed to sharp points. When they passed over the picture, they sliced it to ribbons. The pieces drifted down to the blood-soaked carpet.

His body took him to the front door. His hand pulled on the handle and registered the resistance of the deadbolt. Another pull yanked the door open, splintering the wood around the bolt. As he stepped into the hallway, he heard something below.

"Hello?" a voice called.

He stopped in the doorway, and Carter surmised that his puppeteer was weighing options. "Hello?" came the voice again. "Hey, is everything okay up there? Awhile ago I thought I heard screaming, and just now I heard a crash. Hello?"

As toes and heels tapped on stairs and made them bloody, he seemed to glide down toward the voice that had called in concern. He was moving down the second flight of stairs when he saw the fat man standing in the doorway of his apartment. Hours ago this man had heard screaming, and just now he had heard the sound of a break-in, but he had done nothing but open his front door in response just now. He had decided against making the effort of heaving his corpulence up the stairs to find out whether or not someone really needed help. His inaction – his laziness and apathy – filled Carter with disgust.

The eyes of the concerned citizen began to widen at the sight on the stairs when Carter's hand circled downward and scored the man's front with vertical gashes. Warm wetness surrounded Carter's fingers as they rammed into soft flesh again, carving through the man's middle. Streams of crimson spurted from fresh wounds while the man fell. Carter's fingers passed before his eyes, showing him the bits of skin that clung to their sharp tips – remnants of the man's face.

Carter wanted to take a long look at what his hands had just done. This man was the third human his hands had killed. Killing him had required no reasoning at all. The act was effortless and graceful, power without exertion. It horrified and impressed him at the same time.

His eyes did not grant him the moment of contemplation he wanted. He stepped over the jittery corpse and continued his rapid descent.

The street appeared in front of him. His skin sparkled with the cold, but the sensation carried no unpleasantness. Carter was aware of the cold but unfazed by it. His lungs inflated, and Carter realized that this was only his second breath since awakening. He sucked in the flavors of exhaust and garbage. The tastes were distinct but without quality. His mouth identified them without disgust. Tastes and smells were only raw data.

He paused on the sidewalk and seemed to examine the street. Carter thought he might be preparing to hail a cab. Instead, he started glide-walking in a familiar direction: the hospital. His puppeteer was probably using Carter's memory of his favorite route to reach the endpoint of the ritual. Carter rode along, an observer, anxious to see how he'd accomplish what he was supposed to do when he arrived. He thought of the picture of Caitlin that his fingertips had shredded and felt that what moved him was a singular, all-important aim. A focus on his daughter defined every step.

When he reached the first intersection, the light for the crosswalk glowed red. He didn't seem to hesitate; nimble steps just glided into the lanes. Traffic was light, but several cars came toward him, horns blaring and brakes squealing. Carter felt nothing but curiosity to see what would happen next.

A taxi that had braked too late to avoid hitting him rolled under his feet. He had jumped, gliding upward rather than forward, and he had landed with perfect timing on the yellow roof of the screeching vehicle before pushing off and bolting forward again. Seconds froze in his perception as he soared from the roof of the taxi to the roof of a stopped minivan. His pointed heels left two narrow dents in the metal.

Stride unbroken, he returned to the sky, drifting higher than he had on the long-ago day when Brian and he had failed to span the river with a virile leap. He landed on the opposite side of the street and looked back. The taxi and the minivan still idled where they had stopped. Feeling a smile once again stretch his lips, Carter saw another car smash into the back of the van, pushing it farther into the vacant intersection. He waited a moment. Just as Carter concluded that his spectacular street-crossing would cause no further mishap, his body resumed its direction.

His surroundings whizzed by faster than he could comprehend them. He came to another crosswalk and barely had time to register that it spanned fewer lanes than the last before he leapt, soaring from one street corner to the next. Concrete scraped against the bare bottoms of his bloody feet whenever they landed, but he felt no pain, just awareness of sensation. Carter imagined looking at the scrapes on his feet and watching the formation of a film like the one that had covered him while he was dying.

He sped through a corner of midtown. Here even the late hour didn't keep the sidewalks from being crowded. His quick passing threw people off balance, and sometimes he shoved people down, stabbing them with his touch. Carter wanted to look back at the people he left behind him. Angry, confused, and hurt, they must have glared at him from the shadows beneath flashing neon signs.

Approaching a jammed section of sidewalk, his body turned and directed its glide on a diagonal that looked like it would slam him into the base of a skyscraper. He stepped from the sidewalk onto the building itself, moving vertically, defying gravity as his fingertips and heels pierced and fractured wall and windows. Scurrying squirrel-like and not losing speed, he circumvented the block of bodies at an angle ninety degrees from the ground. Shouts of wonder and appreciation pursued him, but he did not slow. Carter concluded that, for his puppeteer, applause lacked the appeal of destruction.

Carter found himself on the hospital's block, and his body slowed to a human pace before reaching the glass doors. He entered the lobby. The few people milling about on business hushed and froze, staring. Carter remembered his appearance and understood their gapes of horror. He stood still, as if allowing them time to react.

His head turned in the direction of an approaching sound. A nurse had made the bold decision to address him. "Hello...sir...do you need help of some kind? We're not an emergency facility, but if you have—"

A single arm shot out at her, and Carter felt his clawed hand tearing through her uniform as it grasped and lifted her off the floor. He tossed her across the lobby, where she slammed against a wall and bounced to the floor.

Someone screamed, and the sound energized the room. Someone shouted, "Hey!" Someone else shouted, "What the fuck!" He waited, standing still, looking at people as they tried to figure out how to react to what they had just seen. Something bumped him from behind. The collision made him teeter slightly. He turned toward its source. A massive orderly with arms twice the size of Carter's had tried to tackle him. The orderly backed up, his eyes wide, his lips quivering. Carter felt another smile stretch across his face. His fingers pierced the orderly beneath the sternum and lifted him by the bone. A moment later the orderly hit the wall and sprawled next to the dead nurse.

Carter's consciousness bristled: he didn't want to hurt these people. He didn't want any of this.

"Freeze!" a man yelled.

He turned toward the security guard, who stood only a few yards away with a revolver pointed at Carter's chest. Carter heard a click behind him, turned his head, and saw another guard with his gun drawn and aimed. A third joined the first two, completing a tight circle.

"Just...just...don't move!" The first man's gun shook in his hands.

Gunshots filled the air, followed by screams from the onlookers. Carter's body had bolted forward and decapitated one of the guards. The second guard in Carter's field of vision barely had time to see the severed head land near his shoes before clawed fingers slashed his middle and sent him spinning to the floor. He landed face-down and slid on the blood gushing from his stomach.

Carter started to register the two bullets that had hit his body while he spun to face the third guard. One bullet had lodged in his chest, the other in his back. The metal felt hot and itchy where the skin had trapped it. The bullets had penetrated the thick mesh of scars shallowly; the tacky shirt showed far more damage than the skin.

The third guard managed to shoot again before Carter lunged at him. The skin above Carter's stomach caught the bullet, and the impact of the shot was as negligible as that of the orderly who had tried to tackle him. Carter slowed but didn't stop, impaled the guard on his fingers, and sent him flying toward the side of the room opposite where the others had landed. The guard fired again while he flew, and from the corner of his eye Carter saw a woman clutch her side and fall.

The onlookers panicked and rushed toward the exit. Carter felt the stretch of yet another smile, and he mused over the contrast between his hurry to get here and his patient observance of the panic. He had had no reason to waste time on the street, but here time spent was rewarded. The way his eyes followed the panic, the expression on his face, and the tingling of his skin added up to an undeniable sensation: pleasure. His reactions to cold air, rank smells, and gunshot wounds were dull and neutral, but his response to seeing agony, blood, and chaos was keen delight.

This isn't me, Carter thought. I didn't want this.

But you did. You willed this into happening. Pay attention, Carter. All of this belongs to you.

He could hear sounds coming from more distant regions of the hospital. People who hadn't witnessed the carnage were coming to investigate. Carter stood still for a moment more, and he thought he might be waiting to kill again. When he found himself gliding toward the stairwell, climbing toward Caitlin's floor, he felt relieved.

Sounds echoed down the stairs, and Carter couldn't separate the ones originating below from the ones originating above. The first person running downstairs who reached him looked like a doctor. The concern on his face vanished when he saw Carter's shape and color. Carter's lips arced upward for the doctor, who took one step backward, then another. "What the hell happened to you?" the doctor asked. The doctor took another step back, and Carter took a step forward. "HEY!!" the doctor yelled, this time for the benefit of those coming behind him. "There's some guy on the stairs, and he's—"

Carter's fingers tore out the doctor's throat and let the body tumble down.

"You okay?" someone shouted back.

Please, Carter thought. *Please don't come down here.*

He continued his upward climb and reached the correct floor without encountering the voice's owner. If his lungs had been his own, he would have sighed with relief.

At the top of the stairs, he stopped in front of an attractive young nurse. She didn't look up from her clipboard as she said, "Roger, are you getting the coffee or do I have to do—" and then the sight of his face stunned her. She hugged the clipboard to her chest and screamed. He reached out, grabbed her head in both hands, and jerked it to one side. She snapped and crumpled.

The sound made Carter think of the dolls on Caitlin's shelves. They were fragile, breakable. Real people didn't snap like porcelain. Brian had taken time to die. His death had been real. These deaths were only dolls' deaths.

Again at a human pace, he walked away from the crumpled nurse, toward Caitlin. A security guard took him by surprise, appearing from around a corner. He shot once, and then Carter's fingers pierced him below his belt. The expression on the guard's face as Carter eviscerated him didn't register pain: he looked like a child blowing bubbles.

Some of the children who shared Caitlin's hospital room were already up, whispering to one another, trying to figure out what to do. When Carter's shape darkened the doorway, he heard their shrill screams running toward a far corner of the room. Not all of them could run. Most of the ones who couldn't get out of bed were awake. Some of them looked at Carter with expressions of terror and amazement. One or two hid underneath their blankets. One looked at him with calm, puzzled eyes.

He could tell that Caitlin was trying to get up, but she couldn't find the strength. What he first took for calmness Carter soon recognized as a different kind of fear, a fear tinged by accepting that, if the boogeyman had indeed come, she wouldn't be able to do anything about it.

Had he come here to hurt her? Maybe slashing her photograph had been a sign that coming here had never had any connection to the will he had tried to focus during the ritual. Maybe this thing that was moving him had nothing to do with his desires. If it killed Caitlin, then none of the other deaths would be his fault.

Carter felt a twitch in his cheeks, and he knew that the smile he felt forming would be less hideous than the other smiles had been. The steps he took toward his daughter were slow and careful, calculated to encourage calm. The force that moved him didn't seem to want to hurt her. It didn't even want to scare her. The sensations of his body added up to something akin to pleasure, but opposed to what Carter had sensed before. It was tenderness. He was moving toward his daughter with tenderness.

Behind him, his feet left a trail of blood. Carter was ashamed.

"Daddy?"

Forgetting for a moment, he tried to move his mouth, to say something reassuring. He didn't speak, but he moved closer.

"Daddy, is that you?"

He was at her bedside now, and his hand was hovering over her face. She didn't flinch. He caressed her, careful not to let his sharp fingertips harm her fragile skin.

The caress became something more: his fingers moved down her cheek and settled at her mouth. Now she did flinch. She tried to pull away, but his other hand was behind her, holding her in place. He forced her mouth open.

Carter wanted to close his eyes. He was sure that he was about to hurt her, and he didn't want to see it. He did and didn't want it to happen. He remembered Megan begging for sleep, and silently, he begged, too.

His lips touched Caitlin's as if to kiss her, but then something was flowing out of his mouth. It was sweet. Caitlin stopped resisting as it poured out of Carter and into her.

Carter pulled back, leaving a hand behind her head. Her eyes were closed, and her mouth hung open. The change began. New color appeared in her cheeks, and Carter understood that somehow all the distortions of his body had occurred in preparation for that moment, that kiss. What had happened to his outside was nothing compared to what had happened inside. If outside he looked like death, inside he held *life*. He had given it to Caitlin. She was well.

With careful fingertips, he combed her hair.

"Daddy," Caitlin whispered, "*what did you do?*"

He said nothing while he stroked her hair with sharp fingers. Carter thought that the gesture was affectionate.

"Daddy, is that really you? Is this a dream? I feel...."

"Shhhhhhhh." The sound came from Carter's lips. It was harsh and rumbling, from deep inside his chest, but there was nothing threatening about it. "I made you better," he said. "I'll never leave you."

Carter never heard the voice again.

Break

Megan carried Caitlin through the hospital hallway, pressing her daughter's face into her shoulder to keep her from seeing the blood and bodies. When they got to the clean back stairwell, her quivering arms gave out.

"I can walk," Caitlin said. "I want to." Megan watched her daughter walk and gaped at the girl's newfound mobility.

"Are we going home?" Caitlin asked. "What happened to Daddy?"

That question, that name: Megan hadn't thought of Carter as *Daddy* in a very long time. She couldn't take her daughter home. Caitlin would see what *Daddy* had done to his second baby. If they hadn't already, the police would soon come and follow the blood trail up to the apartment. They'd see the footprints – Megan's and those other tracks of red – and they'd start to reconstruct the scene. Both Carter and Megan would be wanted for questioning, possibly for murder.

The plump man in the stairwell, the man who used to help her with groceries, had been *clawed*. What would the police make of *that*? If Megan didn't know what to think, how could they? Megan knew she couldn't explain anything to anyone. She had to hide. She had to get away.

They left the hospital by the back door. Megan steered her daughter through the crowd, which was calmer now, more curious and less confused. The police had arrived. She saw a row of cars topped by flashing lights and a stream of armed men pouring through the hospital's front doors.

Megan tried to put the scene at the hospital as far from her mind as it was from her feet as she trailed her daughter down the subway steps. Caitlin was high on her own new energy. Megan had to call to her, "Wait for Mommy!" Megan hadn't seen Caitlin like this in years, maybe never. She'd been a chipper and buoyant five-year-old, but at an energized seven she moved with extraordinary self-possession. This was a girl who had lived away from her parents for much of the life she could remember. This was a girl who had suffered more than most people did in a lifetime. Trying to keep up, Megan pondered her daughter's psychological age. The girl said "Mommy" and "Daddy" in a way too babyish for a seven-year-old. Caitlin knew how to be independent, but she didn't know how to be a child her age.

Caitlin reached the bottom of the stairs ahead of Megan, stopped, and turned. "Sorry, Mommy, I just feel good. *Better*. Am I better now?"

Megan remembered the girl who had said with mature resignation, "I'm not going to get better." This new Caitlin looked at her mother with hope and wonder. Megan knelt and adjusted Caitlin's knitted hat. "You might be. I really hope so." She kissed her cheek. Everything had been for her. "I really hope so."

They had to wait for the train. Sitting on a bench and feeling out of place among the other shabbily dressed travelers, Megan tried to be attentive to her daughter. There had been days at the hospital when an unusual spurt of energy had made Caitlin chatter like this, but there hadn't been many. Focusing on the stream of words almost required more effort than Megan could muster.

Megan had dreaded some resentment of her long absence, but Caitlin didn't seem to feel any. She commented once or twice on being lonely, but mostly she just did what they had always done when a bit of time passed between visits. She described her daily activities. The teacher in the hospital had said she was doing better with her reading. Caitlin said she still liked looking at the pictures more than she liked sounding out the words, but sometimes seeing the words for the stories she knew by heart could be fun. Caitlin liked reading best. "Math is stinky," she said. Megan mused over her daughter's academic preferences. So like her father.

Until her day-by-day account reached the present, Caitlin's tone was happy and casual, but considering the import of recent events made her serious. "Something bad happened tonight at the hospital," she said. "A lot of the kids were scared. I was only a little scared. And then I saw the blue man."

"The blue man?" Megan asked.

"I thought it might be Daddy wearing a costume or something. He didn't come to visit in a long time, either, but on the phone he said something about maybe you coming too next time because you felt better because you were getting out in the sunshine someplace warm. He wasn't supposed to come in the middle of the night. I was asleep until all the noise in the hall." She looked thoughtful. "I thought it might be Daddy but I was scared anyway."

"What did he look like?"

"He was blue and he had dirt all over him. His shirt was all torn up and funny looking. He walked like an ape-man or something, but he was bald like me. Did Daddy go bald? Daddy used to be kind of hairy. He used to scratch me with his chin sometimes."

"I..." Megan's voice trailed off. She didn't know what to say. Did Daddy go bald? Did Daddy go absolutely fucking insane? Did Daddy turn into a death-monster and cut a swath through the population of the city?

"He came right up to me and I felt scared because he looked so weird but his made-up face looked nice even though it was scary. He had Daddy's eyes, that's for sure." Megan thought of Carter's eyes, their manufactured warmth. "He looked at me like he knew who I was and that made me feel better even though the other kids were all screaming and stuff. He kissed me weird but it felt okay. And then I started feeling really awake, and he said something and then he jumped out the window."

Megan braced herself. 'What did he say?"

"He was doing a funny voice. He said he made me better. And I believed him, kind of, because I really felt better. But then I thought it couldn't be Daddy and maybe I felt better because hospitals make people better and I went to the hospital for a really long time. When he was gone I thought I would wake up any second feeling bad again but then you came and I thought he might really be the one who jumped out the window. It sure is a long way down. I hope he's okay." Caitlin spoke wonders, but she acted like what she reported was no more extraordinary than what she had to say about her reading lessons.

"Did Daddy...did the blue man say anything else?"

"I think so," she said. "I think he said 'I'll never leave you.' Just like that. 'I'll never leave you.' Kind of a funny thing for a blue man to say. And he left right after!"

Megan felt a chill, and she was glad when she heard the squeal of the train stopping. This conversation would end now, and it wouldn't resume until Megan had had some time to think, to figure out what could be happening. Carter. The blue man.

They found seats on an empty train car. When the wheels started rolling, what Caitlin had said repeated in her mind: "I'll never leave you." The blue man had jumped out of the window minutes or maybe even seconds before Megan arrived. He had left – Caitlin found the contradiction funny – but had he really left?

Megan looked left and right, saw only one person through the window that looked onto the next car. Concrete, pipes, and tubes of light rushed by the train's windows. Nothing, no one. She was being foolish. This feeling was exhaustion and paranoia, something milder than what she probably should have been feeling considering the night she had had. She had given birth, lost a baby, forced her distended body to travel all over the city, and seen more blood than splattered the average war movie. Of course she felt strange. She should probably dismiss this feeling, this feeling of being watched, as the product of the amazing, overwhelming twenty-four hours that had just passed.

Her eyes closed, and her mind started painting a picture. The blue man. With claws. The blue man with claws and Carter's eyes. The dirty blue man, covered with blood. The dirty blue man who made a crowd of people think he was an army of terrorists.

"Mommy, are you sleeping?" Caitlin poked her arm.

Megan shook off the image and the haze of overpowering sleep. "Maybe a little," she said. "You make sure I stay awake, okay? I don't want to miss our stop."

"We're not going home, are we?" Caitlin said. She knew.

"No, sweetie, not tonight. We're going to go visit Mommy's friend Gina. You remember Gina, don't you?"

Her shoulders broke out in gooseflesh, and her eyes widened. Three stops had gone by, and the train was still empty. No one could be watching. This feeling was the afterglow of adrenaline, the simmering down of fried nerves.

Caitlin shook her head. No, she didn't remember Gina. "We need to go back to the hospital," she said. "I forgot Katy."

Megan saw tears welling up in her daughter's eyes, and she wondered which of them was more confused. Looking at them, Megan guessed someone would see the daughter as much better composed than the mother, but underneath the shine of new life, Caitlin had to be hiding her own terrors. She said she knew something bad had happened. Did she know *how* bad? She must have heard the gunshots. Did she connect the badness with the blue man who might have been her daddy? "We'll go back for Katy," Megan said, forgiving herself the lie. "Not tonight, but later. I promise."

Caitlin sat back in her seat, quiet, watching her mother for signs of sleep. Whenever the weight of Megan's eyelids brought them crashing down, Caitlin poked her in the arm. They traveled, blinks and pokes, all the way to Gina's stop. With eyes open, Megan could see the emptiness of the train and reason that there was no way someone could be watching them. With eyes closed, she *knew* she was watched and by whom: the blue man. Carter. His eyes had kept her in place for months, and they were still with her now.

Megan looked for an elevator but didn't find one. They'd have to take the stairs back up to the street, one more *long* flight of stairs. "Mommy's so tired. You said you don't want me to carry you. I wish you could carry me!" Megan tried to sound upbeat.

Caitlin took her hand and squeezed it. "I can't carry you," she said, "but I can pull you up. I feel really *strong* right now. Nothing hurts! Not a thing!" Caitlin led her mother up the stairs. With one hand in Caitlin's and the other on the handrail, Megan tried to keep her eyes focused in front of her, but she couldn't help looking back again and again. She heard a noise, an echo of a thump. What was it? Was that shuffling sound a footstep? The platform below was empty, and the turnstile didn't make another grinding noise after the two of them cleared it. Surely there was no one. But there was a feeling of eyes, of a watching shadow, following them.

She hesitated to ring the buzzer for Gina's apartment. She'd be asleep, and the sound of the buzzer would wake her in a panic. Only emergencies come calling at this hour, so close to dawn. But this *was* an emergency. Megan would have to give Gina an explanation, and it would have to be urgent.

She hesitated for another reason. If the feeling that pricked all along her spine had a real cause, if Carter or the blue man or whatever it was really had been watching and following them, she'd be putting her friend in danger. The slain members of the hospital staff flashed before her eyes. She hadn't known them, hadn't recognized them. She barely knew the plump man on the fifth floor who had been missing a face. The baby was another matter, but it had always been abstract, destined to become what it had. She might be able to deal with this horde of dead nobodies, but could she function if her actions led up to a dead somebody?

"Mommy, I'm cold," Caitlin said, and Megan's finger was on the button, ringing.

She rang a second time, a third. Finally a voice came through the intercom.

"Sweet Jesus, who the hell is it? Do you know what time it is?"

Megan pressed the button to speak. "It's me, Gina. Megan. I...can I come in?"

"Holy shit, honey, what's wrong?!"

"I'll tell you when we get inside. I'm sorry it's so late...or early, Gina, but please."

Gina answered with a buzz that unlocked the building's front door. Megan took Caitlin's hand and led her toward the correct apartment. Mercifully, Gina lived on the first floor.

Gina was waiting in the doorway when Megan and her daughter approached. She wore a silky robe over some kind of negligee. "Megan, you look terrible." She stopped herself from saying more when she saw Caitlin, and she tightened the sash around her waist, covering cleavage. "Hey there," she said, bending down toward the child. "I didn't know you'd be here!" Gina's face became soft and bright, and she used her schoolteacher voice. "Why don't you two come on inside where it's warm?" She stepped back to make room and locked the door behind them.

"Thank you, Gina," Megan said. She and Caitlin took the couch, Gina the rocking chair. "You're a lifesaver."

"You've got me really worried," Gina said. Her voice straddled her adult and child registers. She smiled at Caitlin. "It's good to see you up and about. You probably don't remember me. My name's Gina." She offered to shake Caitlin's hand, and Caitlin looked at her warily. Gina's eyes settled back on Megan. "What's she doing, um, out of the hospital? I thought she—"

"It's kind of a long story," Megan said. Think, think, think! Carter would know what to say. These sorts of situations were *his* responsibility. "It's one of the reasons I've been so out of touch." She thought, added some piquing drama to her voice, and then said, "Actually, there are a lot of reasons."

Gina stood when Megan gave signs of settling in for a story. "I need coffee. I have instant. You want some?" Megan nodded. "How about you, sweetie? I think I might have some apple juice."

Caitlin didn't respond.

"I think apple juice would be great," Megan said. "Thank you, Gina. Thank you so much." Gina's wait for the water to boil gave Megan time to plan her story. But she still watched the window across from her, the window that looked out onto the alley – the alley where shadows danced and drifted. By the time Gina came back with two steaming mugs and a plastic cup of juice, Megan had an outline of what she was going to say. "Thanks, Gina, really." She sipped the coffee. It burned her tongue.

"Careful, it's hot," Gina said.

Megan laced her fingers within Caitlin's, ready to squeeze for silence if Caitlin decided to interject. "I'm so tired, I don't know if I'm going to be able to make any sense." Her voice crackled with encroaching tears. Even the lie would be cathartic. "I can't say everything right now." She glanced at Caitlin for explanation. "But to answer your first question, one of the reasons Caitlin is here is that she's doing a lot better. She's in remission. We're even daring to hope that we might have beaten it. She's been in this new test group, with this new therapy, and it's been nothing short of miraculous."

"Thank God," Gina said. "Thank God!" Seeing the look on Megan's face, she cut her elation short.

"She's not supposed to be out of the hospital, though, at least not yet." Megan quieted almost to a confidential whisper. "I took her out just now. I didn't tell anybody I was doing it. I had to get her out, fast. You see..." She looked at her daughter, affecting hesitation. "You see, I was afraid the hospital might not be a safe place for her anymore." The image thrust itself back into her mind: the blue man. She couldn't mention him. She couldn't mention the reason why her eyes kept shifting toward the window. Was the sound in the alley just a cat? Probably. Almost definitely. She had to keep eye contact with her friend.

Caitlin was fidgeting, and Gina noticed. "Hey, I've got an idea. I've got an extra room with a futon in it. It's *really* comfortable. I bet you could lie down on it and go to sleep right away."

"I'm not sleepy," Caitlin said.

"Well, why don't I take you back there anyway? Your mom and I need to have some grown-up talk. There's a lamp right next to the futon. I've got a book or two you can look at, and I bet if you just look at them a little while you'll fall right to sleep." Gina offered Caitlin her hand.

"I won't," Caitlin said, ignoring the outstretched hand. "I won't fall asleep. Mommy, I want to stay with you. Do I have to go?"

"Tell you what," Megan said. "I'll come right back there when we're through talking." Her eyes bounced from her daughter to the window, where a shadow had just passed. "It won't take a really long time. You go back there, and I'll be there soon."

Gina's hand was still outstretched when Caitlin stood, but Caitlin didn't acknowledge it. Gina lowered her hand and led the girl back. The extra bedroom was at the end of the hall, just beyond the master bedroom. Megan remembered that each of the rooms had windows. She wished they had climbed one or two more flights of stairs, putting some distance between them and the alley. Her entire body ached. She needed sleep. Even with the fears buzzing in her brain, her eyelids were closing.

"That little girl seems determined to stay awake," Gina said, sitting on the couch where Caitlin had been. "I've got a shelf-full of things I use in the classroom, so at least she'll be able to stay busy." She took a sip of her coffee. "Now, you can tell me what's really going on. You're a complete mess. Is that...is that blood on your pants? Your face?"

Megan felt tears prick her eyes again. "I'm so exhausted," she said. "It's Carter, Gina. You always knew he was no good. You were right. I just never knew how bad he was."

Gina's face stiffened. "*What did he do?*"

"He...he started hitting me. I think it had something to do with me deciding to quit work for awhile, all that time with the two of us shut up in the apartment. I just started getting on his nerves." Megan watched Gina and saw the reaction she wanted to see.

"Never blame yourself," Gina said. "It's his fault. It's always the fault of the abuser."

Megan detected movement from the corner of her eye, and she tried to ignore it. "I haven't been a dream to live with, let me tell you," she continued. "I thought I was going to snap before Caitlin started this new treatment, and then when we got into the test group, I had this new hope, and instead of being a good thing the hope was just *awful*, it made me worry more and more every day, not knowing if I should dare to really hope or..." Sobs now. Well-timed and natural. Carter would be proud.

"Slow down, take your time," Gina said.

"On top of everything, I...I got pregnant."

"What!"

"I got pregnant, and I...I had a miscarriage when...when he hit me."

"That bastard. That motherfucking bastard! I'll kill him. You should call the police. I'll call them right now if you want me—"

"NO!" Megan yelled. She dropped back to a near-whisper, "No, please, you don't understand. He...he started threatening Caitlin. That's why I had to get her out of the hospital. I think he did something...terrible. I think the police might already be involved."

Gina looked stunned. "What are you talking about?"

"Give me a moment," Megan said. She savored the relief of her half-truths while sipping her coffee. Her nerves started to settle. As she set her cup back in its saucer, she heard a loud metallic bang from the alley. She jumped, sloshing hot liquid on her fingers. She let out a sharp yelp.

"Gina, what is it?" A man's voice, tinged with an accent, came from the bedroom. Stefan's voice.

"Excuse me," Gina said, getting up.

"You should have told me you weren't alone," Megan said.

"Oh, he's here all the time these days. Just give me a minute while I tell him what's happening. Short version, I promise."

Megan watched Gina disappear into the hallway and then let her eyes fly back to the window. She thought of standing, getting closer to the glass so she could see what was outside. What did she expect? A blue Carter-like figure standing in the shadows? Preposterous! Ridiculous! Something was happening, but she wasn't being watched, wasn't being followed, wasn't being *stalked*. Cats or rats were performing one of their elaborate mating rituals. Many things might scurry through urban alleys in the last minutes before dawn.

The master bedroom door clicked shut. Gina had gone in to convince Stefan to stay in bed. Megan imagined Gina loosening the sash of her robe and telling Stefan in her most placating voice that he had nothing to worry about. She wanted this time with Megan, wanted the story that had been denied her for so long. Somewhere underneath her warm hostessing, Gina probably harbored more resentment of Megan's recent estrangement than Caitlin did.

You're tired, Megan. Tired and paranoid. Your suspicions about Gina are as ridiculous as your fears of whatever's beyond that window.

What were those scratching noises? Like a chisel scraping concrete. No, like nails...fingernails scraping along bricks, the bricks of this building, the bricks all around the windows. Not like fingernails. Like claws.

Oh yes, the shadow you were looking at *has* moved. It moved exactly when you heard those noises, the sounds of the blue man clawing his way around the window, clawing, climbing, searching for a way in.

If he wanted in, he would *get* in. Surely the carnage at the hospital proved that.

But he will. He'll get in. You know he's coming. And you're so tired...too tired to move...much less defend yourself...or anyone else.

Stop it, stop it, stop it, stop it!

Imagine Carter trying to climb a sheer brick wall. Preposterous!

Scratch, scratch, scratch, scratch.

The door of the master bedroom clicked open and shut again. Megan heard Gina's voice say, "Honey, what are you doing out here?"

"Going to get my mommy," Caitlin said. "She said she would be right back and it's been a really long time." Megan couldn't see the looks on their faces, couldn't see them at all from where she sat, but she could imagine them. Gina looked pleasant, warm and coaxing. Caitlin looked stubborn, independent but not quite resolved. The girl was feeling insecure. Her mother had abandoned her for months. This was the first time she had had her mother with her in a long time, the first time she'd been out of the hospital in a *very* long time, and she wanted to make sure she got to keep Mommy for awhile, to keep from being alone in a strange place. A strange place full of strange noises where the blue man could be waiting.

Megan couldn't *possibly* be hearing breathing near that window. One long breath, drawn in slowly and then even more slowly released. Her ears couldn't possibly be that good! This was the first time Megan had been out for months, too. She had to remember that the world of city streets had been distant from her seventh-floor prison, distant and quiet. Long captivity had made her unaccustomed to quotidian noises. That scratching sound could just be the wind rustling garbage. It could be anything. Not *claws*. Not the grappling efforts of a creature waiting for the right moment to strike.

"Listen to me, Caitlin. You're old enough to understand that your mommy has had a very rough time tonight, and she's very tired. Do you understand that?" Gina, the authoritative schoolteacher.

"Yes, but—"

"No buts, little lady. I know you've had a really rough time, too. Finish your juice if you want, but when you're done, I want you to go right to sleep. Okay?"

"But I'm not tired! I don't want to go to sleep!"

The whine in Caitlin's voice made her sound sleepy. Even a miracle "cure" couldn't make the girl impervious to the stresses of a night like tonight. She and Megan both needed sleep. Megan imagined curling up with her daughter on the futon. She remembered the way she had sometimes shared a bed with her own mother, the safety, the comfort.

"Well, then, just lie down and shut your eyes," Gina said. "Your mommy needs some rest even if you don't. We're going to talk for just a few more minutes, and then we'll all go to bed, and your mommy will come back and say goodnight. Okay?"

"No!" Caitlin raised her voice. "Don't touch me! I want to go see her now! Get out of my way!"

Megan hadn't heard such a bratty sound come from her daughter's lips in a very long time. She had forgotten that Caitlin could be anything other than the sweet, drowsy girl in the hospital bed. Megan didn't want to deal with her. She cheered Gina on, hoping that her friend would succeed in keeping her daughter away. Her cured daughter. The reason for everything.

"Listen, I'm trying to be nice here, but I know your mommy isn't going to be happy with you if you don't do what I tell you." That's right, Gina! "She said she'd come back and see you soon, and the longer you take getting settled in, the longer it's going to be before she can come back and say goodnight like you want her to."

Scratch, scratch, scratch. Getting farther away from the window. As if it were moving around the building, toward the back bedroom where Caitlin was supposed to be. Such a quiet night – she really could be hearing these things. Not a car on the street or a sound from the sidewalks. Yes, this part of the city could be quiet, quiet enough to hear the scratches of someone, some*thing*, crawling along the side of a building. Scratch, scratch. Barely audible now. Out of range. But still there, definitely still there.

Caitlin coughed, probably to remind Gina of her condition. Like father like daughter: Caitlin knew which buttons to push, even at her age. Caitlin coughed again, hamming it up. "I want to see my mommy now." Her voice was softer but just as defiant. "You're not the boss of me. You're not my nurse. Let me see my mommy."

Megan strained to hear the noises outside. She heard nothing. No cars, no people, no scratches, no cats in the alley, nothing. Caitlin and Gina seemed to be sharing a silence, too, probably a stare-down. Hearing those noises had been bad, but the silence was worse. Hearing noises meant knowing where they were, knowing that what made them was still outside instead of...here. The blue man had said, "I'll never leave you."

"Young lady, are you going to go back to the room like I told you to, or am I going to have to *make* you go there? You've got two choices and about five seconds."

Silence. Megan closed her eyes, straining. Give me something. Some noise, some something. Closing her eyes was dangerous. Sleep could come, and then she wouldn't hear anything at all.

"I'm warning you. One," Gina said.

Silence.

"Two," Gina said.

"*Three*," Caitlin said, mocking. Not like a seven-year-old, like a teenager. Perhaps discipline didn't exist at the hospital. Perhaps after living with the idea of a shortened lifespan for long enough, she had decided to learn a few tricks early.

"Four," Gina said. No scratches. Megan held her breath. Her eyes stayed closed, and she felt a tingling at the edge of awareness. She could sleep right here, sitting up.

"Five," Gina said, and Caitlin screamed.

"LET GO OF ME, LET GO OF ME, LET GO OF ME!!!!!"

Another sound drowned Caitlin's screaming, an explosion of glass. The sound jolted Megan, but she didn't open her eyes. The sound came from somewhere else, from a memory. If she opened her eyes she'd be in her mother's enormous bed, and they'd be coming again, the thieves, not men but monsters, marauding vampires.

A woman screamed. Gina. Megan didn't move. She couldn't bring herself to stand again, couldn't get her legs to get up so she could face what had finally come. She heard the door of the master bedroom fly open, heard grunting and Stefan's voice saying, "What the hell!"

Something stopped him. Megan didn't know what, but something…Carter…the blue man? She heard an *oomph* and a slam, and then there was Stefan's voice again saying, "Get away from me!" He screamed, but something cut the scream short.

Megan heard the sound of something being dragged across carpet. She managed to unglue her eyelids. She heard another sound, the tinkle of more breaking glass. Another sound got her moving: a scream – Caitlin's – not bratty but terrified.

She raced from the couch to the head of the hall and stopped. In the lamplight she saw streaks on the carpet, more blood to add to the night's total. She remembered her hesitation before ringing at the door. She had been right. She never should have come here. She had known.

Stefan lay on the carpet. Blood still gushed from his torso where it had been torn open. His chest yawned away from his abdomen. Something had come close to tearing him in half.

Megan's fist rose and blocked the cry that wanted to burst from her lips. Caitlin stood farther down the hall. Stefan's body bisected the path between them. Caitlin had stopped screaming; she just stared at the bleeding dead man. Megan had spared her the scene at the hospital, but Caitlin was getting the full force of this.

Another thought occurred to her: "Gina, where's Gina?!"

Caitlin looked at her mother but didn't respond. Megan went to her, stepping over Stefan. She looked in the master bedroom, which was empty, and then she looked down at her daughter. "Where is she?!"

The girl was crying now. "I didn't mean it! I didn't mean it!!"

"Caitlin, answer me!" She tried to sound calmer. "Where is Gina? Is she hurt?" Her mind continued, *where's the thing that did this?* She'd just rushed in, not thinking that she'd be risking—

"He took her! The blue man took her! I didn't mean it!" Megan dropped to her knees and hugged her wailing daughter. Ahead of her she saw the bedroom where Gina had wanted Caitlin to sleep. Her eyes took in the sight of yet another trail of blood, this one leading up to where the bedroom window had shattered. Megan needed sleep, but not yet. First she needed to go, to get her daughter out of the city and as far from here as possible.

The Descent of Carter Anderson, Continued

The glass rolled off his skin like water as Carter smashed through the window. He didn't look down, but he could sense the street far below, and he thought that his body, even now, might not withstand the crushing combination of gravity and asphalt. The strange skin that covered him was not invulnerable. Bullets had made dents. His reinforced bones might shatter if he fell.

The city street didn't rush to crush him. Carter found himself clinging to the side of the hospital building, and instead of going down, he went up. Fingers and heels pierced brick and lingered near the broken window he had used as an exit. He sensed that he was waiting for something. Soon he heard Megan enter the room, and Caitlin asked her if the thing she had just seen had been Daddy. Carter felt proud: his daughter could recognize him even in his altered form.

Megan was carrying Caitlin out of the room when Carter started climbing again. He reached the roof in seconds. A breeze flecked his skin with particles of dirt and ice. On the rooftop's edge, he took in the impressions of the night – the lights, the quiet city. He didn't know why he had stopped moving, but he was grateful for the respite. The shock and ache of having seen his own hands slash through uncounted lives subsided while he stood still.

The skin around the bullet holes in his back, chest, and stomach pulsed. The itchy, hot feeling that reported damage intensified. It approached pain without producing pain's debilitation. Carter couldn't see what was happening. The holes in his skin felt like they were moving without the aid of his muscles. The edges of the wounds felt like lips in an intimate act. The lips spat out the bullets, closed, and disappeared.

Megan's voice floated from the sidewalk to his ears, and his attention focused. She and Caitlin emerged from the back of the building, which the police hadn't yet secured. Without taking a step, he watched their progress. They were headed toward the subway. Carter expected to scurry down the side of the building and follow them. Instead he stayed still.

After his wife and daughter had gained a lead, Carter found himself running across the roof in Megan's direction. He reached the ledge and leapt from it without a pause. As he moved from rooftop to rooftop, jumping and scaling walls, Carter felt as if he were riding on the shoulders of a comic book superhero, a webless Spiderman. The power wasn't his, but he got to sense it. The working of superhuman muscles felt better than thinking, better than guilt.

His feet returned to the ground. Carter understood: since Megan and Caitlin had descended into the subway, he, too, would descend. His wife and daughter were his puppeteer's purpose, so they were his purpose. The suture of the seeker had joined them in an eternal act of will. He had heard himself say it: his will – their will – was to make his daughter better and never leave her.

As his body glided down the subway steps, Carter slipped into thought. He and Brian couldn't have concocted a neater philosophical conundrum. Independent of his puppeteer, Carter somehow *was*, but did a being with no independent will – no capacity to act, interact, or be perceived – have a proper claim to existence?

Megan and Caitlin sat on a bench at one end of the train platform, and Carter hid in the shadows at the other. He hung from the ceiling, and when a rag-bundled woman sat nearby, she carried on the heated debate she was having with herself without noticing him. When the train came, he lurked two cars away from the quarry. His only fellow passenger stared at him. Carter expected to kill the man, but his attention never diverted from his wife and daughter.

Sticking to the streets, Carter trailed Megan to Gina's. Megan had capitulated to captivity and worn filthy pajamas day after day while she was pregnant, but now she was somehow strong enough to keep going. Carter felt awe. Megan had never been more like Susan Penser than at this moment. Lingering in the alley by Gina's apartment, he listened to his wife tell beautiful lies.

Despite the elegance of Megan's lies, Gina should have called the police and an ambulance. The blood on Megan's clothes and skin should have overpowered the lies. Carter remembered that Gina was, and had always been, selfish, stupid, and hopelessly oblivious.

He didn't think much about the altercation between Caitlin and Gina until he was smashing through more glass and taking another victim. He hardly looked at his daughter while he killed Stefan and dragged Gina out through the window. Caitlin screamed in terror, but he didn't touch or even acknowledge her. At the hospital, Carter had assumed that his puppeteer was trying not to frighten her, but now he thought otherwise. His movements were mechanical.

Megan and Caitlin fled the apartment, and Carter didn't follow. Clinging to the side of the building with an unconscious, but still living, woman on one arm, he watched his quarry go and made no move to pursue them. Carter was perplexed as he carried Gina back into her apartment, stepped over the corpse of her boyfriend, and set her down on her own bed. He reasoned that he must have some other purpose, a motive beyond the girl he had promised never to leave.

He had only bumped Gina against the wall, knocking her unconscious. Her flesh was still intact. His eyes looked at her form, at the rise and fall of her breasts as she breathed. Gina had never seemed particularly attractive to Carter, but as his eyes traced her curves, he found a new appreciation. He remembered that his new body had no sex organs. Though he couldn't *want* her, not in that way, the way his eyes devoured her reminded him of lust.

Soft pokes on his sandpaper tongue – he was licking his teeth.

She started to stir, to wake. He stood on the bed. His heels dug into the mattress, and his knees hovered just an inch above the blanket as he arched his body over her. One of her arms reached out beside her, brushing past his leg. Her searching arm probably expected to find Stefan lying beneath the rumpled covers. Her eyes opened and froze. Carter could read her thoughts by the expressions on her face. No, she hadn't been dreaming. The thing that had come through her window and murdered her boyfriend was standing over her. He reeked of rot and gore; he looked like Nosferatu on steroids.

Gina raised an arm to bat him off her, but he caught it with a foot and shoved it back on the bed. Still crouched over her but not touching her, he gave her an opportunity, which she took. She rolled away, and she almost reached the side of the king-sized bed before he grabbed her, picked her up, and threw her back down in the bed's center. With the grab he broke her skin for the first time, sinking his fingertips into the flesh of her sides.

She screamed and sat up, her feet pushing her back toward the headboard as her arms locked in front of her in combat position. This woman taught at a public school in the city: she knew how to fight. Carter thought he might give her a chance for some hand-to-hand, but then he yanked her ankles, making her back flop down on the mattress. She swung a fist. He caught it, squeezed until it opened, and severed one of her outstretched fingers with one of his own. Her detached pinky dropped on the bed.

Straddling her waist to keep her from getting away, he gave her a moment to howl over the loss of her finger. "Oh, God!" she screamed. "I'm bleeding!" And then, "Carter! Carter! Carter! Stop it, stop it, stop it! SOMEBODY HELP ME!"

Try FIRE, Carter thought.

He lifted the detached digit from the bed and examined it. While Gina wriggled beneath him and tried to staunch the bleeding with the hand that was still whole, his sharpened fingertips flayed her severed finger.

He showed no interest in the pinky's paltry bit of meat. Fascinated, Carter watched himself strip the bone and pop it into his mouth. Gina had quieted; she was watching, too. His new teeth crunched through bone.

Crunch, crunch, crunch.

Gina began gibbering, her struggles growing weaker. She passed out again after he started to slice open her left leg.

Starting with the knees, he ate cartilage, ligaments, and bone. Carter prayed that he couldn't digest these things, prayed to be sick. He tried to escape into thought. He tried to classify his new form; just when he had concluded that he was a Bone Monster, he started devouring Gina's lungs. His fingers picked out bits in selective order, and when he started to eat what he thought might have been lymph nodes, he understood: he was eating the parts most ravaged by his daughter's cancer.

At one time or another, though, the cancer had been almost *everywhere* in Caitlin's body. Quite a bit of time passed before he was done. Carter couldn't close his eyes or nose or ears. He couldn't shut off his tongue. He couldn't turn his stomach inside out. He could only wait for the experience to end.

It finally did. From the corner of his eye he saw a mirror, and he feared that his body would go over to it and show him how his face and neck looked now that they were caked with more than blood. He felt happy when he sat down in the leftovers at an angle that obscured the mirror. The tacky shirt and dark slacks he had donned just hours ago had become unrecognizable from the gun blasts and carnage. New stains wouldn't matter, but he longed for the sensations of a shower and a change of clothes. Stefan was a big guy. Maybe he had something here that would fit.

Trying to frown at the ridiculousness of thinking about clothes when he was sitting on someone's entrails, he realized how little his face had moved since his death. There had been a few smiles, but he hadn't even closed his eyes since their first post-mortem opening, not even to blink. At the moment the stillness of his eyelids struck him as inhuman, they squeezed shut.

Carter welcomed sensory oblivion. When his eyes closed, the rest of his senses seemed to shut off, too. The sounds of the new day dawning outside the apartment were gone. He didn't smell rot. He didn't taste the bits of flesh that clung to his teeth or feel the squishiness beneath him. He exulted.

Was this sleep? Deprived of sense, he was drifting, and he could imagine himself, a bodiless non-thing, floating through a dark void. He felt light and free, no longer tied to his puppeteer. Movement through this non-space had a direction, but he had no way of knowing where it lay.

Gradually, he began to sense his surroundings again. Morning light started to press against his retinas, and in the blurriness he became aware that he was cold, hungry, and tired. He was standing next to someone who was impossibly tall. A big, soft hand enclosed his own. It was dirty and trembling. The hand was feminine, definitely feminine, despite the grime.

A brick wall stood in front of him, and in it he saw a metal frame around some kind of machine. He recognized it – an ATM. The buttons seemed to be placed at a height appropriate for the giant beside him. The giant was getting cash.

"Damn it! Come on, just do this for me. Work, work, work. Come on! It's *my* money! You can give me more than two hundred fucking dollars of it if I tell you to!" Carter didn't place the voice until it spoke again. "I'm sorry to talk that way, sweetie. I guess Mommy's got all the money she's going to get." Megan. The "giant" was Megan.

Megan gave his hand a little reassuring squeeze. The warmth of it felt good. He felt a sudden desperation for her not to let go, and as if in response, he wrenched his fingers away from her. His small fingers. His child-fingers. No razor-sharp killing tips and no blue and bloody skin. Five healthy fingers of a healthy little girl.

He was tired, hungry, and cold, and dried tears made his cheeks feel sticky, but he was well. He was Caitlin.

"Mommy, can we get something to eat?" He said it without volition, driving home the understanding that he could control Caitlin's body no more than he could control the one that had been his. Feeling the hollowness of his tummy, though, he decided that Caitlin had said just what he would have in her position.

Megan's exasperated expression asked how Caitlin could possibly think of food at a time like this. Carter could understand Megan's look, but he guessed that Caitlin couldn't. He feared that Caitlin would glean Megan's disapproval not from Megan but from him, and he waited for a clenching of muscles or some other physical sign that his daughter had understood his thoughts. He received no sign; Caitlin didn't seem to notice him inside her head. For Caitlin, he did not exist, and he was glad.

"I bet you'd like to get something better than all that icky hospital food, huh?" Megan's tone was controlled and affectionate, bearing no trace of the exasperation that Carter had sensed. Even after the ordeal of the last night, she was able to be a mother. Carter's awe resurfaced.

He nodded at her with enthusiasm.

"I think there's a McDonald's on the way to the car rental place we're going to. Does that sound good?"

"Uh-huh." He couldn't remember the last time his daughter had had a Happy Meal.

When Caitlin started to eat the Egg McMuffin, Carter's mind made an unwelcome connection. The warm bread and egg squishing around his dull teeth contrasted with the other things he had recently felt in his other mouth, but not enough.

The connection of textures and flavors bore no bodily consequences. While his thoughts were revolted, his mouth and stomach were overjoyed. Again Carter felt glad that his daughter showed no awareness of sharing her senses with him.

Megan was eating, too. Carter could tell from her face that the food felt like chalk in her mouth, but she chewed and swallowed all the same. Her eyes kept closing from the weight of exhaustion. Even adrenaline had to run out sometime, and her face and posture told him that the collapse was near. When she looked over at him – he had to remind himself that she was seeing Caitlin, not Carter – the sight seemed to give her a boost, to perk up her posture. The way his eyes kept looking from his food to her told him that Caitlin was also happy to be with Megan. Not long ago, the girl had seen a horrible monster tear a man in half, but now she could manage to be happy. Caitlin had been through many different hells. She'd survive this one.

Carter watched his wife and estimated her thoughts. Megan ate because she needed strength. She hadn't seen Carter, or the thing that Carter had become. She only knew that *something* was after her. Caitlin might have described the Daddy-like thing she had seen, but Megan still wouldn't know for certain what that thing really was. The only thing she could know with certainty was the need to escape. To run.

"You finished?" she asked.

He had finished the sandwich and the hash brown and was just sucking the last drops of orange juice through his straw. The meal seemed tiny to Carter, but it had made him feel quite full. He gave Megan a little-girl nod.

After filling out the paperwork, Megan hesitated about how to pay for the car she was renting. Her purse had credit cards and cash, and Carter could see her fingers going back and forth between the two options. The sales rep behind the counter eyed her. Megan's smell and ragged appearance didn't seem to bother Caitlin, but they bothered the sales rep. Megan had gone into the bathroom at McDonald's to freshen up, but she hadn't gotten the blood out of her pants and sweater. Seeing the rep's suspicion, Megan had to be doubly concerned about using a credit card. Would he call it in? And even if he didn't, had the police gone to the apartment she and Carter had shared, found the mess, and put out some sort of APB that would make her card raise a red flag? Could the police work that fast? Carter didn't know, and he was sure that Megan didn't know, either.

His body fidgeted at Megan's side, expressing Caitlin's blissful ignorance.

The need to conserve cash for later must have outweighed worry about the card. Megan handed the plastic over, and the man ran it through without a problem. Minutes later Megan was driving a shiny new sedan off the lot. She and Carter both hated driving in the city, and as Carter looked up at her from the passenger seat, he could see the new tension in her overstressed brow.

Caitlin couldn't have seen the tension. When she looked up at her mother, she must have been seeing something else. Caitlin's body – his body – gave him no clues about what she saw or felt.

Was it admiration? Wonder? Curiosity? Or was she just looking up at Megan because there was nothing else more important to draw her attention?

Megan drove across the bridge. Traffic was thick, but once she got beyond the city limits, she'd be going opposite the bulk of morning commuters, and that would be a relief. He blinked a few times, and Carter worried that Caitlin might be going to sleep. He wanted to keep watching Megan, to keep following her progress on the highway, and he had no idea what would happen to *him* while Caitlin slept. The closing of these eyes didn't send him drifting into a void the way the closing of those other eyes had, but still he doubted that he'd experience sleep while Caitlin did. Would Caitlin's sleep send him back to the other body?

He had been thinking of Caitlin's body as his body the whole time he had been sharing her senses, and he realized now that it *was* his, or at least as much his as that other body. He possessed either, or he possessed neither. There wasn't much of a distinction. The only significant difference between the two places his mind had been since his death was that he felt fairly certain Caitlin didn't detect his presence while the other thing – the puppeteer – did. That difference didn't indicate rightfulness of place, though. Even within a body, Carter was disembodied.

His thoughts took a turn: since Caitlin didn't detect him, would he be able to detect someone or something else? What if more than one thing shared the senses of his daughter? Had his puppeteer's consciousness traveled with him? Or stranger still, what if an entirely different consciousness dwelled here as well? What if disembodied minds like himself could set up colonies in people's brains? What if they were everywhere?

The equivalence struck him. He must have become what the puppeteer had once been, the sort of thing that Dr. Fincher had called a disembodied will. Had the puppeteer once had a body of its own? Had it ever lived powerlessly in his body like he had started doing after he had invited it to take over? Had it started out as human? Had it come from somewhere else, or had it always been a part of him? Had he and it merely traded places?

"MOMMY, LOOK OUT!" he screamed.

Megan slammed on the brakes, and the tires screeched to a halt, bringing the front bumper within inches of the stopped car in front of them. Carter hadn't been paying attention to what he was seeing, but Caitlin had seen her mother falling asleep at the wheel.

His eyes stayed glued to Megan with a definite purpose now: he was on sleep-watch. Caitlin had a job. She had to keep Mommy awake. Carter's smart, responsible daughter would make sure they got where they were going without causing a seventeen-car pile-up. Carter's attention stayed as fixed as hers did for the rest of the ride.

Once they cleared the city, they took the first exit with a motel sign visible from the turnpike. Carter saw the exit number, and he saw the motel's name. He saw Megan turn in and park.

Abrupt blackness overtook him, and he was again drifting in the senseless void. When his sight returned, he could also smell and taste and feel. He was back in the putrid body, the one sitting in the mess that had once been Gina, the one with the taste of her in its mouth.

He climbed off the bed and went over to the mirror. After the experience with Caitlin, Carter felt better prepared to take in the horror of his reflection. The work his hands began to do puzzled him. They wiped some of the gore away from his cheeks, and then they started taking off the tattered, matted shirt. Not only was he undressing, but he was showing himself that he was undressing. A minute later he stood in Gina's shower, washing bits of Gina down the drain.

Megan was probably showering at that moment, too. As Carter welcomed the sensation of the warm, cleansing water, he imagined inhabiting his wife. He wished he could see her soft, human skin instead of the coarse blueness that was his own. He remembered the two of them showering together. Carter felt a yearning for his wife, an echo of his lost sexuality.

He found some of Stefan's clothes and put them on. Nothing tacky this time, just a pair of jeans and a sweatshirt. He was doing exactly what he had wanted to do before the act of closing his eyes had sent him to Caitlin. At first he thought it was a coincidence, but he soon reasoned otherwise. Though he was trying to concentrate on memories of his wife in the shower, he felt the image of the exit ramp Megan had taken coming from memory into consciousness. He saw the motel sign again and noted where Megan had parked.

He understood what had happened. When Carter had closed his eyes, his consciousness had been sent on a mission to find the charge he had let slip away. Maybe his puppeteer had been able to watch through Caitlin's eyes as he had, or maybe it had needed him to come back before it could gather the information it wanted from his memory. The timing of his return suggested the former, but the informative images erupting from his memory suggested the latter. He couldn't decide.

The one thing he did know was that his consciousness had been used as a tool by the will that controlled his body. It must have been listening to his thoughts and desires from the beginning. It knew that the shower and clean clothes would be a fitting reward for his good service. He didn't have a choice in the matter, so the reward served no purpose. Maybe the puppeteer did it out of compassion, or maybe it did it to mock him. Or maybe it was a coincidence, and it never really heard him at all. Carter's reasoning was impotent. His thoughts spun like a wheel in a hamster cage.

Direction

The distance between Megan and the city wasn't large enough, not nearly large enough, but she decided to stop at a motel anyway. A near-collision told her that driving on would be more dangerous than stopping. She got a room with two double beds, and seconds after tossing the key on the dresser, she flopped onto one of them. Caitlin would figure out that the second bed was for her. She'd go to sleep, too, and when they awoke refreshed they'd be able to face their situation, find some sense in it, and make a plan.

Megan slept, and despite complete exhaustion, she woke again in a few hours. She tried to blame the sunlight pouring around the edges of the room's cheap curtains, but she knew the real reason. Fear wouldn't let her sleep. At any moment, one of these windows could explode, and she'd finally see it. *It.* The thing responsible for the massacre at the hospital, for hacking Stefan to death, for Gina's disappearance. The blue man. Carter.

Once she had confirmed that Caitlin had gone to sleep and that the room remained as secure as it would get, she closed her eyes again. She had never experienced fatigue like this before. Even maintaining a heartbeat seemed to require effort. The pervasive weariness should have let her drift away again, but it didn't. She was here. She was here in this strange motel room by the highway, and whether or not her situation made sense, she had to make a plan.

She had to shower, and she had to get new clothes for both of them. After the shower, as she got back into last night's crusty pants and sweater, she realized that getting new clothes would mean going outside. She wanted to flee, to go miles and miles away, but she didn't want to go outside. So far this room had been safe. Maybe the blue man didn't know they were here. Maybe if they stayed here, he or it would never find them.

No sense trying to dismiss her sense that something stalking her had led to Stefan's death and probably Gina's, too. However much the fear she felt seemed like paranoia, she had to rely on it. Relying on it would be easier if it weren't telling her two opposite things. The fear said *run*, and the fear said *hide here*. She couldn't do both. Sooner or later, they would have to leave. She understood that. Sooner or later the impulse to run would win out.

Where would they go? She had taken the way out of the city that she knew best, and that had pointed them south. Toward Susan. Susan wasn't like Gina. Susan would know what to do. Susan had ways of getting things done. Megan imagined adding her mother's face to the crowd of the dead that appeared on the backs of her eyelids when they closed. She shuddered. Carter would know that Susan's house would be a likely place to find her. Carter often said that because Megan always had Susan to fall back on, she had never experienced true independence. She had never had to grow up, he said.

Carter said a lot of things. Like, "I'll never leave you." *Was* that Carter?

She couldn't pick up the phone to let her mother know she was coming, and she couldn't fathom getting up and going as far as the nearest store to get clothes. She was weak. A few hours of sleep had turned her back into the powerless, mindless wimp who had let a year of indecision and inaction put her in this horrible position. Soon the weight of the horror would crash down on her, and she wouldn't be able to move.

NO.

Megan tapped her daughter on the shoulder. The child grunted, rubbed her eyes, and looked up. "Mommy's got to go to the store," she said. "We've got to get you out of these clothes into something nice and new, and I've got to get out of this stinky sweater." Megan sniffed her arms and wrinkled her face in disgust. Caitlin sniffed the air and mimicked her mother's expression. They both smiled.

"I get to go with you, right?" Caitlin asked.

"Of course you do," Megan said. "We're a team now. All that stuff about you and me spending lots of time apart is over. You're going to stick close to me from now on, okay?"

"O-*kay!*"

While Caitlin beamed at her, and she beamed back, a little voice told her that Caitlin would be just fine in this secure motel room. Why bring her back out into the world where the blue man could be waiting? Leave her alone. Go by yourself. Be rid of her, of all of it. Be *free*.

No, no, no.

She had spotted a strip mall full of discount outlets near the motel as they turned into the parking lot. She worried about leaving a credit card trail that someone – maybe Carter or the police – could follow, but since she had already used it for the room, she'd use it again now. She had seen an ATM on the strip. She'd get more cash if the machine would let her, and she'd use only cash for the rest of the trip. That little bit of carefulness would be all she could manage. Other worries – like that someone might have seen her picture on the news or that someone might recognize the stains on her dark clothes – she had to table.

She no longer knew what sizes her daughter needed. Seeing the way Caitlin's face turned dark during quiet moments, Megan decided to make trying things on a game of dress-up. In-store dress-up was something Caitlin had been too young to enjoy before the diagnosis. Caitlin had no experience, but television had taught her what her mother meant when she told her to pretend like she was a model. Caitlin marched with flair between her mother and the mirror, but Megan told her she wasn't convinced. Megan tried on a pair of the pants she had picked out and strutted catwalk-style, walking with exaggerated bounces of her hips. Mommy's funny walk got Caitlin giggling, and the next time she tried on a shirt, the seven-year-old vamped.

Good, Megan thought. She had managed to distract Caitlin. She had even managed to distract herself until Caitlin's knitted hat slipped off.

At the register, during the anxious seconds that passed while the clerk eyed Megan and the machine authorized the credit card, Caitlin asked, "Mommy, how about some candy?"

The pucker of sour candy had been a revelation after Caitlin's first Halloween haul, and she had never lost the fascination. Megan had brought Sour Patch Kids for special occasions at the hospital. Now, Caitlin could pick out candy *herself.*

"Okay," Megan said, "but only a little. We've got a long drive ahead of us, and I don't want you bouncing all over the car."

"I won't," Caitlin said. "Are we going back to get Katy? Or Daddy?"

"I think there's a drugstore next door," Megan said. "I'll let you pick out some candy if you want." Megan had to jog to keep up with Caitlin as she dashed to the store and honed in on the candy aisle.

They went back to the motel, got cleaned up, and put on new clothes. They decided to throw away everything they had been wearing except for Caitlin's hat. Her scalp was downed with new growth, but it still needed extra protection from the cold.

Behind the wheel again and merging into southbound turnpike traffic, Megan lost the comfort she had felt during the mother-daughter bonding. Megan once again became not just Caitlin's mother but the woman who had conspired to murder Caitlin's sister. Caitlin, in turn, became the motive behind that murder.

Megan could think matter-of-factly about the act that would define them both in her mind for the rest of her life: I bore a child so my husband could kill it. HER. Kill her for Caitlin's sake. She could think matter-of-factly because she still couldn't comprehend it. When comprehension threatened, Megan simply changed lanes.

She watched her rearview mirrors almost as much as she watched the road in front of her. Caitlin's eyes wandered between the windows and Megan, and when they landed on her, Megan thought she detected distrust. After all, Megan had almost killed them yesterday – just this morning – when she had fallen asleep at the wheel. And she had shown herself capable of participating in the death of one child already. Caitlin was wise to keep an eye on Mommy's driving.

Megan thought that increasing the distance between her and the city would allow her to loosen her grip on the steering wheel, but distance and time only brought more tension. The mirrors taunted her. She didn't know what to look for, but she had to look. Her imagination suggested the bizarre blue man of Caitlin's description, but she kept checking the men behind the wheels of surrounding vehicles to see if their shoulders and heads favored the Carter she knew.

She wanted normal Carter, jailor and murderer, to be the one chasing them. The abnormal, supernatural explanation was unacceptable, but the way Caitlin bounced in her seat to the music on the radio insisted on it. The girl beside her had been more than cured: she had been reset, returned to health as if cancer had never marched through her body on a Sherman-like path of total destruction. Nothing pure, nothing natural had brought that girl back. Caitlin defied nature with every breath. She lived because Carter had become more than a killer. Megan wanted to search for regular old Carter in the mirrors, but Caitlin's breathing said she should look for a blue, clawed monster whose shape only echoed her husband's.

Flashes yanked her eyes toward the mirrors, a van changing lanes behind her, a bird circling around an overpass. Each time she tried to dismiss her fears, she remembered the sounds in the alley she had dismissed at Gina's. She had to look at every object that might be a threat. She had to be ready.

Two hours into the drive, Caitlin said she had to go potty. Megan's first reaction was to refuse – they couldn't stop, not now! He could be waiting at the rest stop! The idea of the Carter-thing's omnipresence seemed absurd, but she had to be on her guard. Megan didn't have to use the toilet, but she went anyway so she could stay in the stall next to Caitlin for as long as the girl needed. The creak of another stall door almost made her yelp. Footsteps, the squeaky turn of a faucet...she hoped the bathroom would sound empty again by the time Caitlin was ready to leave the stalls. Then it sounded empty, and Megan feared what she couldn't hear while Caitlin flushed.

If Carter or whatever it was wanted to hurt Caitlin, he, it, could have done so already. But could Megan be sure? He might have been waiting for the moment his demented mind thought *right* for killing them. She didn't know. None of her ideas made sense. She could explain nothing. She could only stay on her guard, ready to jump at the slightest sign.

Back in the car again, Megan forced herself to take three long, deep breaths. She couldn't yield to the panic that scratched at her nerves harder and harder with each second that passed. For Caitlin's sake, for her own, she had to stay calm.

When the overcast sky opened up and started pouring, Megan punched the dashboard with a trembling, frustrated fist. Traffic slowed, which meant she had to slow. Raindrops in the mirrors provided millions of distracting sources of threatening motion. That movement – there! – was that...? Each blast of thunder could have been the shattering of her back windshield. Her heart pounded in her chest.

"I've got an idea," she said to Caitlin. "Let's play a game. How about something like 'I Spy.' We'll take turns watching for neat things outside, and then one of us will have to guess what the other saw. We can get ideas by looking all around all the time."

Help Mommy WATCH, Caitlin!

Caitlin was at first uneasy about the mobile version of the game that Megan had concocted, but she soon got into it. "I spy something...brown," she said on her second turn.

The sound of the B almost made Megan slam on the brakes. Instead of "brown," she had expected "blue." Carter-shaped blue. Normal, abnormal, whatever: menacing. After them.

"Was it a tree?" Megan asked.

No, not a tree. A billboard? Nope. A car? Close, but no. A truck? Bingo! Cars and standard roadside images came up repeatedly. Neither one of them thought it much of a game, but they played it anyway. They searched the roads again and again, Caitlin looking for a stumper of an object, Megan looking for a monster of a man.

Traffic was light for a while, unusually smooth for the weather, but it slowed to a crawl when they approached another bulging metropolis. The lane next to Megan's seemed to be going faster than hers, so she flipped on her signal and waited for an opening. Once there, a different lane seemed the one to be in, so she made her way over to it. She knew the switching was pointless, that she should stay in place and wait it out, but all the signaling and steering distracted her from the mirrors. She kept hunting for the perfect spot until finally she was trapped, stopped completely, glued to the reflections of the street behind her.

"Uh-oh," Caitlin said.

Uh-oh. Shit, shit, shit! They needed to keep going. Fatigue was threatening, and dusk had come, and they needed to go, to get past this city so they could find another out-of-the-way motel and stop and hide for the night. Not a traffic jam like this, not now!

The rain poured down. She turned on the radio, switched to AM, and searched for information. She found it. A trailer had jackknifed on a bridge up ahead. Traffic wasn't going to budge until a clean-up crew could get there. I hope you didn't have hot plans tonight, commuters, because you're in for one hell of a wait!

Megan rubbed a hand on her forehead and shifted to park. Not going to move. Going to sit here. Exposed. Waiting. Mirror, mirror, mirror. Rain.

"Mommy, what's that man doing on top of that truck?"

The words hammered on her spine. Which man, Caitlin? You mean the blue one? Megan looked in her mirrors again. Her sedan sat in the second lane from the right in six lanes choked by vehicles of varying shapes and sizes. Behind her, she saw two enormous trucks. Sheets of rain on the mirrors made them blurry, but she could make out the roofs of their trailers. She didn't see any man, blue or otherwise. "What man, sweetie?"

"He's bent over kind of funny on that truck over there. He's kind of hard to see, but he's there all right." Caitlin twisted her body further around so she could point through the back windshield. Finding her angle insufficient, Caitlin unfastened her seatbelt, turned so she could kneel facing backward, and pointed again. "*There* Mommy. Do you see?"

The mirrors had failed her. Megan would have to twist around like Caitlin had. She didn't want to, didn't want to unfasten her seatbelt and turn, but she did.

There, three lanes to the left, sat a truck with a long orange trailer. Through the heavy rain Megan could make out a shape on its roof, a shape the angle of her left-side mirror had concealed. It looked like it could be a man. She couldn't make out any color, but the man-shape did seem to be facing in her direction.

"Isn't he *cold* and *wet* out there?" Caitlin asked.

Megan twisted around further and knelt on the seat. She had to be sure she wasn't hallucinating, had to be sure she was really seeing—

"I don't know, Caitlin."

He was there. There, looking at them. Cold and wet and watching. The looking was the important thing. It didn't care about things like comfort. It only cared about them. It wanted them, and had waited for the moment its demented mind deemed right. Not Carter, not normal. A monster, a stalker, a bringer of death with an inscrutable scheme and calculated timing.

She placed a hand on her daughter's back. "We've got to get out of here, Caitlin." They didn't have an umbrella. "We're going to get cold and wet, but we've got to get out of here."

"Why, Mommy? Is it the blue man? Is it Daddy?" Caitlin had seen it. Caitlin had seen the thing up close and had seen it tear Stefan in half. She had to understand the urgency, had to feel the panic in her stomach like her mother did, had to know the need to run with every fiber of her supernaturally repaired little being.

Megan looked to the sides of the sedan. In each car that flanked her, a woman sat alone at the wheel. One nodded her head with rhythm. The other smoked a cigarette and tapped at her dashboard. No help. No one *could* help. Anyone who tried would just end up another dead face on the back of Megan's eyelids. The blue man was an army of terrorists. The blue man was unstoppable.

The blue man was three lanes away. Maybe they could run. They had no other choice. They had to try. Megan faced forward, and Caitlin did the same. "Caitlin, do you see that road that goes off to the side up ahead of us?" She pointed to an exit ramp on the right, and the little girl nodded. "I'm going to count to three, and then I want you to open your door and get out of the car. I'm going to climb out right behind you, and then we're going to run toward that road as fast as we can."

"But it's raining and I'm scared!"

"I know you're scared. I'm scared, too. But the man over there is a bad man and we have to get away, okay? Okay Caitlin? We can do this together. We're a team, and we're going to get away. Okay?"

Caitlin nodded, a tear dripping down one soft cheek.

"One," Megan said. *Oh, God. I can't do this. I can't.* "Two." In her mind, she heard a child's voice, whether her own or Caitlin's she didn't know, say *Two and a half, two and three quarters....* "THREE!"

Caitlin opened her door, and Megan was up and pushing at her daughter's back before even one of the girl's feet hit the road. Megan grabbed Caitlin's hand and started running, weaving around the car with the smoking woman, bumping against an SUV as she dashed by, and almost tripping on a shred of tire in the road. The exit ramp was a hundred, maybe two hundred yards away. Caitlin could keep up. They would make it.

Thump, thump, thump, THUMP. Megan heard it coming, didn't know how it made the noises but heard and knew that the blue man had seen them and was closing the distance far faster than they could hope to move. She was almost lifting her daughter off the ground as she swerved around another SUV. Looking to both sides, she took a second to consider which way to run. If they got to the breakdown lane, they'd have a clear path.

"Mommy, you're hurting my arm!"

The whiny sound broke her concentration, and she looked down at her daughter. Rain had already soaked through her hat and her new clothes, and it obscured the tears that Megan knew were flowing. And in the corner of Megan's eye, behind Caitlin—

A line of vehicles with dented roofs marked the path that the Carter-thing was taking. It *was* the Carter-thing, the blue man. She could see the blueness and the hint of her husband in its shape. She couldn't see more than that, not yet, but she didn't need to. Some of the drivers whose cars had been used as stepping stones pressed hard on their horns, adding their blare to the drumbeats of the rain. They didn't know what they honked at. If they did, they would be fleeing the scene like she was.

She was about to start running again when she realized that the blue man wasn't moving. Finding its shape on the roof of an SUV, she saw that as she stood still staring at it, it stood still staring at her. As a test, she leaned forward like a runner about to dash. It made a similar motion. It was waiting to see what she'd do next before it took another leap.

The driver of the SUV the Carter-thing stood on decided to get rough with the intruder. Megan could see the tire-iron in his hand as he opened his door and stepped out into the rain. "Hey, motherfucker, what the hell do you think you're doing? Get the hell down off my car!!!" The man waved the tire-iron for emphasis. The rain had already soaked him by the time he had finished barking his order.

The Carter-thing turned away from Megan to face the man. Megan watched it step toward him as he swung the tire-iron toward the high roof and missed. The Carter-thing leaned over farther than it should have been able to and swiped at the man with one of its feet. As the man grasped at his spurting throat and collapsed into a puddle, Megan realized that she was missing her moment. The Carter-thing was facing the other direction. She squeezed Caitlin's wrist to let her know they were going to move again and lurched toward the breakdown lane.

She felt the shadow passing above her while she tried to run. A thump and the shattering of glass made Megan look at the car she had been running by to get to the empty lane near the exit. Inside the car, a young man crouched beneath his dented roof, helpless and screaming. On top of it stood the Carter-thing, ready to block Megan's retreat.

Without thinking, she turned and pulled Caitlin in the opposite direction, back toward the sedan and the orange truck where the blue man had started. As she weaved through stopped cars with blaring horns and slack-jawed drivers, she expected to hear the thumps and smashes of her roof-hopping pursuer, but she heard nothing. She crossed one lane, then another and another until the only thing between her and the breakdown lane on the left was a tiny two-door.

The thing landed on its roof, which crumpled beneath the impact. Megan screamed, releasing Caitlin as she lifted her hands to block out the sight.

"Mommy, Mommy, Mommy!" Caitlin screamed. The sounds that followed were as incoherent as the bellowing from Megan's lungs, but they worked. Yanking her daughter's other wrist, the one she hadn't yet bruised, Megan started back toward the right, weaving forward this time, hoping to cover some distance toward the exit while the Carter-thing volleyed back and forth.

The blue man's next leap cut them off before they reached the second lane from the right, pushing them back toward the middle. Its next leap cut them off even closer to the center. Megan tried to go straight ahead through a narrow aisle between car doors; it cut them off in front. She turned and ran the other way, cutting left and right and left in attempts to get the thing to make a leap in the wrong direction and lose time.

Thump, smash, the blare of horns, the screams of drivers, rage and terror and pounding rain and pearls of glass on the hard, wet street, Megan navigated and ran, toting Caitlin, feeling clothes clinging tight and wet to her freezing skin, cut off again, again, and again.

She found herself only two cars away from where she had started, close to her own rented sedan. She tried to run left, and the blue man cut her off immediately. Time and again it could have done more than just cut her off. A swipe of its sharp heel or its claws could have killed them both, but each time it landed on a roof, it stopped and waited for Megan to make the next move. Its leaps became swifter and shorter, boxing Megan in. She realized where it wanted her to be: back at her own car.

Caitlin must have reached the same conclusion. She slipped her injured wrist away from Megan's wet and slackened fingers, opened one of the sedan's rear doors, dove in, and covered her head with her arms. Still wanting to run, not wanting to be where the Carter-thing wanted her to be, Megan started to pull her daughter back out.

The blue man landed on the street, its bare feet hitting pavement for the first time that Megan had seen, and slammed the car's rear door shut before Megan could reach it. Megan stood just a few feet away from the thing that had been hounding her, *herding* her back to this spot. Buried beneath a hard, twisted mesh of blue and grey tissue, she recognized the structure of her husband's face. Peering out beneath the ledge of its bare brow, she saw her husband's eyes. They bore into her, cold and angry.

She took a step backward without thinking, and it grabbed the back of her neck. Its grip was tight, but Megan sensed that it could have been tighter. The sharpness of its fingertips grazed, but didn't split, her skin.

It pulled her closer, close enough to kiss. Terror caused her entire frame to shake with spasms, and her legs threatened to give out beneath her. Even with the drumming of the rain, Megan was close enough now to hear the thing take in a long breath. The sound was familiar: she had heard the thing breathing outside Gina's. One breath, only one. She waited, panting, for the thing to breathe again. It didn't.

The air rushing through her nostrils carried the putrid scent she knew from her apartment. It was the final connection, the last piece of evidence her brain needed to dismiss the hope of normality and sanity forever. This *thing* had come from her apartment. It looked like her husband. Carter had cut up her baby and put its pieces into little jars, and doing that had changed him into what his cured daughter called the blue man. She thought of a group of blue-painted performing artists she had seen advertised on an old billboard in the subway, and the image allowed her to smile at the strange thing that held her by the back of her neck.

It didn't smile back.

"Carter," she whispered. She hadn't been sure if her vocal cords would respond to her brain's request for sound. "Carter," she said again, this time with a volume that could be heard over the rain. "Carter, please let go of me."

The repetition of Carter's name got no reaction from the thing that looked like him, not a blink or a move. It held her and stared. Water streamed down its face and into its eyes, but still it did not blink.

"Carter, don't hurt me," she said.

No reaction.

"Please, Carter, please!" Her eyes shifted from side to side. An audience of mesmerized travelers gazed at her from both dented and undented vehicles. Those who couldn't have seen this monster slay the one man who had dared to oppose it budged no more than those who had. They were all going to watch. Even if this thing started tearing her to pieces, they were only going to watch. Horns had stopped blaring. All Megan heard was the rain.

"Okay, Carter," she said. The hand at the back of her neck seemed to have frozen there. "Okay, if you're going to hurt me, then hurt me. Do it now. Kill me. I deserve it."

The thing tilted its head to one side, as if considering Megan's offer. Its grip tightened, and Megan felt its claws pierce skin.

Another shift of her eyes showed her that Caitlin was no longer hiding her head beneath her arms. Like all the others, she watched the scene from behind a pane of glass.

The Carter-thing released her, and she almost fell. She stood frozen while it walked around her, up to the driver-side door. It opened the door and waited. Unbelieving, she stared at it while it did nothing. She stepped toward it, toward the open car door. Her wet bottom touched the car seat, and she heaved her legs inside.

It closed the car door behind her and brought its face up to the window. If the glass hadn't intervened, husband and wife would again have been in kissing range. Megan's eyes moved from the Carter-thing's face to its uplifted hand. A lone, pointed finger poked toward the sky, and when the thing saw her looking at it, the finger started to wag. Megan read the signal: *Naughty, naughty*, it said.

"Caitlin, climb back up front," Megan said. Her eyes did not move from the Carter-thing.

Caitlin just sobbed.

"Caitlin, I'm sorry I hurt your arms. Get up front. *Now.*"

The girl obeyed, crawling into her seat. Megan looked at her daughter while she buckled her own seatbelt. Following her mother's demonstration, Caitlin fastened herself in. When Megan looked back at her window, the Carter-thing was gone.

Through all the windows and in all the mirrors, Megan saw nothing but halted traffic and rain. Megan turned up the volume on the AM station that was giving constant traffic updates. She thought that at any moment someone would tap on her window to see if she and her little girl were all right, but no one did. The woman on one side was still smoking, but she no longer tapped her dashboard. The woman on the other side had lost her nodding rhythm. They were both staring at her. Megan tried to ignore them while her fingers dabbed at the shallow cut on her neck. Like the members of her audience, she waited, too stunned to do anything else, until traffic finally started to roll.

The Descent of Carter Anderson, Continued

Carter and his puppeteer followed Megan and Caitlin along the highway, riding behind them atop trucks and vans where he wouldn't be noticed. The rides were monotonous, so Carter strained to hear his drivers' radios whenever he detected a faint hum. He caught news more often than anything else, so often that he wondered if his puppeteer were seeking it out.

The puppeteer seemed to have a taste for violence and mayhem, so listening to the news made sense. While waiting in an electronics store next to a shop where Megan took Caitlin to get candy, he walked past a screen flashing images of corpses from the Middle East. Instead of pausing to appreciate the gore, he stood near a screen full of pundits discussing the implications of the violence for the next round of elections. Nothing distracted him until Megan and Caitlin reappeared and headed back to the motel. Carter did not understand.

Riding down the highway with freezing air whipping his bare scalp, Carter mused over his puppeteer's interest in politics. A single vote, an act of will, could hand control of a political body to a madman who, regardless of the desires of the body's constituents, could wreak havoc around the globe. The analogy between Carter's condition and the state's was entertaining, but it didn't explain why his puppeteer seemed to pay closest attention to reports about a new grassroots movement gaining energy in southern churches. This particularity suggested a personality for the puppeteer, a purpose in excess of the will to help Caitlin that had brought it into power. Carter wondered if someday he might participate in a drama other than the life he had left behind.

Staying far enough behind Megan and Caitlin to keep them from seeing him meant letting them get away from time to time. When that happened, Carter's eyes closed, and he soon found himself sharing his daughter's senses. His puppeteer cast his consciousness back and forth like a fishing line. Carter kept track of his wife and daughter through two sets of eyes.

Sitting in a traffic jam during a thunderstorm, Megan spotted him. Carter saw her looking his way but wasn't sure that she had seen him until his legs had pushed off from the top of the truck and he had come crashing down on a nearby vehicle. She and Caitlin had burst from their car into the rain, and he was chasing them. He had no idea why he was doing it; if they got away, he could find them again by closing his eyes. After a spell of jumping around in the stopped traffic, crushing vehicles beneath his feet, Carter understood: he wanted his wife and daughter to get back into their car. Apparently he didn't like the idea of his recently ill daughter being dragged around in the rain.

Megan looked at Carter and called him by name. Hearing her say "Carter" had the opposite effect of hearing Caitlin say "Daddy." His daughter's acknowledgment made him feel alive and human, but his wife's made him feel dead. As he raced behind Megan and directed her behavior, he understood something new about "the suture of the seeker." Threads tied him to his puppeteer, and they tied him to his daughter. Similar threads tied him to his wife. Since she was Caitlin's mother and protector, all four of them were sewn together, a diabolical image of a close-knit family. When Carter got Megan and Caitlin back into the vehicle, he held up a single finger as if to say *one*. He wagged it at his wife to show disapproval of her poor maternal management.

After the episode in the rain, he let Megan and Caitlin get away again. He ran up an exit ramp, sprinted down a four-lane road, and found himself in an office park. Grassy islands made muddy by the downpour freckled the parking lot, which was surrounded by naked trees and somber five-story buildings. Carter thought that another of his puppeteer's inexplicable interests could be revealing itself – what the hell was he doing here in this isolated pocket of corporate buildings?

He spotted a man walking toward a Mercedes, briefcase in one hand, black umbrella in the other. He wore a long grey trench coat and a mismatched brown hat. In seconds Carter had snapped the man's neck. Carter felt perplexed while he stripped off the businessman's coat, but when he put it on and covered his bald head with the hat, he understood. He wanted to diminish Megan's chances of spotting him again; he wanted a disguise.

He distanced himself from his latest victim and closed his eyes. Carter saw Megan driving, and he felt the familiar sensation of tears drying on the cheeks he shared with his daughter. Megan looked frazzled, but she seemed to be in control. Carter's heart rate suggested that Caitlin was still trying to process what had just happened. His wrists hurt where Megan's grip had bruised him, and his wet clothes were itchy. He leaned forward to get closer to the heat pouring from the vents, and he imagined Caitlin hoping that dryness would make her terror go away.

Soon Carter found himself back in his original body. He ran toward the highway, and his new coat floated out around him like a cape. Carter remembered the comic book silhouettes he had loved as a kid, Superman and Batman in heroic profile. He was amused, and he hoped his puppeteer could sense, perhaps even share, his amusement. He found himself laughable until he wondered when he would have to eat someone again.

To close the lead that Megan and Caitlin had gained while he was fetching his new costume, he alternated between running and shutting his eyes. He stayed in Caitlin long enough to glimpse a road sign in the dark, and then he resumed his inhuman form and speed. He noted that Megan's eyelids were drooping more and more, which meant she'd be stopping and looking for another motel soon. The chase reminded Carter of Van Helsing using Mina to track Dracula to his Transylvanian end. The characters didn't match, but the comparison amused him nevertheless. When he closed his eyes and saw the lobby of a Super 8 motel, Carter knew his destination.

They stayed a full night at the motel. Carter watched in the parking lot. When Megan emerged the next morning with a steaming cup of coffee in her hand, some of the darkness under her eyes had vanished. She got on the southbound road again, and Carter felt sure that they would end up at Susan's house before nightfall. He knew his wife well enough to guess where she'd go, which meant that the puppeteer probably knew, too.

Carter got through most of the morning without being cast into Caitlin. He stayed close enough to keep tabs directly, clinging to the bottoms of trucks instead of their tops to ensure invisibility. The sun was high in the sky before Megan had to make her first stop for gas. She chose a station in the crook of another highway, facing a strip mall. Caitlin stayed in the car while Megan pumped gas and walked over to pay the attendant, and even when Megan walked farther away, toward the mall, Caitlin didn't move.

They had traveled far enough south to find temperatures above freezing, but an overcast, windy day didn't seem like a good time to leave a seven-year-old alone in a parked car at a gas station. No time was good for doing such a thing. This was un-Megan-like behavior. She walked away from the gas station without looking back, as if she were glad to be leaving Caitlin behind. Her path would take her to the doors of a clothing store plastered with sale signs. Carter remembered that they hadn't bought enough outfits at the first mall to last more than a couple of days.

He crawled away from his holly-cloaked vantage point and stood as erect as his new shape seemed to allow while he crossed the street. Walking at a human pace with hands in the pockets of his buttoned coat, Carter thought that he might have looked like a bad *noir* detective, out of place but human. He closed in on the gas station, on the parked car where his daughter waited for her mother.

The passenger-side door opened, and Caitlin got out. Carter stepped forward as if to go to her, but then he retracted his naked foot and leaned on a signpost. Caitlin looked all around her, hesitating before she moved away from the car and toward the larger mall lot. Carter watched her small stride gain speed as she moved toward her goal: a shop called The Jellybeanerie, a few doors down from where her mother hunted for clothes.

Carter wanted to wrap his hands around his own neck, to throttle himself and scream *Go after her!* A few steps out of a car onto a highway in a rainstorm sent him rushing to Caitlin's side with superhuman car-leaping panache, but the sight of his daughter alone and wandering into the parking lot of a place totally unknown to her didn't even make him pull away from a goddamned signpost. He was supposed to be her father, wasn't he?

Was he? The expectation that he would act like a father struck him as odd.

Caitlin disappeared into The Jellybeanerie, and Carter stopped leaning. His posture collapsed into its customary stoop as he crossed the parking lot, dispelling the gumshoe aura. He moved from parked car to parked car, obscuring himself at angles where he could see either door that could open and emit one of his sutured charges. The Jellybeanerie's door opened first, and Caitlin emerged accompanied. A woman in a frilly blouse and long skirt held his daughter by the hand.

Carter could hear them. "My car's parked just over there," the woman said. "I've got a box of change I use for parking meters in the glove compartment, and we can use some of that to get you some of those sour apple jellybeans, okay?"

"Okay!" Caitlin said.

His daughter was only seven, and she had spent a lot of time locked up in a hospital, but hadn't someone taught her better than to walk off with strangers offering candy? Surely Megan had taught her better? If Carter had had control of his neck, he would have shaken his head in disapproval and vexation. Instead, he stood still and observed, moving closer only when he needed to hear them better.

The woman led Caitlin down a lane of cars that took the girl even farther from the gas station where she was supposed to be waiting for Megan. After covering half the lane, Caitlin stopped and said, "Maybe I should go back and wait. My mommy'll be mad if she comes back and sees I didn't stay where she told me to."

Releasing Caitlin's hand, the woman bent down and whispered something in her ear. Carter couldn't hear; he moved a few cars closer. Caitlin giggled. The woman rested her palms on her thighs and said in a normal voice, "I'll get you right back in a hop, skip, and a jump, and you can share some of the jellybeans with your mommy. She'd like that, wouldn't she?"

"I guess so," Caitlin said.

Carter expected to rip the woman's throat out. He thought he would find such an act acceptable.

The woman took his daughter's hand again and kept leading her in the wrong direction. Carter trusted that his puppeteer would never let anyone hurt her, so he felt more rage than fear, rage that, after only two days with Caitlin well and back in it, the world would send a woman like this after her. The vulnerability of "the children" that people like Gina railed about in PTA meetings was supposed to be an exaggeration.

"That's a cute hat you've got on," the woman said. "It looks like it might be a little warm, though."

"I wear it because my hair hasn't all come back yet," Caitlin said.

"Come back from where?"

"I was sick, and they had to make my hair fall out to make me better. I'm okay now. The hair's already coming back. Wanna see?"

"That's all right," the woman said. "You're sure you're better though, right?"

"I think so."

Carter could feel himself straining to hear what Caitlin said next.

"I think my daddy made me better."

"Your daddy, huh? And where's he?"

"He's a bad man now. Mommy says so. He looks funny. We saw him yesterday." Caitlin scrunched up her face, troubled. "I don't want to talk about it."

"Well, okay, you don't have to. As long as you're all better, right?"

"I guess so." She still sounded troubled. The quest for candy had made her forget everything, but this woman's questions had brought the worry back.

"Here's my car," said the woman. She pointed at a long Cadillac with a "Jesus Loves Me" bumper sticker. "I tell you what. Why don't you get in the front seat over on the other side, and you can help me look for the change we need for that candy."

"I'm not supposed to get in the car with you," Caitlin said.

"Why not?" asked the woman. "Don't you want your jellybeans?"

"You're a stranger."

"I'm not a stranger!" the woman protested. "I thought you and me were already friends. Aren't we friends now?"

"I guess so," Caitlin said, "but I don't want to get in the car. I'm sorry."

"Well, don't be sorry! You're a smart young lady, and I probably shouldn't have asked you to get in my car. Why don't you just come around to the side with me, and I'll get in and look and hand the change-box to you when I find it." Pulling Caitlin, the woman circled around to the passenger side.

"Ow, my wrist hurts! Let go of me!"

The woman loosened her grip, but did not let go. She drew Caitlin toward the car door and opened it.

Carter abandoned the SUV that hid him and walked toward the woman. He was in plain view, and the woman saw him coming. Her eyebrows shot together, trying to make sense of the figure that lurched toward her. With clawed blue hands, Carter unbuttoned his coat and took off his hat. The woman's eyes grew wide.

"Good Lord, *what is that!*"

Caitlin slipped away from the woman and started running, moving in Carter's direction without seeing him. Having dashed a few yards, she faced forward and stopped so abruptly that she almost fell. Turning back around, she cried, "It's the blue man! My daddy!"

Carter thought Caitlin would run from him back to the woman who apparently wanted to abduct her, but she didn't. She stood motionless, indecisive, suspended between them.

"Your *daddy*?" the woman gasped.

Yes, her daddy, Carter thought, *and he's a very, very bad man.*

He walked around Caitlin and grabbed the stunned woman by the shoulders. He shoved her through the open car door, got in after her, and pulled the door closed behind him. His fingertips split her open in less than a second, and he exited the car on the other side, dragging the bottom of his coat through blood. When he looked at Caitlin, he smiled the smile he had used at the hospital, the one with tenderness.

Caitlin started to back away. Carter felt something in his throat and thought he might say something, but he stayed silent and immobile, lips stretched in a smile that Caitlin seemed to find tolerable. Caitlin halted her backward retreat and stared. "Is that really you, Daddy?" she asked.

Carter wanted to nod, speak, shout YES, but he did nothing.

"You scared me when you hurt that man. Why did you hurt that man? Why does Mommy say you're bad? Why do you look like that?"

Carter wanted her to run from him. If he wasn't going to speak to her, to answer her questions and calm her fears, then she *should* run. Had that woman really been an abductor, or had she simply been an oblivious, overbearing troll? Carter couldn't be sure, and Caitlin couldn't know at all. She had far more reason to fear Carter than to fear the woman he had just killed. Maybe Caitlin was too young to understand what she had seen Carter do. Maybe she was too confused by all that had happened in the last two days to know which of her experiences to believe or trust.

She didn't budge when he took a slow step toward her, and she remained still when he took another. Her lips moved like she wanted to ask him something else, but she didn't make a sound.

SCREAM! Carter thought. There's a monster walking toward you, Caitlin, SCREAM!

Carter walked up to her, and she did not move. He reached down and scooped her up in one arm.

Her nose wrinkled; she grimaced. It was the smell. Carter didn't need to share her senses to know that his smell revolted her, and he didn't need to call her chest his own to feel her heart hammering out the extremity of her fear. She was afraid of him, and part of her did want to scream and run. Another part of her must have seen enough of her father within his new features to counteract her panic – she was his child, and even after everything he had done, she trusted him.

He carried her back to the gas station. Carter felt as if hours had passed since Megan had abandoned Caitlin in the car. The position of the morning sun in the sky said that a full hour couldn't have passed since Caitlin had first set out for The Jellybeanerie, probably not even a half hour. Megan wasn't waiting at the car or searching around frantically yet because she hadn't finished her shopping. But she *had* been gone far too long not to have taken Caitlin with her.

Carter set Caitlin down on the passenger side, put his hat back on his head, and walked around to the driver's side. The two of them opened doors at the same time, and they both got into the car, sitting next to each other.

Caitlin stared at him. Carter remembered looking through her staring eyes and seeing Megan, and he wondered if the expression on her face – his face – had been anything like what it was now. There might have been uneasiness, distrust, or maybe even something as powerful as terror, but above all there was a look of expectation that bordered on reverence. Carter's daughter waited for his cue, the signal that would determine the next event of her life. Sick or well, she was helpless, utterly dependent. Carter remembered a wriggling thing on top of a tiny coffin and wanted his heart to register the shock of emotion.

His body sat sessile and cold. Caitlin looked away from him and down at her lap. She starting singing, half mumbling. Carter didn't recognize the tune. It was something about a pineapple under the sea.

Carter's head turned. He thought he was going to look at his daughter, but instead he looked at the window over her shoulder. In the distance he saw Megan walking across the parking lot with a bag in each hand. She was stepping into the marked area around the gas station when she noticed him. She dropped the bags. Her eyes did not widen, her jaw did not drop. She saw him, and she saw Caitlin sitting next to him, and the images had turned her to ice. Gradually, she bent her knees and picked up the bags. As she walked toward the car, she switched both bags into one hand and picked up speed. Soon she was running.

Almost tackling the car, she grabbed the handle, yanked open the door, and screamed at Caitlin, "GET OUT OF THE CAR!!!"

Caitlin looked at her like she was crazy. "What?" she said.

Megan looked from Caitlin to Carter, and then back to Caitlin again. The look in her eyes was beyond panic, beyond incomprehension. She looked like her brain had an uncontrollable case of the hiccups.

"Caitlin." Megan said. "Carter?"

Neither of them responded.

Megan seemed out of breath. "Caitlin, honey, I'm sorry I took so long at the store and left you...I don't know what I was thinking. I just...Caitlin, honey, please get out of the car." She paused. "Caitlin, you have to get out of the car and get *away* from him."

Caitlin looked confused. "Why?"

Carter imagined what Megan wanted to say. Because he's bad! Because he kills people! Because, because, because – that's right Megan, *why?* He had never hurt their daughter, not this one. He looked monstrous, yes, and he had hurt someone in front of her, but he had never hurt *her*. He had never really hurt Megan either, for that matter, at least not that Caitlin had seen. Explain it to her, Mommy. Why?

"*Why?*" Megan echoed.

"He got me away from this weird lady," Caitlin said. "He doesn't talk much, though."

"*What?*"

Carter got out of the car and walked around to where Megan stood. She looked at him, and he could see the terror in her eyes. She was too stunned to move. He raised a finger like he had in the rain, the finger that had said *one* before it had wagged at her in disapproval. He raised a second finger. *Two.* Carter felt the scowl on his face and saw it reflected in Megan's eyes. They both understood what *three* would mean.

Connection

Megan couldn't drive any further. The sight of the Carter-thing sitting in the car with her daughter had sapped her will to continue, and after five minutes of riding in the very seat it had occupied, she knew she had to stop. She exited the highway and pulled up at another chain motel. When she used her credit card, it felt like a rebellion. Let them come. She couldn't surrender, not yet, but if she just happened to end up in someone else's custody, she wouldn't complain. It would relieve her of the need to figure out what to do.

Standing face to face with the Carter-thing had jolted and rearranged her thinking. She couldn't keep grasping at the comforting fantasy that the monster wanted them dead. The evidence pointed too clearly in the opposite direction. It wanted them, or at least Caitlin, alive and well, which meant *their* wellness and *its* wellness were connected. Ever-helpful, after Megan had abandoned Caitlin in the car, it had shown up to babysit. The Carter-thing wasn't working against them: it was *in league* with them. In a way, Megan had always been its co-conspirator.

She told Caitlin to watch television while she lay on the lumpy motel bed and watched the ceiling. The daydream that had engulfed her during childbirth returned: an impish Caitlin, excited and giggling, jumping up and down on the bed and on Megan's stomach. A happy, healed Caitlin tearing her baby sister apart.

But none of this was Caitlin's fault. Caitlin was the only innocent one among the surviving members of her family. Nevertheless, the daydream persisted, and Megan kept staring at the ceiling to avoid seeing the capped little girl who sat too close to the TV. Caitlin and the Carter-thing. Inseparable. Megan's head hurt. She didn't know if her vision would ever feel clear again.

For lunch and dinner Megan brought fast food back to the motel room. Otherwise she stayed on the bed, and Caitlin kept watching television. The girl was used to not being able to do much more than stare at a screen. Megan welcomed the opportunity to let her mind travel elsewhere, to a place uninhabited by Caitlin and the Carter-thing.

A second full night's sleep left Megan feeling worse. No longer having exhaustion to blame for the world's increasing blur, she knew the time to decide about the future approached. It approached, but it wasn't yet *now*. She could give herself more time. They could leave the motel and continue southward. They would reach Susan's country estate sometime in the afternoon if Megan indulged in no more stops.

Flashing lights greeted her when she opened the door. Three police cars and an ambulance crowded the motel's parking lot. With bags of their few outfits in hand, Megan thought she and Caitlin would march over to the police and announce themselves. Her credit card rebellion had worked!

Relief didn't have time to set in before Megan realized that the police were not interested in her or Caitlin. The people exiting the room next door held their attention – EMTs carrying a stretcher covered by a bloody sheet shaped like the body of a woman. Megan watched the procession for less than a minute. She logged another anonymous entry in the mental record of her victims. Megan's victims, Caitlin's victims, the Carter-thing's victims, they were all the same. The three of them were in league, a team. It had to stop. Carter had convinced her that their love for Caitlin could justify anything, even murder. But seeing murder after murder after murder had made Megan's head hurt so much that love was beginning to feel like a memory, or a dream, receding in the blurry daylight hours, which had a way of making such love look like something monstrous.

Back on the highway, Megan tried to escape the pounding in her head by driving fast. Traffic was light, and Megan found herself speeding down the highway in the far left lane unimpeded. She could have reached her mother's house long before nightfall, but she didn't. Instead she lingered in the place she considered her hometown, the place where she had gone to a little private elementary school before being shipped off to a more prestigious academy farther away. It was the closest thing she had ever had to a neighborhood, where she had spent time with the people who were the closest things she had ever had to real friends. Driving down some streets that were familiar and some that were not, Megan tried to point out personal landmarks to her daughter. The locations of scant memories failed to give her a sense of a life lived apart from Carter and all the rest.

Awhile after the sun finished setting, Caitlin asked again about when they would get to Grandma's. The question needed an answer. The journey needed an end. In half an hour, she was pulling into her mother's driveway. The long gravel trail concealed the extent of the house from the few drivers who went by on the narrow two-lane road. The structure at the end of the driveway didn't sprawl enough to be divided into anything as lofty as *wings*, but the time necessary to walk from one corner of the asymmetrical house to another made a statement about Susan Penser's resources. The clustering of areas most often used toward the center of the house – Susan's bedroom, Megan's old room, the main stairs, the kitchen, the dining room, and the den – allowed the house to feel cozy. The guest suites, the back stairway, the nanny's old room, the office, the fitness room, the library, the room Susan had recently outfitted as a "media room," and the chamber she simply called "the gallery," considered as a whole, could make the house feel Gothic and grotesque.

Susan was already standing in the house's front doorway when Megan walked around to help Caitlin out of the car. Light behind Susan made the woman's shape into a shadow, and the house looming above made her look tiny. Megan had often worried about her single, aging mother living in such an enormous, secluded house alone. She worried, but she said nothing. It was what Susan desired, and little could stand between Susan and what she wanted.

Usually composed, Susan stood in the doorway shifting from foot to foot in an awkward display of anxiety. Holding Caitlin's hand, Megan walked up the front steps and said, "Hi, Mom."

Susan put on a smile. "Hello there, Meg. And hello Caitlin! It's good to see you!" Worry and sleeplessness marred Susan's face, which Megan thought had gotten very old very suddenly. The grandmother beamed at her granddaughter.

"Hi, Grandma!" Caitlin freed her hand from Megan's and held up her bruised arms to be hugged.

Without a pause or a groan, Susan lifted the girl and squeezed. "You look so wonderful," she said. She stared at Megan but addressed Caitlin. "I'm really at a loss for words. When did you start looking so *good* again?"

"I got to leave the hospital!" Caitlin said.

Susan continued to look at Megan while she spoke to Caitlin. "I can see that." Despite the way the light behind Susan obscured her face, Megan could tell that tears glazed her mother's eyes. "You're like an answered prayer," Susan said. The word "prayer" sounded foreign on her lips, but it also sounded comforting.

Susan set Caitlin down and addressed Megan. "How did this happen?"

"It's a long story," Megan said. "Can we come in?"

"Of course you can," Susan said, taking a step back. "You're always welcome here, you know that. In fact, I've been expecting you."

Megan felt the blood rush from her face. "Why's that?"

"I'll tell you once we've got this one settled in," said the grandmother.

Somehow Susan had the strength to carry Caitlin upstairs. Caitlin said she wanted to stay with them, but she didn't resist Susan like she had resisted Gina. Even though Gina had been an accomplished schoolteacher, she had never learned to put the right amount of authority in her voice like Susan could. Susan told Caitlin that she could watch TV or read for a little while, but that it was important for her to get to bed early after such a long trip.

"If you really are well," Susan said, "then you've got to *stay* well, and that means doing what your grandma says." She offered Caitlin Megan's old bedroom like a special treat, and Caitlin received it as such. After getting the girl under the covers with an old book and a remote control, Susan went downstairs and made her a sandwich. Megan wasn't used to seeing her mother serve anyone.

Back downstairs in the den, a cup of tea in hand, Susan's face changed from grandmother to mother, her expression more severe. "Megan," she said, "I don't know where to begin."

Megan laughed, and Susan looked puzzled.

"Neither do I, Mom. I really don't. I don't even know if I should be here." Megan heard the sound of her own laughter, imagined listening to it from her mother's position, and understood the look of concern on her mother's face. "The last person I tried to turn to...something terrible happened."

"You mean your friend Gina," Susan said.

The shocking statement came out of her mother's mouth as if it were a simple, well-known fact. "How do you know about Gina?"

"The news, mostly. I'm afraid the case has received some national attention, especially in the light of what followed."

"You mean they...they *found* her?"

Susan looked discomposed for a short moment before replying, "You mean you didn't know?"

"I knew...I knew she was missing...and I saw...what happened to Stefan, her boyfriend."

"Yes, I heard about him, too. It's all too horrible for words. They found her in her bedroom nearby. It seems strange to me that you would know about one and not the other."

"I guess I knew that Gina was dead. I don't know how she ended up in the bedroom. She wasn't in the apartment anymore when...when I left."

"I see. Well, if you saw Stefan, you won't be surprised to know that they didn't find quite *all* of her—"

"Mom!" The pain in her head got sharper.

Susan folded her hands in her lap. "I'm sorry. I don't mean to be gruesome. I just *can't* understand what you possibly could have gotten yourself involved in. The police want you and Carter for questioning. After the first time I heard your names on the news, I decided to make sure they wouldn't be mentioned again for awhile. It's been difficult. Since the report only said you were missing, I wasn't even sure I'd done the right thing – not until I found out that you were heading in my direction."

"How did you know that?"

Susan smiled. "I have my ways, of course, but again I can say that it's mostly the news. All the events are being tied together because of the *way* the people were hurt. Surely you know how brutal and strange it all looks."

"You have no idea," Megan said. She stifled a laugh. Her mother, if convinced of the need, wouldn't have Megan committed to a mental hospital, but the house was large enough, and the bank accounts ample enough, to accomplish a private equivalent.

"I *do* have an idea. People are saying that you and Carter and Caitlin are missing and that you're somehow involved, but that you couldn't be to blame because the man people had seen do these terrible things didn't match Carter's description, didn't match *anyone's* description. And people are telling me to prepare myself for the worst like you're dead and I don't know what to think or do or say because I know at least one of you is alive and—"

"How many?" Megan asked. Hearing her mother's uncharacteristic blubbering was a unique experience, but it did not interest her.

"I'm sorry," Susan said, "how many what?"

"How many people are dead, Mom?" The question's urgency now outweighed all others. It alone loosened the axe cleaving her skull. "You seem to know so much more about all of this than I do. How many people are dead?"

"I'm not sure. I think the number was up to seven at the hospital, with one or two people in critical condition. There was the man in your apartment building, which is how your names got mixed up in it all. Add in Gina and her boyfriend, and there was some sort of traffic incident with another body that looked like the killer had used the same M.O., and there was another man found not too far away from that, and then just this morning I heard about a woman at a motel in...Meg, are you even listening? Why am I telling you these things when *you* should be telling *me?*"

Her thoughts had become stuck on what her mother had omitted. "There was the man in your apartment building," she had said, and that was all. What had happened to the little jars on the coffin? To the rest of it? Did the police find it all and keep the information from reporters to minimize the frenzy, keep it from Susan to minimize her suffering? Or had something else happened? Megan didn't understand. She saw the way the room had looked, the streaks of blood that had now become features of her daily life. She started to cry, the blade sliding more deeply into her throbbing brain.

"Meg, honey, you *have* to tell me what's going on. I can do a better job of protecting you and Caitlin if I know what I'm protecting you from. What happened to Carter? How is he involved in all of this?"

Megan looked up at her mother through tears. The lie she had told Gina tempted her. She could blame it all on Carter, frame him as an abusive madman, spin a tale more believable than the truth. "Carter," she said, hesitating, "I think Carter's dead, Mom." What she said had nothing to do with what she was thinking. She hadn't ever thought it before, but when it came out, it sounded like truth.

"I'm so sorry. I'm so, so sorry about everything." Susan handed Megan a tissue. "What happened to him? What happened to all of you? How does Caitlin fit into all of this? Why is she here? Why does she look like she's the healthiest girl alive?"

"Mom, you won't believe me. I can't tell you." *Because I'm a madwoman. Because you'll know. And because you might end up resenting your granddaughter as much as—*

Susan shook her head. "I didn't want to believe it when I heard about the murder in your building having something to do with you. I didn't want to believe when I connected the dots and saw that a trail was leading from you to me, when I realized not only that you were coming but that death followed you. I didn't want to believe it, but I did. Now I want desperately to have something new to believe because I can think of no explanation for what I already know."

"It's too horrible, Mom. I...I'm so ashamed of my part in it." As she wiped her face with the tissue, Megan knew she was about to tell her mother everything.

"Megan," Susan said, "What happened to the baby?"

The last shock Susan had given her had not been intentional, but Megan's mother shot out this question like a torpedo. "What...what baby?"

"Come on, Meg. I played dumb then because it was obvious you didn't want me to know. I figured you were trying to decide whether or not to keep it and didn't want input from a meddling grandma." Susan stared at Megan, waiting. "Okay, I'll say it. Megan, the last time I saw you, which was far too long ago, you were pregnant."

"I...I was?"

Susan rolled her eyes. "Yes, Meg, you were. I knew it before I even saw you, and seeing you just confirmed it. What happened? Did you have an abortion? Did Carter pressure you into one, and does that somehow have something to do with all of this?" She took a deep breath and continued. "You say Carter's dead, and I don't quite believe you. Is he the one responsible for all of this?"

"Yes!" Megan yelled. She cupped her hand over her mouth afterward, afraid of summoning Caitlin, and whatever new disaster Caitlin might bring. "Yes, he is. And so am I. We're both responsible. Really...I did, Mom. I did it. I murdered my baby. For her."

Susan looked down at the floor and took another deep breath. "No, Megan, abortion is not murder. It's perfectly natural for a woman to feel—"

"It wasn't an abortion, Mom! I killed her! I killed my baby girl so that Caitlin could get well! I did it! I carried it all those months and then had it in my own bedroom – and then handed it over to...."

"Megan," Susan said, "you're not making any sense. Take things one step at a time. First tell me about Carter."

"Carter's not alive anymore, Mom," Megan said, "and it, or he, I don't know, could be here any minute. I don't know what to do. Tell me what to do."

Megan dissolved into tears, and Susan sat flabbergasted. They waited there, together, for their composure to return. Susan's came first, but she didn't say anything. Megan knew her mother was waiting for her to recover from her collapse. When Megan couldn't cry anymore, she felt calm enough, barely, to narrate through a veneer of sanity. She let the story come out of her, and while she spoke, her thoughts went elsewhere. While the past came out – all of it, about Jess ten years ago, about the baby and the hospital and everything after – her mind went decisively and irrevocably into the future.

"It *is* far-fetched," Susan said at last, "but I can believe it on some level, for now at least. I can believe everything but the part about you allowing Carter to kill my granddaughter. An abortion I could understand, but how could you do...*that*? No daughter of mine could do that. I understand wanting Caitlin to live. I probably understand that better than anyone other than you and Carter. You know how much that girl means to me. I always thought that...the Foundation, everything I've built...it's all nothing...*she* was going to be my legacy. When I heard her prognosis, her death sentence...I...I broke a little bit. I turned into an old woman. But don't you see that you had another chance? You say the thing turned Carter into a monster. I don't know. I think both of you were already something worse."

Megan closed her eyes. "Mom, please don't look at me like that. Please. I need you. I need you to tell me what to do. It's out there, Mom, and it's going to go on hurting people unless...unless there's something else I can do." *Unless I stop it. Unless I stop its reason for being. Unless I stop* her.

Carter had lied about love. The Carter-thing had to be stopped, and that lie about love is what let it be, what let it *feed*.

"I don't know what you can do," Susan said. "If I hear you correctly, I should probably expect a blue thing that looks sort of like Carter to jump through one of these windows at any moment and cut me to ribbons. Isn't that right?"

"It could happen," Megan said. "I knew I was taking that risk when I came here, but I came here anyway, and I'm sorry for that. You don't seem to believe you're in danger, but you are." The words she spoke sounded miles away. Megan was elsewhere. Everything her mother had told her, everything she had told her mother – it all added up to something: the future. Her actions had caused one death, the murder of her second child, but her inaction had caused many more deaths than that. "Death follows us, Mom, just like you said. Everywhere Caitlin and I go, someone dies. It's because of what Carter and I did to make Caitlin survive her cancer. All these deaths...because of what we did for her." Caitlin owed her existence to the Carter-thing, and its existence sprang from her.

"Yes," Susan said, "I suppose you're right about that. In one way or another, you're right."

"I know what I have to do," Megan said.

"Do *nothing*," Susan said. "I have to make some phone calls, and then—"

Her voice trailed off when the lights went out.

"Oh, God," Megan said. It was here. The Carter-thing, the blue man. "Mom, I'm so sorry. I'm so sorry I brought it here." She had known this would happen, but she had come anyway. Her indifference to the lives she had risked just by moving, just by *being*, astounded her. But she had to dismiss the past. All that mattered was what she did next. She had to end this, and she thought she knew how. Whatever punishment she got she would deserve and accept.

Susan set down her tea and stood. "Nonsense," she said. "The power lines out here are ancient. Not the first time this has happened. I've got some kerosene lamps in the pantry, and I can find my way there in the dark with no problem. Stay where you are. Drink your tea."

"Mom," Megan said. The protest was weak. Susan would go where Susan wanted to go just like she would believe what she wanted to believe. A small part of Megan thought that keeping her mother near would keep her safe, but the rest of her knew that her presence didn't matter. She'd never had any power over the Carter-thing. It did what it wanted to do. The *why* of it – the why of Gina, of all the people at the hospital, of everyone – did not have to make sense to her and would not. Susan was going to the pantry, and if the Carter-thing wanted to kill her, it would.

Susan's shuffling steps went in the direction of the kitchen. Megan waited for shattering glass, a scream, or one of the other horrific sounds she had come to know so well. The footsteps became inaudible, and Megan listened to silence. The power failure would have cut off the TV, so if Caitlin were still awake, she would probably make some noise soon. A girl her age, after all she had been through, alone in the dark – if she were awake she'd be screaming.

Susan must have made it to the kitchen. No sound, no sound at all.

A breeze made the house crackle. Dead leaves and pine needles the gardeners had missed rustled, and there was a whistling somewhere, maybe a bird. No rain or thunder, nothing but the sounds of a quiet winter night in the country. She had longed for nights like this when, after going off to school, she had realized that true quiet could be hard to come by. Now the quiet stifled her, magnifying the faintest noises, the whistling outside and the screeching of her nerves.

Shuffle, shuffle, shuffle. She didn't know what the Carter-thing's footsteps would sound like coming down the hall. These were not its footsteps – these were Susan's, returning.

"I've got three of them, fully loaded," Susan said when she came into the room. Megan's eyes had adjusted. The uncommon starlight and the sliver of moonlight gave shapes blue outlines in the dark, and the burst of orange that accompanied Susan splashed everything with writhing shadows. "I'm going to leave one lamp with you, and then I'm going to take one up to Caitlin. You'll be okay, won't you?" The question sounded perfunctory.

"I'll be fine," Megan said, "it's not me I'm worried about. Be careful, Mom. Don't fight it if you see it. Run."

"You sound fairly confident that I'm going to be attacked by this thing you describe. You're lucky my doctor says I have the heart of a woman half my age. Thank God for the 'Get Physical' craze of the eighties." Susan was probably trying to be funny. Megan blinked at her, seeing more and more of her in the dark, which was somehow less blurry than the daylight had been, even as it pulsated with the throbbing in her brain.

"Anyway, I'll be just fine," Susan continued. "I don't know about this running business. It's more your flaw than mine." She cleared her throat and exited.

While Susan shuffled away, Megan pondered. This running business, her flaw. How far back did her mother's judgment of her go? Just to the point where she and Carter had made their decision about curing Caitlin, or back to a time in her childhood that only Susan could remember?

If the axe in her skull allowed, she would think about all that later. She knew what she had to do now, and she would do it. She stood, took the lamp in her hand, and started searching the room. Several figurines of varying worth caught her eye, none heavy or solid enough to suffice. The lamp she already held could do it, but that seemed too cruel. The poker next to the fireplace might work, but it also seemed too violent, too unwieldy. The Carter-thing used parts of its body for weapons, and it performed with swiftness and grace, unhampered by a sense of horror. Megan envied it.

The Carter-thing might be unstoppable. She had seen men, large men with guns, that it had torn to pieces. She had heard people talk about how it absorbed bullets as if armored, and she had seen it move in impossible ways. Physically, she'd be lucky if she could slow it down. Stopping it would require more than using direct force against it.

Megan's searching eyes settled on the telephone. Her mother had said something about making phone calls. Had she sneaked off to do that instead of bringing the lamp to Caitlin? Stumbling over a corner of the coffee table, Megan made her way to the phone and lifted the receiver. She did not hear her mother's voice, or anyone else's. She heard nothing. No voices, no dial tone. The line was dead.

Lights out. Phone dead. The Carter-thing had lurked in the alley by Gina's without taking any of these steps. Carter had a history of cutting Megan off from the outside world, but the Carter-thing did not. Cell phones didn't get service this far out, which Carter would know. Did *it* know? Carter would know about the house's electronic security system – did the Carter-thing know, too? Did the Carter-thing even care about the possibility of an intervention from the outside? Carter would care. If Carter wanted to trap Megan in her mother's house, he'd create conditions exactly like these, isolated, safe for the predator and hopeless for the prey.

How much did her husband have in common with the thing that had his eyes? She didn't know, and she realized she didn't care. She wanted to grind every part of it, especially its eyes, into dusty oblivion. She wanted to kill it with her bare hands. What she had to do instead revolted her, but everything revolted her now. Her life had become a symphony of revulsion. She would kill it, even if it meant she had to die, too.

Megan unhooked the phone cord and gathered it in her hands. She stretched it as taut as she could, testing its strength. The coil of coated wire would leave a pattern on the flesh it pressed against, but it would be strong enough. It would be as strong as Megan could be, and Megan thought she could manage enough strength to be effective and quick.

A popping noise, maybe the wind again or maybe the Carter-thing coming, grabbed her attention. She imagined wrapping the cord around Carter's neck and pulling its ends with all her might.

The Carter she had known might have grasped at the cord, pitting his strength against hers as his face turned red. The Carter she had known might have died that way if she had tried when she had had the chance. All those nights that he had slept next to her – she had had such chances! But those chances had come and gone.

She might have been able to strangle Carter, but the thing that had his eyes could break the cord with a flick of its sharp finger. It used its fingers for all kinds of things, like counting. She hadn't understood until the thing had held up *two* fingers, and then the *one* that had wagged at her made sense. One strike, two strikes. The thing was judging, evaluating, scoring her behavior.

Strangling it would be a pleasure, but she couldn't do that. It hardly even needed to *breathe*. No, she couldn't stop the Carter-thing with this cord, not directly. She couldn't stop him through any direct means at all. Stopping him would require something more. It would require an act of will. It would require a sacrifice. Carter, the man she'd loved before that love had turned out to be a lie, might have called it "fearful symmetry."

Megan navigated through the den with the lamp in one hand and the cord balled up in the other. Both hands shook, and the spasms of light made the writhing shadows more sinister. Would she go upstairs and find her mother already dead? She listened, thought she heard a creak, and then nothing. The only sounds were the noises outside, breezes, rustling, and suffocating country quiet.

Would the sight of her mother's body – torn or dismembered like any one of the other corpses she'd seen in the last few days – blast her senses with enough power to wither her resolve? Or would her conviction grow stronger? She didn't know. She had to keep moving. She stood at the bottom of the stairs; she took the first step.

One more, two more, three more deaths would not matter. Not in this house, not tonight. What mattered were all the deaths that could happen tomorrow, or the next day, or the next. Each day that she continued in her passivity would add to the tally of her crimes, which the love-lie would no longer excuse. The blade in her head pressed deeper into her brain.

On more than seven hundred mornings she had woken up, and her first thought had been, "What if today is the day my daughter dies?" The question had once been so compelling that she had agreed to do something that should have been as unthinkable as it was absurd, as impossible as it was preposterous. Now the question of all those mornings did not matter. The answer she had feared had turned into hope.

Today will be the day my daughter dies.

And then the Carter-thing would be gone. And then Megan could die. Nothing more would matter.

Moving up the stairs, trying to be quiet, she winced when the floor squeaked. The effort to be quiet was pointless – the lamp in her hand would give her away. They'd know she was coming. They'd know, but would they care? Even if they saw the cord in her hand, wouldn't they just be bewildered?

Susan might suspect. If Susan lingered in the bedroom, Megan would have to ask her mother to give her a moment alone with her daughter. Susan would try to stop her if she could.

She didn't want to do it. If she succeeded, if she survived the night, she wouldn't live much longer with what she had done, but the conclusion she had reached was irresistible: as long as Caitlin lived the life won through her parents' murderous ritual, the longer the list of deaths would become. When Megan had asked her mother *how many*, she had gotten a sense of the true sacrifice she and her husband had offered up for their daughter's cure. The baby had only been the beginning. The sacrifices would continue as long as Caitlin breathed. Tonight the breathing and the killing would stop.

Megan turned the corner at the top of the stairs, telephone cord in her hands. She reached the open doorway to her old bedroom, where her daughter would be sleeping. She stepped inside.

The room hadn't changed much since she had called it her own. Being in her room's pulsating darkness, speckled with flickering lamplight, she felt suspended in time, simultaneously the little girl and the mother. The transient décor of teenage fashions had gone, but the fundamentals – the shelf with the dolls, the desk, the bed, the curtains – remained the same. The bed was against the far wall. Its covers were rumpled. On the nightstand next to it, the lamp Susan had brought burned. The window that the burglars had escaped through a lifetime ago overlooked the bed.

The bed was empty, and the window was open.

The Descent of Carter Anderson, Continued

Megan's decision to stop at another motel after their encounter at the gas station made Carter want to wring his hands in frustration. Something important – he didn't know what – was going to happen once they got to Susan's house, and he wanted to be there. He spent most of the day on the motel's rooftop. Two jaunts into Caitlin's senses showed him little more than a cartoon-filled TV screen. He watched Megan walk to the fast food restaurant next door twice, but he didn't follow her. Perched on a rooftop, camouflaged by his coat, Carter waited.

After nightfall he took a new position in the parking lot. Carter didn't understand why: his puppeteer might have wanted to watch more carefully in case Megan had some plan to sneak off under cover of darkness, or it might have hoped to catch news reports through someone's window. For whatever reason, Carter made himself vulnerable to suspicious eyes, which soon found him. A woman emerged from the room next to Megan's.

"Hey, you. Creepy guy in the trench coat. Yeah, I'm talking to you." Her accent was much farther north than she was.

Carter stood as erect he could, letting light from the streetlamps give the woman a glimpse of his pallor. She stepped back. Shaken but resolved, she spoke again, "I don't know what the hell you think you're doing out here, lurking, but beat it or I'll call the cops."

Carter wished the rude woman could find his next move as predictable as he did. If she knew what was coming, she might make an interesting countermove. Her creative response wouldn't be effective, but it would be *something*. Carter killed her, and he did it quickly, but first he did something unusual: he clamped a hand over her mouth and rushed her back into her room. With surprising thoughtfulness, Carter closed the door behind him before the evisceration.

Carter was pleased that his puppeteer had tried to conceal the crime. He realized that he had done the same thing earlier with the female abductor in the parking lot. The killings in the car and at the motel were signs of increasing wisdom. The gumshoe costume and the two attempts at corpse-concealing pointed toward a new era of subtlety. The puppeteer had a personality, and it *learned*.

Carter resumed his roof-perch for the rest of the night. Boredom consumed him; even his hamster-cage ratiocination lost its attraction after a few hours of nothing but twinkling stars. He wondered if the puppeteer might be bored, too.

The learning curve hadn't reached the sophistication of using a "Do Not Disturb" sign to ward off discovery, so the early maid service found the body. The police arrived before Megan and Caitlin set out for their car, but they took no interest in anything but the corpse. Soon, Carter thought, the authorities would figure out that Megan had been here and connect this murder with all the others. Soon there would be an APB out for Megan Anderson.

He followed Megan's car by clinging to the bottoms of trucks like he had the day before. Always close and invisible, he had no need to put on his daughter's senses for updates on her position. He only found himself cast into the void once, after an hour of circular driving around the town closest to Susan's house. The puppeteer must have been as mystified by the circling as Carter was.

Through Caitlin's eyes he saw Megan staring at the windshield and strangling the steering wheel in her fists. Megan looked at the landscape, but Carter couldn't be sure that she actually saw it. From time to time, she pointed out landmarks. He only glanced in each indicated direction. Caitlin seemed to share Carter's lack of interest in these monuments from Megan's youth.

Carter studied the expression on Megan's face when she looked at her daughter. In the squint of Megan's eyes and the tilt of her lips, he thought he saw an explanation for why she had left Caitlin alone at the gas station the day before. The curve of her lips revealed both distaste and disbelief. Her eyes oscillated between affection and revulsion. The woman he had known and maybe loved had disappeared. She had become someone new.

Caitlin showed as little interest in her mother's expression as she did in the landmarks. The child, at least, saw nothing of what the father saw in the mother's face. Carter reasoned that if Caitlin could look at his own pale and perverted body and see her father, she wouldn't detect her mother's transformation.

When he returned to his original body, Carter abandoned surveillance and set out on his own. The puppeteer knew what he knew, so it knew which direction to take. He shed his coat and started out for Susan's estate at top speed. He ran through woods and fields, plotting a direct route between winding roads. After arriving at the head of Susan's long driveway, he circled the massive house twice, creeping around pine trees and bushes. He looked at all the windows long enough to match them up with the rooms Carter remembered as Susan's, Megan's, and the guest suites where they usually stayed during their visits. A study of the house's exterior summoned enough memories of the interior for Carter to sketch a map. He didn't have the power to sketch, but he guessed that the memories he pieced together would serve the puppeteer just as well.

With the survey of the house completed, he wandered farther out onto the grounds. He relearned the paths that led through the gardens and into the thicket of pines. He noted the power and phone lines, and he observed the road. No cars drove by. After he had learned the area around the house and all the things that connected it to the world beyond, he crawled into a ditch by the street. He waited. No Megan. His eyelids squeezed shut, and a few seconds of seeing through Caitlin told him she and Megan were on their way.

Megan pulled into the driveway and led Caitlin to Susan. Carter moved toward the house, almost slithering, until he got close enough to hear their conversation. Susan wanted information, but she wouldn't drill for it until Caitlin was tucked away out of earshot.

Carter's ears honed in on the women's voices, and he followed their movements from outside the house. When they took Caitlin upstairs, he scaled the wall. They moved to the den, and he planted himself upside-down above one of the room's many windows. The two women sat together, sipping tea, and Megan confessed, telling her mother everything she and her husband had done. Throwing out questions and affirmations to move the story along, Susan's voice conveyed belief. Carter knew better than to take Susan's tone as a reliable indication of her feelings.

Megan whined about not knowing what to do, and Susan stayed quiet. Carter wished he could make himself peek into the room to see the expression on the older woman's face. When she spoke, he heard vague derision. Whether or not she believed in the more fantastic elements of Megan's story, she clearly believed in Megan's guilt.

"I know what I have to do," Megan said.

Carter felt the change in Megan's voice with his entire body. It moved him to action. His body dropped to the ground and glided to the telephone pole. He leapt up and severed wires that spat sparks as they fell. The lone streetlamp went out, and the house he turned to face became almost invisible. He rushed to the place he had held over the den's window and listened. A breeze buffeted his skin, which remained unaffected by the cold. The wall he clung to crackled, and Carter thought the sound might alert someone to his presence. No one came to investigate.

He heard the sounds of moving feet. One woman was alone in the den now, and her pacing announced her as Megan. Carter dropped silently to the ground and sped to Megan's car. Quick thrusts of his fingers penetrated its rear tires. He pulled his hands away from the rubber slowly, allowing no noise beyond a hiss and a whistle. Carter understood that he was cutting off Megan's chances of escape; he would not give her another opportunity to make him catch up to her.

The resolve in her voice came back to him – she knew what she had to do – and he remembered the way she had looked at Caitlin in the car. A deduction his puppeteer had already responded to finally occurred to him. All the violence she had seen in the past few days had led this new, unfamiliar Megan to make a decision. She blamed herself, and she blamed Carter, but most of all she blamed Caitlin, the center of everything.

Carter understood that Megan meant to murder their daughter, and he understood that he meant to stop her. He didn't need to feel his fingers gesturing to know his wife had reached *three*. Tonight he would kill her.

He heard voices in the den when he moved back toward the house, but instead of crashing through the window and ending it with a quick swipe at his wife's throat, he scaled the wall, climbed over the roof, and found the window that looked over Megan's old bed, where Caitlin was sleeping. His hand crept down over the glass, got a hold, and prepared to pull. The muscles in his arm had already begun to gather the force that would split the wood around the lock when he withdrew and retreated up the wall. Concealing himself in the trellis, he pushed his head out in front of the window just enough to see what was happening inside.

Susan entered the room, carrying a kerosene lamp in each hand. The light from the bobbing lamps made hectic, shimmering patterns on the walls. Susan tiptoed across the carpet, fixing her eyes on Caitlin, and set both lamps down on the nightstand. Seeing the way she guided her trembling hands away from the lamps, Carter could tell that she feared knocking over one of them and making a sound that would waken her granddaughter. Megan's story had affected her. The formidable Susan Penser was tired, anxious, and afraid. After hearing everything that Megan had to say, Susan was afraid for Caitlin. She gazed down at the sleeping little girl and moved a hand over her peaceful cheek. Carter felt a new affection for his mother-in-law.

A smile stretched across his face, radiating the warmth of Carter's affection. He remembered Megan's warning about what "the Carter-thing" might do to Susan and realized she was right. The last two killings had involved less gusto but no less bloodlust. At any moment he might break open the window and kill Susan while his daughter watched. Carter – or his puppeteer – was certainly capable of killing Caitlin's grandmother on its way to killing her mother.

Desperate, Carter tried something that hadn't occurred to him before. He thought that if he could focus his thoughts, concentrate all of his paltry essence, he might achieve something like telepathy. He could send out a message to warn her. She would hear him, look up, see him, know the whole truth, and save herself.

Run, Susan, run! He summoned the words and thrust them out of his mind, silently chanting like he had chanted before but with more hope and commitment than he had ever felt, thinking, knowing that if the power of his thoughts could accomplish everything it had in all those rituals, it could accomplish this one little thing. He banished even that thought and let the message alone occupy him. "RUN!" He thrust, he sent, he poured everything he had into the single silent syllable.

Susan bent over Caitlin again and kissed her cheek. The girl stirred but didn't wake. Smiling with uneasy lips, Susan picked up one of the two lamps she had set on the nightstand, turned, and walked out of the room with no urgency. She didn't scream, didn't run, didn't even look up at the position Carter had tried to give away. His effort at action had failed, and his lips seemed to stretch into an even wider smile in response.

Carter knew he deserved the mockery. He was pathetic. He started to spin his hamster wheel, contemplating his non-existence, but the sight of Susan's light disappearing down the hall snapped him out of it. She hadn't done so by Carter's intervention, but Susan had gotten out of the room. She was farther away from him, moving toward her own bedroom, and that meant that at least for a little while longer Carter wouldn't feel her blood on his hands. Self-pity turned into relief.

His hand reestablished its grip on the window. His arm tensed, and the window popped open. The sound wasn't as explosive as Carter had thought it might be, but it was enough to make Caitlin come back to consciousness. The window was open by the time she sat up, turned her head, and saw him. She opened her mouth to speak or scream, but he covered it with his palm, keeping his sharp fingertips as far from Caitlin's delicate skin as they could stretch. With his free hand, he held a finger up over his twisted lips.

Shhhhhhhh.

Caitlin nodded. She understood. He removed his hand from her mouth, and she made no sound. When he scooped her up in his arm, she did not resist. Blinking sleep from her eyes, she stared at him. Her forehead wrinkled in worried confusion, and Carter wished he could say something to her. He had no idea what he was doing; he watched, his mind as quiet as his footsteps.

He carried her into the hallway and turned in the direction opposite where he had seen Susan go with her lamp. The hall was dark, but his steps were sure. He grasped the dangling cord that would bring down the ladder to the attic. The ladder creaked as he pulled the cord and unfolded the ladder. Caitlin shifted in his arm while he climbed the rungs. Carter could tell that she didn't like where he was taking her, but she didn't resist.

Making another shushing gesture, he set Caitlin down on the attic's plywood-covered floor. She opened her mouth to speak, and he shushed her again. Frowning, she sat down. Carter's eyes traveled around the dark space, seeing piles of boxes by the starlight coming through the attic's single, large window. He spotted a box labeled "Christmas lights," took it down from the stack, and opened it. He pulled out a sheet, the one Susan would drape around the trunk of the Christmas tree to simulate snow, and tossed it over his shoulder. He pulled out a string of lights, coiled it around his arm like a rope, and went back to Caitlin.

Before she could register the meaning of his movements, he had a hand over her mouth again, and he pushed her up against a roof beam. She wriggled, struggled, tried to get away. With the hand not stifling her screams, he used the string of lights to tie her to the beam. The knots were not tight, just secure enough to keep her from getting away. He gagged her loosely with a shred of the white sheet and left her, gliding down the ladder and closing the attic with another soft creak.

When he bound and gagged his daughter and abandoned her in the dark attic, he felt even more like a monster, but he understood why he was doing it. Part of parenting was the pain of doing things for his child's own good even though they hurt her. She'd be safe in the attic, safe from Megan and safe from the sight of what he was going to do. Megan was planning to kill Caitlin. He needed to go beyond just preventing the act: he needed to keep Caitlin from ever thinking of the act's possibility. He needed to shield Caitlin from her mother's intentions, and he needed to spare her another glimpse of her father's hands covered with blood.

A sound on the stairs — footsteps. He backed down the hall, feet barely touching the carpet, and hid himself in the darkness. Megan reached the top of the stairs. She looked right and left, probably checking for Susan. Carter didn't know where Susan had gone, maybe down to the first floor. The possibility of hurting Susan occurred to him again, and he dreaded it. Megan turned the corner, walking toward his hiding place in the darkness. She didn't see him. Her eyes were fixed on the doorway to the room that had once been her own, where she expected to find their daughter sleeping. She disappeared inside.

With slow, silent steps he followed her. In the room he heard Megan say, "Caitlin?" The searching question came out with a tremor. Carter knew that his wife was seeing the empty bed. She was looking at the open window, and when she saw the splintered wood around the lock, she would think of the splintered door to their apartment. She would know he was there. She would know he was coming.

He stood in the doorway, filled it. Megan didn't turn around. Still staring at the bed, she took a backward step. Her left hand squeezed something. In the lamplight Carter saw coils, a phone cord. She wanted to use the cord to strangle their daughter. He knew her reasons, understood them. He might even have approved of them if he and Megan hadn't done so much, sacrificed so much, to save their little girl. He was what he was, and Megan was what she was, and everything that had happened had happened, all for Caitlin. Megan wanted to destroy all of that by destroying their daughter. Carter hated his wife, and he longed for his puppeteer to feel that hate and respond.

Megan took another backward step away from the bed, toward Carter. The flickering lamplight cast out multiple shadows, and one of them covered him. He raised a hand to the doorframe and punctured it with four fingers. He pulled them downward, his skin deflecting the splinters but not the sound they made. Megan turned around and said, "You're finally here."

End

The thing that looked like her husband had climbed up the side of the house, forced open the window, and whisked Caitlin away to some safe place. The Carter-thing had saved Caitlin from Megan, whose plan to sacrifice her daughter it had anticipated. It had anticipated it, and it had judged her for it. One, two, three strikes. Megan sensed judgment like a stench, like—

That smell. She knew it. She had been close to it. It had filled her nose when the scar-plastered features of her husband had been close enough to kiss her, and it had turned her stomach when she had gotten back into the car where the thing had waited with their daughter. The Carter-thing left dead bodies and a putrid stench everywhere it went. She knew its signatures. She could detect it as easily as it seemed to detect her. It was standing behind her, in the doorway, looking at her unguarded back.

One second passed, two. Megan's eyes shifted left, toward the nightstand. One lamp there, and one in the hand not holding the phone cord. The cord would be useless; her mind had already gone over that. But *fire* – hadn't Carter told her to yell fire when she needed help?

She had seen how the Carter-thing could move. Faster than she could blink, it would be able to leap from the doorway and split her in two. Another second passed, another. The thing didn't pounce. It was just looking at her; she could feel its stare gnawing at her spine. It had a chance to kill her now, but perhaps Megan was not the only one who let chances to strike slip away. She remembered how it had chased her through the rain, how it had paused before each leap to see what her next move would be. It waited now for the same reason: the next move would be hers.

Megan took a step backward. The step brought her closer to the Carter-thing, but it also brought her closer to the nightstand. She already held a lamp in one hand. In the other she held the phone cord. She squeezed it, wishing she didn't have to let go. Her next backward step moved on a more pronounced diagonal, bringing the lamp on the nightstand within arm's reach.

Behind her, she heard the sounds of crackling wood. She didn't turn toward the crackling – the sounds continued, wood splitting, bursting in the doorway. The Carter-thing wanted her to face it. It was trying to get her attention. She'd give it what it wanted, more than that, in just a moment. She calculated; she got her left arm ready for the quick movement she needed it to execute. Now or never. She turned to face the monster.

"You're finally here," she said.

The Carter-thing had dug its fingers into the doorframe and carved four trails. *And you call me melodramatic*, Megan thought, and she smiled. The pleasure of another perfect reproof that she wouldn't voice to her husband was all she needed. In a fast swipe, she dropped the cord and picked up the lamp. Before the thing could take a second long stride toward her, she threw the lamp at its feet. The lamp shattered, spilling oil, and a wall of flame leapt up between them. Still watching the figure moving through the growing light, her right hand released her second missile, which splashed flame on its chest. She couldn't tell if the Carter-thing's flesh ignited, but the clothes it wore did.

The second lamp succeeded in stopping the creature's rush toward her. Megan saw its arms flail out, bat at the flames, and start to tear at its burning clothes. The attack had worked, but it had only bought time. She had two options: She could run around the creature, through the flames that grew faster and faster as they spread along carpet to furniture, or she could climb out the window.

She sprung toward the bed, and her arms were reaching through the window into night air before she knew if they'd have something to grab. With her blind reach she found the trellis, and gripping it as tightly as she could, wincing at the pain as metal and dead vines cut into her hands, she pulled her body away from the bed, the fire, the thing that wanted to kill her.

With agonized hands, she tried to use the trellis as a ladder to lower herself. Beside her and above her she felt heat pouring from the window, and a quick glance upward that she should have denied herself showed her the peering head of the Carter-thing. Flames surrounded it, but its expression was calm. Snapping noises brought her attention back to her hands. The trellis was separating from the wall. Of course, a house so well-secured wouldn't have a sturdy ladder right outside the window that—

Flimsy metal bent outward as the trellis's supports broke one level at a time. Megan tried to hold on, lacerated fingers oozing blood, but she couldn't. She dropped the remainder of the distance to the ground, landing on her feet and then slamming down on her backside. She sat stunned but uninjured on the dead grass and soft soil. Dizzy from the fall, her head tilted upward again.

The Carter-thing had its eyes fixed on her. It thrust its bare and charred upper body through the open window and launched into the air. Entranced, Megan watched it soar up and fall down, down, and while it fell her mind half-articulated the hope that it would be hurt or stunned by the impact. Its feet smashed into the dirt, poised and balanced. Blinking back panic, Megan stood on unsteady legs, clutched her pounding head, and ran away from the house, toward a trail she remembered that led to the woods, where she might be able to lose him.

In her periphery she saw the thing watching her. It did not speed toward her, not yet, but it seemed to evaluate her progress and direction, to divine her plan. She knew she couldn't outrun it, but she ran anyway, hoping that darkness and the skull-seeping childhood memories of this area that the Carter-thing didn't share would give her an advantage.

She lost sight of it as she dashed down the trail, didn't see it coming until it landed on the path in front of her. She screamed, and the waste of breath cost her. When the thing had landed, it might have been fifty yards away. In the short seconds of her scream, it closed the distance between them by more than half.

It paused again once she started running toward a different trail. Once more it evaluated her, seeming confident that it didn't need to chase her, that it could cut off any vector of escape with its acrobatic leaps. Maybe its confidence would be its weakness, if only she could run fast enough. This trail would take her on an indirect route toward the street, where maybe a passing car would stop and help her. Trying to keep focused on what lay ahead rather than what trailed behind, Megan pushed herself faster, faster.

The Carter-thing landed in front of her, cutting her off with a thud and a spray of dirt. Without hesitation, she turned, choosing to run alongside the house. She darted by a lawn chair and tossed it behind her without slowing. Maybe it would trip the thing, maybe it would – but the thing was in front of her again, so close, too close. She stood near the back door that led to the kitchen. She grabbed at the doorknob, panicked for an instant when it threatened not to turn, flung the door open and slammed it shut behind her. Shaking hands threw two bolts before she turned to run into the smoke-filled house.

A voice, her mother's, screaming: "MEGAN!!! CAITLIN!!! WHERE ARE YOU?!!"

The sound came from the den, not from the conflagration upstairs, where Megan had feared her mother would be trapped. Her mother had another lamp in the den; its light reached the kitchen. Going from the kitchen to the den would bring her closer to the front of the house, toward the front door. If she could get out of the house she could dash to the car and maybe get it started and on the road before the Carter-thing could stop her again. She ran toward the light – but why? Wasn't she supposed to....

"SOMEBODY ANSWER ME PLEASE!!!"

"MOM!" Megan yelled as she bolted into the room. "Come on, it's here, we have to get out of the house!"

"There's a fire upstairs! Where's Caitlin?!" Susan sounded out of breath; she had been running around, frantic, trying to find her granddaughter.

Megan grabbed her mother's arm and pulled. "We can't help her! Come on, we've got to get out of the house!" Her head pounded as the flames behind them seemed to encroach from all directions. She pulled hard enough to make Susan move her feet toward the exit. When she got to the front door, she heard a loud crash. The Carter-thing had burst into the house through the heavy kitchen door.

Susan strained in Megan's grip but yielded to her momentum. Leaving the front door open behind her, knowing the time necessary to close it would be better spent sprinting toward the car, Megan prodded her mother down the front stairs and then dragged her. Susan yelled Caitlin's name again and again as they covered the distance to the sedan.

The sight of the car stopped her, and Susan slipped from Megan's grasp. The sedan's rear bumper was touching the gravel driveway. The Carter-thing had made a preemptive strike against the tires. The power, the phone, the tires – the Carter-thing had planned all of it. It had foreseen everything Megan might do, and it had cut off every chance Megan had to escape or to finish what she started.

Not every chance. There was still the fire. Had the Carter-thing left Caitlin somewhere in the house? The fire might get to Caitlin even if Megan didn't. The fire could stop Caitlin, stop the Carter-thing, stop the stream of sacrifices.

Susan stopped yelling for Caitlin and just screamed. Megan saw why her mother was screaming: the Carter-thing had landed on the driveway between the sedan and the road. Soot smudged its skin, everywhere bare, nothing but twists of grey-blue scars in the starlight. The nakedness of its body canceled whatever humanity remained in its face. Megan and her mother confronted clawed hands, pointed feet, twisted spine, and vacant groin. Susan would believe her now. Carter was not alive, but he was here.

"BACK TO THE HOUSE!" Megan ordered, and Susan obeyed. Split skull or no split skull, Megan was in control. She would lead them back to the house, back to the fire, back to Caitlin. Getting away and getting to Caitlin were all that mattered.

Megan dashed through the open doorway with Susan trailing behind. She had crossed through the foyer toward the stairs when her mother's voice made her look back. Susan stood in the doorway yelling, "CAITLIN!!! CALL OUT SO WE CAN FIND YOU!!!" There wouldn't be, *couldn't* be a response they'd hear over the pounding in Megan's head and the raging of the fire on the second floor, but Susan called out anyway, wasting time, wasting her chance to get away from the thing that was coming up the front steps behind her.

The Carter-thing knocked Susan to the floor as it came through the doorway. Megan didn't see if it stepped on her mother as it came toward her. Remembering the man it had slashed on the highway, Megan knew that even this thing's feet could kill. She didn't have time, couldn't go back to see if her mother were dead or alive. The stairs were close. She had to go up, to lure the thing into the flames and pray that fire would do the rest.

The thing cut her off again, reaching the foot of the staircase before she did. Without looking at her, it stood on the bottom step. She wasn't sure, but she thought she saw the thing close its eyes. It was hesitating – it could have killed her then, but it hesitated to choose between its prey and the stairs. Megan knew. Caitlin *was* in the house, hidden somewhere upstairs, and the Carter-thing had to decide whether to be first the destroyer or the protector. The time was a gift. Megan ran away from the stairs, into the kitchen.

Her movement must have made the decision for it. Lunging through the kitchen, Megan could sense her pursuer closing the distance behind her. She found herself by the sink, by the knife rack. Seizing the biggest blade, she turned around. The Carter-thing stood a few feet away. Something, maybe the threat of the knife, halted its progress.

Waving the knife at the remnants of her husband, Megan felt a kind of familiarity. The familiarity gave her a charge, made her ready to fight. Was the memory of their standoff in another kitchen, of the duel of knife and words that she had lost, slowing down her opponent while it invigorated her? A smile stretched across the Carter-thing's loathsome face, and the darkness of the room did not shield Megan from seeing the sharp points of its teeth.

Swinging the blade to from side to side, carving a protective barrier between them, Megan maneuvered away from the sink. From the kitchen she could run to another side of the house, to the back staircase that connected the first and second floor guest suites. She could get upstairs, get to Caitlin, if only she could make it out of this room.

The Carter-thing was too close for her to run. She had to attack. The bulletproof thing she had heard about at the hospital wouldn't fall by a knife, but the panicked reports she had heard could have been wrong or exaggerated. Maybe Megan could do with a knife what those men hadn't been able to do with their guns. In that other kitchen months ago a plunge of the blade would have brought her husband to his knees. She couldn't be sure if she could even hurt what her husband had become, but she had to try.

The thing was missing an opportunity to tackle her, to end the confrontation. It stood watching for her next move as she swung the knife in air-splitting arcs. The potential of the blade at least made the Carter-thing hesitate, and that meant she had a chance. She got far enough from the sink to make a strategic strike, to stab and dash. Risking a closeness that threatened to overwhelm her, she dove at the stooping Carter-thing and drove the blade straight into the side of its neck.

Its arms clamped down on her sides like a sprung mousetrap as the force of her charge pushed it backward. With all her strength, Megan struggled to keep from falling in the same direction, to keep her body from colliding with and pressing close to the thing before her. Wriggling away between squeezing arms, she kept her hold on the knife handle, pulling it within the hard flesh, hoping to slice outward through the throat. They pulled in opposite directions, and she lost her grip before she could wrench the blade free. The thing's arms slid by her, and its fingers ripped into her sides as she pushed away from them.

Backing up, stumbling, feeling the blood run down from her open sides onto her stomach and back, Megan couldn't help watching, vision shaking to the rhythm of her headache, to see how and *if* the Carter-thing coped with the metal driven into its neck. A stab as lucky as the one she had made would have killed any man, any beast, any form of life she had ever known. The Carter-thing didn't collapse, but it stumbled as far back as the kitchen counter and dropped to its knees. Megan thought she should see blood spurting from the artery she must have severed, but in the gathering smoke she saw no sign of the wound beyond the knife itself. Even when a clawed hand pulled the blade from its flesh, she saw no blood.

No more watching – she ran away from the center of the house, toward the outer rooms, past the gallery, into the guest suite. Panicked, unthinking, propelled by echoing drumbeats inside her, she slammed the bedroom door, locked it, and with adrenaline-strength swung a heavy chair up against it. Spiral stairs through another door linked this room with the room above it. Unable to manage much speed as she grinded her jaw against the pain in her sides, Megan climbed the stairs, opened and closed the door at the top, and stumbled into the second floor bedroom identical to the one below.

She stopped to breathe, to clench her sides, to think through the skull-splitting haze about how to buy more time. The smoke was thick, hurting her lungs, clouding her thoughts with a thicker black. In the dim light from the windows she could see that a television sat on a heavy table next to the stairwell door. Megan moved toward it. Expecting the strength she had had with the chair below, she yanked at the table, using all her might to try to get the heavy furniture to block the door. It did not budge. Her legs wobbled, sent her sprawling to the carpet. From her prone position she looked at the door she had failed to barricade, thinking it would fly open now and end the chase.

No movement. No sound.

Consciousness ebbed. The scratches on her sides weren't severe enough to kill her, but the pain and the smoke menaced her with faintness. She knew if she gave in now, if she let her narrow, pulsating vision rush her into oblivion, she would die. She would die not knowing if the fire she had started had finished the work she had to do. She didn't care if she died, but she did care that she might fail to *act*. Caitlin was all that mattered now. All that had ever mattered. Tilting, wavering, she stood.

Her eyes settled again on the nearby door that she expected the Carter-thing to come rushing through. It didn't open. Had the knife stopped it? Was it unable to keep chasing her? Would it come bursting through the door any second?

Or was it coming around to the other staircase?

"CAITLIN!!!" she yelled. She used her strongest mother-voice. She strained to hear a noise in the chaos, the sound of Caitlin answering, leading Megan through the smoke to her location. Nearly blinded by smoke and darkness, Megan wouldn't have been able to see Caitlin if she were sitting in the same room with her. She wouldn't see, but she would hear, and that meant Caitlin was somewhere else. *The girl* will *answer me*. She made her way to the hallway, yelling again, "CAITLIN! Answer your mother!"

With arms folded across her chest and hands clutching at her sides, Megan lurched down the hot, smoke-filled hallway. Fuzziness gathered at the edges of her distorted vision, unconsciousness threatening, tempting. She would not yield. The strength she had used to get through so much in the last few days would *not* fail now. If the Carter-thing appeared at the other end of the hall, in the flames at the top of the main staircase, she would face it. She'd use her last bit of strength to keep it from saving her daughter and itself.

In the smoke something brushed against her face. She couldn't see it, but her fingers caught it – a cord dangling from the entrance to the attic through the ceiling. A sound reached her ears. It sounded like Caitlin, and it came from above.

"CAITLIN!" Megan directed her voice upward.

Faint and desperate: "Moooooommyyyyyyyy!"

Caitlin was in the attic. When Megan pulled at the dangling cord, she half-expected her daughter to drop with the ladder. She saw and heard no further sign of the girl, so she called again, "Caitlin, are you up there!"

Waiting for an answer, she imagined how the fire had spread from the bedroom to the center stairs. The initial blast had devoured the kerosene, and then it had slowed, but soon new fodder of carpet and wood had let it multiply. It spread to the hall, to the stairs, and now it was coming toward her. She could feel the heat against her back. In a moment she would be burning.

"Moooommyyyyyy! Daaaaaddyyyyyyy!"

She climbed the ladder up to the attic. The flames would not let her come back down. She knew, but she climbed toward the sound of her daughter, the only thing that mattered.

Billows of smoke preceded her into the attic, and when she reached the top, she was almost as blind as she had been at the bottom. Shielding her eyes with a blood-soaked arm, Megan scanned through the density of darkness and spotted a writhing shape near one of the roof beams. She walked closer, hearing child-coughs getting louder and louder.

"Caitlin!"

"Mommy! I'm over here! Help me! I can't get loose!"

A white gag hung under the girl's chin, and what looked like a string of Christmas lights secured her to the beam. Without thinking, Megan started to loosen the string, to free her daughter. She worked quickly at first, but the motion of her hands soon slowed, then stopped. No. She was here for a different purpose altogether. Her heart and instincts could revolt, but the axe in her head insisted that she *would* succeed.

By leaving Caitlin up here, the Carter-thing had almost done Megan's work for her. She wondered whether the girl would have perished in the flames if Megan hadn't discovered her in the attic. If so, then she had come up here and allowed the flames to consume her last hope of escape for nothing.

No, not for nothing. For Caitlin. Everything was for Caitlin.

Megan took part of the loose string of lights into her hands, looped it around Caitlin's neck, and started to pull. Smoke stung her eyes – she couldn't look, didn't have to look. She just had to pull at the string of lights until it was over. She would feel nothing then. She would feel nothing, and the list of her victims would end with herself. Megan and her daughter would die together.

Sounds on the ladder, someone climbing up. The Carter-thing could stop her now. If it could find her in the smoke, it could stop her, save Caitlin, and ruin everything.

"Megan, is that you?" The voice was Susan's. Megan's arms relaxed, and she heard Caitlin gasping for air. Megan would ignore her mother. She would ignore her mother and pull. Feeling the blood from her scratched hands slick along the wires, Megan pulled the string, tightening the loop around her daughter's throat.

"The main stairs are out, but we can still get down through the guest rooms! I forced the door, there's a way! We've got to go now!" Her mother coughed. "I can't see you! Is Caitlin with you? What happened to...to...the thing that was after us? Megan, answer me!"

Susan was coming closer, finding her way through the smoke. Megan's arms wanted to relax again, and her lips wanted to answer her mother, but she wouldn't let them. Just this, this one last act, one last exertion, and it will all end, it will all be over. One last—

"Oh, my God, Megan, stop!"

Susan grabbed her from behind, yanked her away from Caitlin, who once again started gasping for air, struggling through sobs and smoke. Megan slipped from Susan's hands, turned, and flailed her arms wildly in her mother's direction. An arm made contact – she hit her mother's face, and the woman crashed down onto the plywood-covered floor.

Megan wanted Susan to be able to get out of the house, to save herself, but there was no time to help her. Caitlin was more important. Megan stumbled back toward her daughter. Through the smoke Megan could barely make out the girl's continuing struggle with the string of lights. Between coughs and sobs, Caitlin managed to scream as her mother approached. Megan knelt, made another loop, and started pulling. She cut off her daughter's sound.

"Megan, stop! Stop now! MEGAN!" Susan's voice.

Don't look. Don't listen. Don't breathe. Just *pull*.

A sound stabbed Megan's eardrums – gunshots. As she collapsed to the floor, the last thing she heard was her daughter sobbing.

The Descent of Carter Anderson, Continued

The person that Megan had become was capable of more than Carter had ever thought possible. Their struggle should have ended when he found her in the abandoned bedroom. He lunged at her, but she anticipated the move and hurled two kerosene lamps. The fire caused no pain, but it nibbled at Carter's flesh while it ravaged his clothing, causing damage that his senses registered in blinding pulses. Flailing arms stripped off the burning clothes and patted down flames. Megan climbed through the window, and he followed her with a leap that brought a cooling rush of air to his skin.

The chase led them around and around the house. They ended up in the kitchen, and she waved a knife with uncharacteristic conviction. She rammed it into his neck, and for a moment Carter thought she would cut off his head. The feeling in his neck made his other senses blank; Carter thought she might have found a way to cut through all the sutures, to kill him. By the time the wound started sealing itself, she had vanished.

He stood and glided back to the central staircase. The flames that had spread to the stairs might have had the power to damage him, but they didn't deter him. He ran into fire, reached the top floor, and saw through clouds of smoke that the ladder to the attic where he had left Caitlin was both lowered and burning. He heard something he couldn't understand: gunshots.

Swift bends of his knees launched him into the attic. Thick smoke surrounded him, but he could still make out three distinct shapes: Susan, Megan, and Caitlin.

Susan had seen Megan tightening the noose around Caitlin's neck, and when Megan failed to heed her commands to stop, Susan had shot her more than once. Carter heard Caitlin coughing and sobbing, and then he saw Megan topple onto the floor, dead.

Susan hadn't heard him enter, and though she looked back over her shoulder, she didn't see him standing in the smoke.

Carter could barely see Susan, but he could hear. A low moan escaped her throat between coughs. The sound quaked, and he imagined the woman's entire body quaking around it. He knew he hadn't heard the sound of the gun hitting the plywood-covered floor, which meant she still held it in her hands. Realization of what she had just done caused shockwaves to wrack her entire body, but she didn't let go of the weapon she thought she might still need to defend her granddaughter.

Taking two silent steps closer, Carter saw Susan bending over Caitlin and freeing her from the string of lights he had used to bind her. While he was chasing Megan, he had checked through Caitlin's senses several times to see that she was still okay, but he hadn't done so since Megan had stabbed him. Carter realized that, through carelessness, his puppeteer might have made him responsible for another daughter's death. Susan had saved Caitlin from Megan, and now she was saving her from him.

Susan found the white sheet he had used and wrapped it around Caitlin. "Breathe through the cloth," she said, "and I'll see if I can figure out a way to get us out of here." Despite fits of coughing, the girl was pliant in her grandmother's arms. She had seen her grandmother kill her mother, but she cooperated. Carter wondered how seeing this latest killing would affect his daughter. Perhaps her brain quarantined it, leaving it to be uncovered in some distant future therapy session, or perhaps the girl had simply become used to death.

Carter took another step forward and started to tense his arms at his sides. He was getting ready to make a move, and he felt terrified that he was about to kill Susan. He had to do *something*: the flames had reached the attic, and soon the fire and smoke would overwhelm them both. Susan would die even if he made no move against her, and Caitlin would die, too.

His next step alerted Susan to his presence. When she turned and saw him, she moved in front of Caitlin, pointed the gun and fired. The shots slowed but didn't stop him. He continued approaching while bullet after bullet slammed into his body. When pulling the trigger made only dull clicks, she threw the gun at Carter's face. Disarmed and helpless, she backed up as if to hide Caitlin behind her. Coughing, wheezing, searching the attic around her for some other means of defense, Susan said, "Carter."

She seemed to use the name like a talisman to ward him off, to use it in the same unbelieving way Megan had used it, attempting to access the humanity she knew she would not find. She said "Carter" again, and he heard a different tone altogether. Her voice was pleading. "Carter," she said, "help us." She coughed, doubled over, almost collapsed. She fought to keep standing, to raise her head again and address him: "Carter, help Caitlin."

His hand was on Susan before Carter could register the movement of his arm. He grabbed her and expected to feel his fingers tearing into her, ripping her open and flinging her into a heap with her dead daughter, Carter's dead wife. Instead, he used caution with his fingertips, handling Susan like he had handled Caitlin. He picked the woman up and slung her over his shoulder. With his other hand he grabbed Caitlin, wrapped and coughing in her white sheet, and tucked her under his arm. He turned toward the large attic window, ran, and jumped.

Glass showered his skin. He twisted his body to protect the people he carried, saving Caitlin from all the shards and saving Susan from most. He landed on his feet and glided away, to a place within the thicket of pines far enough from the burning house to be safe. He set down Susan and kept Caitlin under his arm.

Dazed but conscious, Susan looked up at him. Carter saw resolve and relief in her expression. Together, they had ensured Caitlin's safety. Even in the presence of a monster, she could relax now that she knew her granddaughter would live. She knew him, knew what he was, and knew what he would do. He might kill her, but he would protect Caitlin. Her face showed more gratitude than fear.

Carter set his bundled daughter down in her exhausted grandmother's lap. Caitlin worked her face free from the sheet, and he saw her take in gulps of the night air. The air made her cough, and the breaths that followed the cough told Carter that she would recover. His eyes made contact with Susan's. He wondered if he would speak. There were things that Carter wanted to say.

His lips did not move, but soon Carter understood that they didn't need to. The only sensation in his face came from his eyes. They gazed at Susan with warmth, genuine warmth. The thread that had tied him to Megan was broken. With that look, he sutured himself to Susan, his daughter's new protector.

Susan understood his meaning as well as Carter did. She looked at him, nodded, and kissed the top of Caitlin's head, where the new growth of hair, soaked with ash and grime, told them both about the future. Megan had once told Carter of the fantasies she had had about Caitlin's ascent to womanhood, fantasies destroyed by cancer. Those fantasies would live for Susan now, and they would live for him.

Epilogue

Carter wondered what would happen once Caitlin grew old. Would she grow infirm and die, or would he somehow keep that from happening? If she died, would he die with her? Or would he go on forever, trapped inside this body, the ghost of Carter Anderson, serving out the eternal sentence, the never-ending paternity, he had requested?

His thoughts never stopped spinning certain questions, but he did eventually learn to enjoy his existence, cursed as it was. He didn't spend every moment following his daughter, but she was still his main purpose. He learned to savor the details of her life; they were all he had. He hoped that the puppeteer was capable of sharing his pride.

Carter followed Caitlin, so death followed her. Since he shared Carter's knowledge that his legacy would hurt her, the puppeteer seemed to try to keep from being too much of a burden on the girl. After transferring Caitlin into Susan's capable hands, he started keeping more of a distance, allowing Caitlin to learn to fend for herself. He was always with her, but he strove for invisibility. Nevertheless, some encounters were unavoidable.

She was fourteen and going on a date that Susan hadn't approved. The boy taking her to the movies, Brad, was seventeen. He drove a pick-up truck and liked to drink beer. Susan didn't know, but Carter knew, and he watched from a shorter distance than usual when the two teenagers were together.

Brad started groping Carter's daughter in the movie theater. Experiencing this sensation from Caitlin's point of view was uncomfortable, but it did not summon him to action, even though Carter wanted to run in and stop it. When the two teenagers walked into the parking lot afterward, he watched but did not disturb them.

Brad made Caitlin laugh, and Carter thought that, at least, was good. Caitlin had many troubles, far too many for a girl her age. She saw the best psychiatrists, but some wounds therapy and drugs could not heal. Carter didn't have access to her thoughts, but he knew they must have been haunted by images of him, her mother, and a night of strangulation and gunshots.

He didn't sneak into Caitlin's senses to listen to her conversation with Brad once they were sitting in the boy's truck, but he wanted to. He nagged at his puppeteer for showing too much restraint. The truck pulled out of the parking lot. Carter wanted to ride beneath the truck, but he didn't. Instead he glided alongside the road, catching inconspicuous lifts when chances appeared. His daughter got out of his line of sight, but she never got away.

The truck pulled into a public park. Carter noted the "Closes At Dusk" sign that Brad seemed to ignore. Brad parked his truck, the sole vehicle in the lot. He climbed out of his side, walked around to Caitlin's, and opened the door for her. The mock-chivalry did not fool Carter, but it enchanted Caitlin. They walked hand in hand through the recreation area and onto one of the nature trails. Carter followed on high tree branches, far enough behind for his rustlings to be dismissed as the night-errands of squirrels and mice.

Carter's body had continued to evolve. His sight had kept improving way beyond the point of not needing glasses: he could see minute movements and objects at great distances. Even on the moonless night when Caitlin and Brad walked through the park, he had no problem seeing every gesture and touch from high in the treetops.

Caitlin and Brad found a bench to sit on and started kissing. Carter felt glad that he did not have to feel the sensation of Brad's lips on his daughter's, on his, but he still felt the urge to cringe. Addressing his puppeteer in a way that had become customary, he suggested varying strategies for interrupting the too-young lovers. He could have broken into the truck and started pressing on the horn. He could have uprooted a tree and let it crash down near them, providing a providential sign that they should not be doing such business here or anywhere. She was only fourteen. Brad needed to leave his daughter alone.

The puppeteer did not follow his suggestions.

Brad's hands wandered into Caitlin's shirt. Carter griped that Caitlin hadn't even *had* breasts for very long, and already some guy was feeling her up. His thoughts were squirming, but his body stayed perfectly still. Brad moved his hand down between Caitlin's legs, and she inched backward without breaking off their kiss. Carter would have cheered for his daughter's display of prudence if he had been capable.

Caitlin's resistance did not daunt her suitor. After his hand failed to get access between her legs, it moved down between his own. At first Carter thought the boy was only adjusting his erection, but soon he realized that Brad was unzipping his pants. Caitlin didn't see. She was wrapped up in the kiss, in the romance of nighttime and trees. He pulled her close to him again, and she didn't resist. He pressed on her chest until she lay back on the bench. As he unbuttoned her shirt, Carter could tell that she was getting uncomfortable. She *must* have been getting uncomfortable, but she didn't say a word. Brad moved over her, rubbing against her, groping and fondling.

Do something! Do something now!

Carter kept watching, only watching until the boy shifted his body so that his weight covered Carter's much smaller daughter. He blocked her from Carter's view, and Carter jumped down from the tree and moved closer. The sound of movement made Brad look over his shoulder, but soon he was kissing and rubbing again.

Brad slid down his pants, and without seeing, Carter knew that Brad was grabbing for the button on Caitlin's jeans. Their movements became less fluid now. Caitlin wriggled underneath him, and he bore down on her, still kissing, still squeezing. He was probably forcing open Caitlin's pants when she shouted, "No!"

Carter pounced on him, grabbed him, and carried him into a treetop before Caitlin could get more than a glimpse of her father. Despite his learning curve, the puppeteer didn't cut off the boy's ability to scream before he tore into him. Caitlin heard Brad's cries and ran to the bottom of the tree where Carter held him. Carter could see her from his branch. With her pants fastened and her shirt open, she screamed, "Brad, Brad, Brad!"

Some of the blood pouring from the gashes that Carter was inflicting rained down from the tree, splashing Caitlin's face. She screamed Brad's name a few more times, and then, after emitting something that sounded like a roar, she screamed, "DADDY, NO!!!"

Hearing her say "Daddy" jolted Carter's emotions: confusion, guilt, happiness, and rage overwhelmed his thoughts. His hands stopped tearing. The fingers slipped out of the wounds and hovered in front of Carter's eyes. Once more he had traumatized Caitlin, and the gestures of his hands might have reflected recognition of the error. Brad had died before Caitlin had started yelling his name, so there was nothing he could do. Carter stopped moving, holding the body and himself motionless on the branch. Caitlin collapsed in a fit of howling and tears.

She didn't go on another date until she was sixteen.

Carter kept his distance. He didn't have to eat very often – only once or twice a year – but he did eat, and there were news reports about victims that Caitlin saw from time to time. He varied the patterns of mutilation as much as he could, and sometimes he used fire to destroy the evidence. The media didn't connect many of the killings to one another, so to most eyes other than Caitlin's and Susan's the strange bulletins looked like random murders or animal attacks.

Caitlin learned at a young age not to bring Carter up in therapy sessions or anywhere else. Susan prepared how Caitlin would respond to questions about her past, and the two went over the script so many times that to Caitlin it probably felt as familiar as truth. Caitlin deviated from the tale only once in a confidential session, and that night Susan got a call from the therapist, who worried that Ms. Penser's granddaughter might be delusional. Susan and Caitlin had a long talk, and Caitlin never repeated the error.

The official story of what happened to Carter and Megan painted them as run-of-the-mill lunatics. Susan shot Megan when Megan tried to burn down the house and strangle Caitlin. It was a horrible but necessary intervention. Susan told the police that Carter was also in the house; his remains, she said, must be mixed with the ashes of her property. He was into heavy drugs; he and Megan were responsible for all the mayhem that had torn through the country. The story was close enough to the truth to satisfy most authorities, and Susan's lawyers were enough to satisfy the rest.

Caitlin started out in the best private schools, but teachers branded her a troublemaker, so she ended up in a lower-tier academy by her junior year in high school. At sixteen, after two years without seeing Carter, she got her life together, and she made good enough grades to get into a decent liberal arts college. She wanted to study creative writing, and Susan encouraged her. Susan wanted her to have "outlets" for the truths that Caitlin could only express through fiction.

Late in her freshman year, Caitlin saw Carter again. She was walking home from a party by herself. She often did dangerous things like that, which caused Carter endless frustration. He thought that a past like his daughter's should have made her afraid of everything. He thought her experiences should have turned her into a babbling neurotic frightened by her own shadow, far too frightened to walk down urban streets alone at night.

Instead, she had become a young woman who seemed to have no concept of fear.

He was watching from the top of a tall hotel a block and half away from where she walked, a distance that even he would need time to cover. A man jumped out at her from an alley. He had a knife, and he knocked her on the pavement before demanding that she hand over her money. Carter heard him and rushed down the side of the building, but the mugger had her wallet in his hands when Carter was still a block away. He demanded Caitlin's diamond earrings and held the knife to her throat. While her trembling hands tried to unfasten her earrings, his knife made a shallow cut on her neck.

Caitlin might have thought that the blood spattering her face was her own. Carter had reached the man who was menacing his daughter, and without a pause he had shoved his hand into the mugger's back. Carter impaled him on his fingers and lifted him up, away from his daughter. Caitlin probably knew why the man rose into the air before Carter tossed him, giving her a clear view of Carter's hunching posture and bloody hand.

Carter turned and was about to glide away, hoping, perhaps, to spare his daughter a longer glimpse of him than was necessary. He was taking the first few steps of his retreat when he heard Caitlin's voice.

"Wait," she said.

He turned toward her. She was still down on the sidewalk, using her sleeve to wipe off her face. She struggled to her feet. With fingers dabbing at the shallow cut on her neck, she started walking toward him.

Carter wanted to run. After all the years of watching, he had come to see his life's mission as saving his daughter from seeing any more horrors in the world, including himself. Again, she was all he had.

"Wait," she repeated. She closed the distance between them, and he did not move.

She reached up and touched the side of his face. Her hand was warm. When he had felt the world through her fingers, he had never felt her warmth, not like this. He was on the other side of her touch. He realized that no being had willingly touched him – not *him* – in a long, long time. His daughter touched him, looked from his stooping body to his eyes, smiled, and spoke.

"Thank you."

About the Author

L. Andrew Cooper thinks the smartest people like horror, fantasy, and sci-fi. Early in life, he couldn't handle the scary stuff—he'd sneak and watch horror films and then keep his parents up all night with his nightmares. In the third grade, he finally convinced his parents to let him read grown-up horror novels: he started with Stephen King's *Firestarter*, and by grade five, he was doing book reports on *The Stand*.

When his parents weren't being kept up late by his nightmares, they worried that his fascination with horror fiction would keep him from experiencing more respectable culture. That all changed when he transitioned from his public high school in the suburbs of Atlanta, Georgia to uber-respectable Harvard University, where he studied English Literature. From there, he went on to get a Ph.D. in English from Princeton, turning his longstanding engagement with horror into a dissertation. The dissertation became the basis for his first book, *Gothic Realities* (2010). More recently, his obsession with horror movies turned into a book about one his favorite directors, *Dario Argento* (2012). He also co-edited the textbook *Monsters* (2012), an attempt to infect others with the idea that scary things are worth people's serious attention.

After living in Georgia, Massachusetts, New Jersey, and California, Andrew now lives in Louisville, Kentucky, where he teaches film studies at the University of Louisville. *Burning the Middle Ground*, his debut novel, appeared in 2012 and introduced the world to the insidious Dr. Allen Fincher. *Descending Lines* is a standalone tale within Dr. Fincher's vast legacy of horror.

Also from BlackWyrm...

Burning the Middle Ground

by L. Andrew Cooper

This dark fantasy about small-town America transforms fears about the country's direction into a haunting tale of religious conspiracy and supernatural mind control. Burning the Middle Ground has as much appeal for dedicated fans of fantasy and horror as for mainstream readers looking for an exciting ride. [Spiritual Horror, ages 14+]

VINE
an urban legend
by Michael Williams

An amateur theatre director's sensational production starring an eccentric fly-by-night cast and crew draws the attention of ancient and powerful forces. Vine weds Greek tragedy and urban legend with dangerous intoxication, as the drama rushes to its dark and inevitable conclusion.
[Modern Mythic Fiction, ages 14+]

www.blackwyrm.com

Remnants of Life: Legends of Darkness

by Georgia L. Jones

Samantha Garrett lives and dies a good life in the human world. She awakens a new creature, Samoda, a vampire-like warrior in the army of Nuem. She is forced to realize that she has become a part of a world that humans believe to be only "Legends of Darkness." Samoda finds her new life is entwined with the age old story of greed, love, betrayal, and vengeance.
[Urban Fantasy, ages 14+]

DARK HALO

by Christopher Kokoski

A winged stranger appears during a violent lightning storm, chasing Landon Paddock out into the maddening night with his estranged 15-year old daughter.

As layer after layer of reality is dissolved by a series of violent encounters, the only way to survive might be for Landon to band together with the family he destroyed to make one last stand against a sinister army of unthinkable magnitude.
[Supernatural Horror, ages 14+]

www.ingramcontent.com/pod-product-compliance
Lightning Source LLC
Chambersburg PA
CBHW070456260626
47161CB00004B/1322